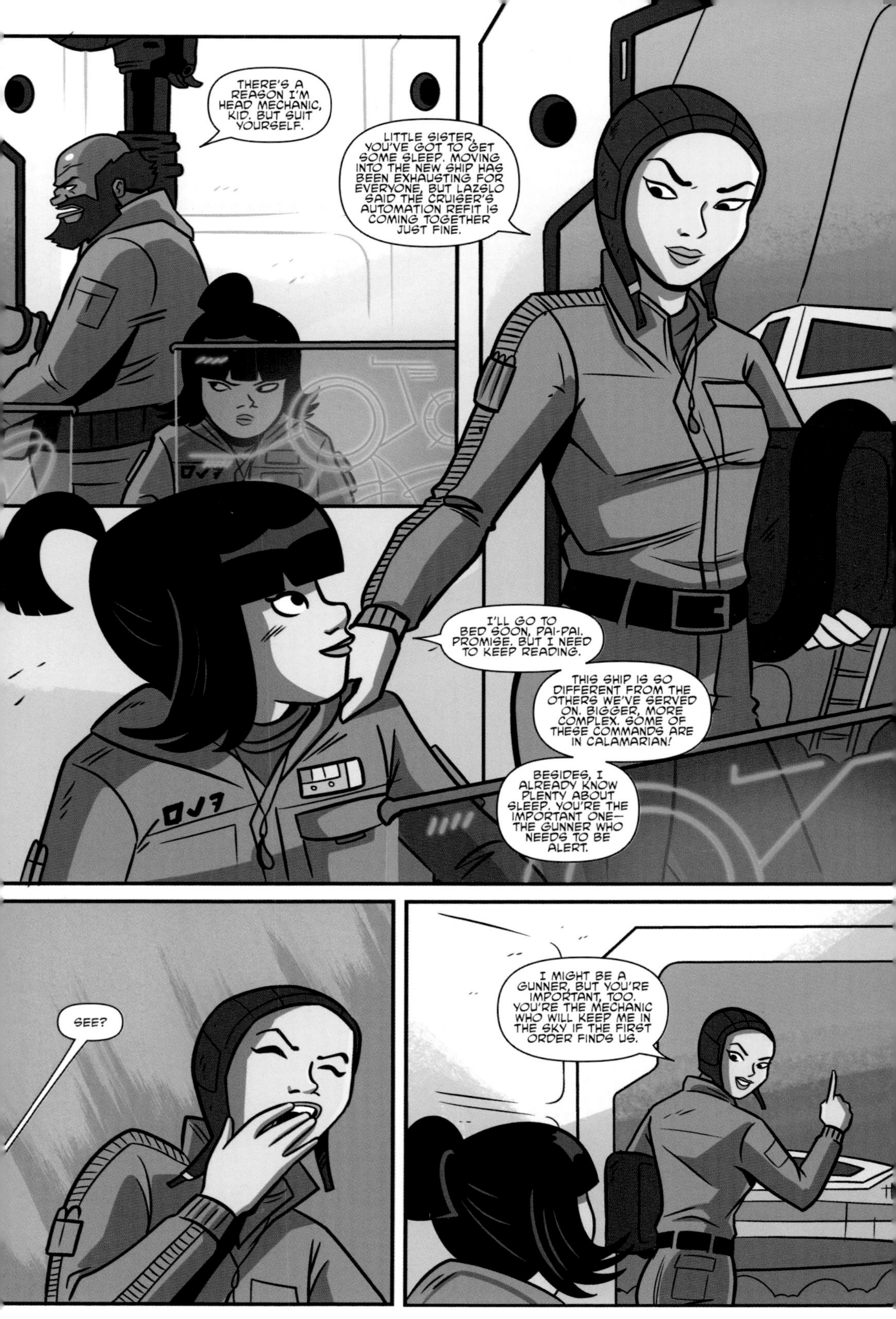

THERE'S A REASON I'M HEAD MECHANIC, KID. BUT SUIT YOURSELF.
LITTLE SISTER, YOU'VE GOT TO GET SOME SLEEP. MOVING INTO THE NEW SHIP HAS BEEN EXHAUSTING FOR EVERYONE, BUT LAZSLO SAID THE CRUISER'S AUTOMATION REFIT IS COMING TOGETHER JUST FINE.
I'LL GO TO BED SOON, PAI-PAI. PROMISE. BUT I NEED TO KEEP READING.
THIS SHIP IS SO DIFFERENT FROM THE OTHERS WE'VE SERVED ON. BIGGER, MORE COMPLEX. SOME OF THESE COMMANDS ARE IN CALAMARIAN!
BESIDES, I ALREADY KNOW PLENTY ABOUT SLEEP. YOU'RE THE IMPORTANT ONE—THE GUNNER WHO NEEDS TO BE ALERT.
SEE?
I MIGHT BE A GUNNER, BUT YOU'RE IMPORTANT, TOO. YOU'RE THE MECHANIC WHO WILL KEEP ME IN THE SKY IF THE FIRST ORDER FINDS US.

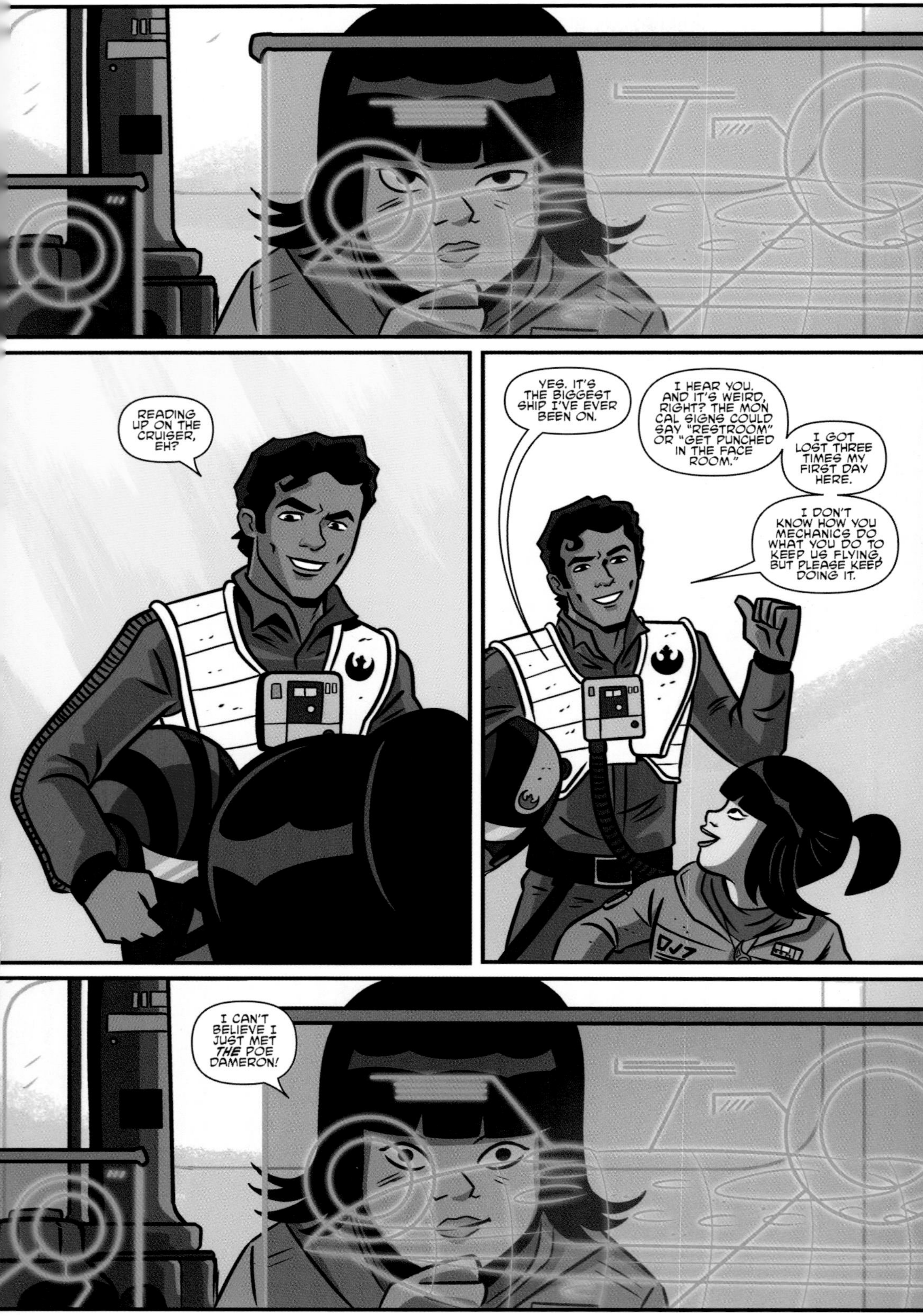

READING UP ON THE CRUISER, EH?
YES. IT'S THE BIGGEST SHIP I'VE EVER BEEN ON.
I HEAR YOU. AND IT'S WEIRD, RIGHT? THE MON CAL SIGNS COULD SAY "RESTROOM" OR "GET PUNCHED IN THE FACE ROOM."
I GOT LOST THREE TIMES MY FIRST DAY HERE.
I DON'T KNOW HOW YOU MECHANICS DO WHAT YOU DO TO KEEP US FLYING, BUT PLEASE KEEP DOING IT.
DJ7
I CAN'T BELIEVE I JUST MET *THE* POE DAMERON!

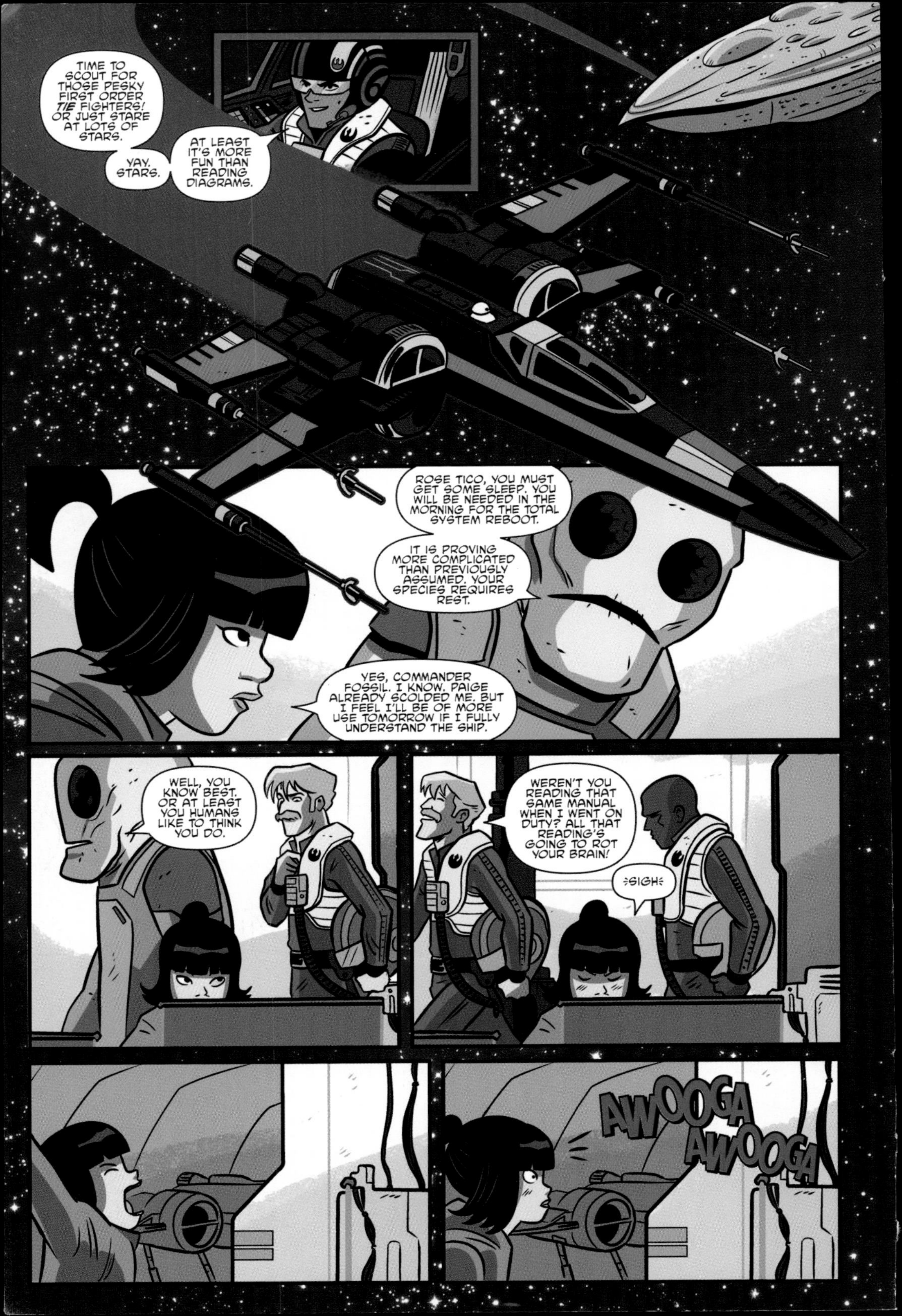
TIME TO SCOUT FOR THOSE PESKY FIRST ORDER TIE FIGHTERS! OR JUST STARE AT LOTS OF STARS.
YAY. STARS.
AT LEAST IT'S MORE FUN THAN READING DIAGRAMS.
ROSE TICO, YOU MUST GET SOME SLEEP. YOU WILL BE NEEDED IN THE MORNING FOR THE TOTAL SYSTEM REBOOT.
IT IS PROVING MORE COMPLICATED THAN PREVIOUSLY ASSUMED. YOUR SPECIES REQUIRES REST.
YES, COMMANDER FOSSIL. I KNOW. PAIGE ALREADY SCOLDED ME. BUT I FEEL I'LL BE OF MORE USE TOMORROW IF I FULLY UNDERSTAND THE SHIP.
WELL, YOU KNOW BEST. OR AT LEAST YOU HUMANS LIKE TO THINK YOU DO.
WEREN'T YOU READING THAT SAME MANUAL WHEN I WENT ON DUTY? ALL THAT READING'S GOING TO ROT YOUR BRAIN!
SIGH
AWOOGA AWOOGA

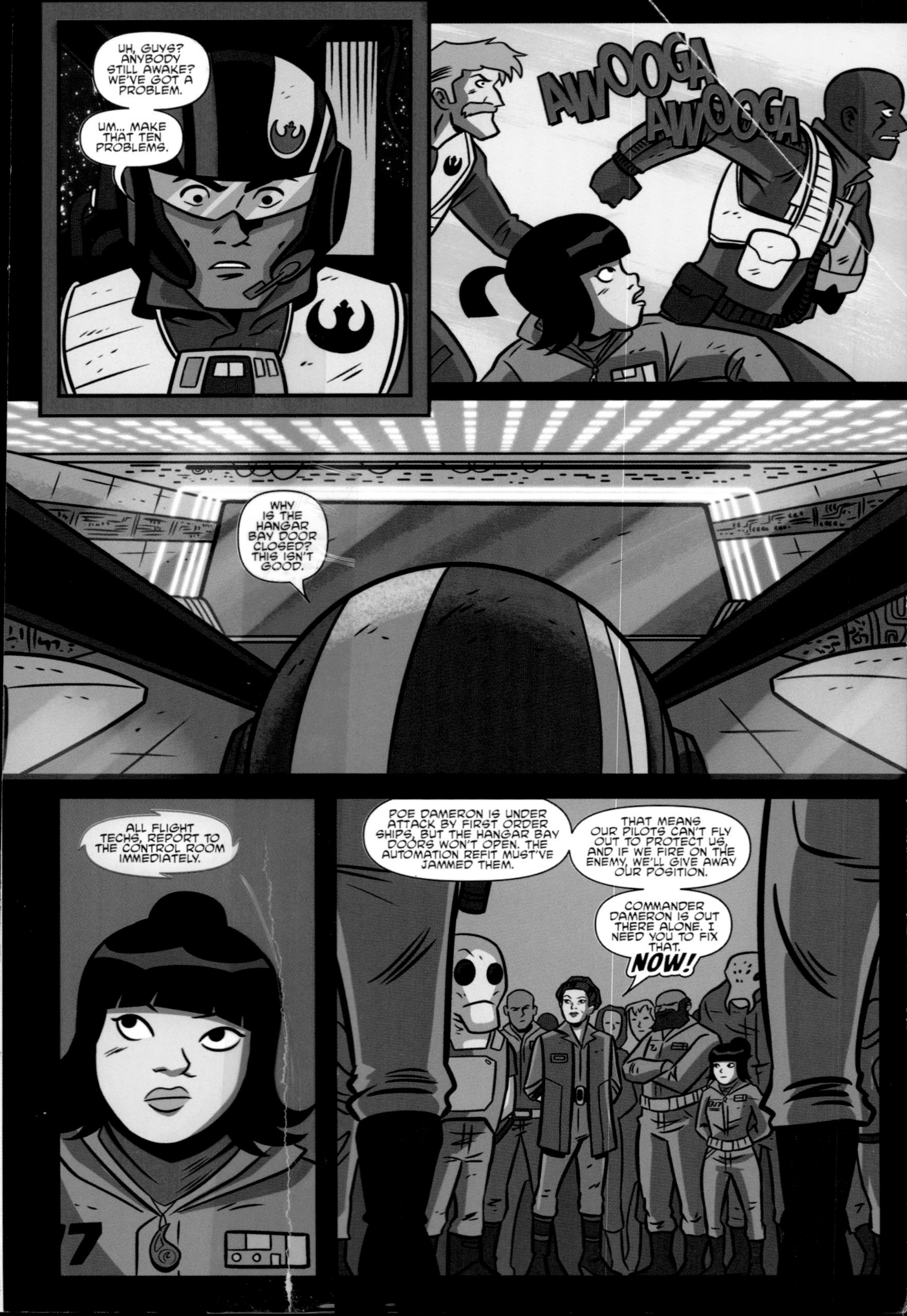
UH, GUYS? ANYBODY STILL AWAKE? WE'VE GOT A PROBLEM.
UM... MAKE THAT TEN PROBLEMS.
AWOOGA AWOOGA
WHY IS THE HANGAR BAY DOOR CLOSED? THIS ISN'T GOOD.
ALL FLIGHT TECHS, REPORT TO THE CONTROL ROOM IMMEDIATELY.
POE DAMERON IS UNDER ATTACK BY FIRST ORDER SHIPS, BUT THE HANGAR BAY DOORS WON'T OPEN. THE AUTOMATION REFIT MUST'VE JAMMED THEM.
THAT MEANS OUR PILOTS CAN'T FLY OUT TO PROTECT US, AND IF WE FIRE ON THE ENEMY, WE'LL GIVE AWAY OUR POSITION.
COMMANDER DAMERON IS OUT THERE ALONE. I NEED YOU TO FIX THAT. NOW!

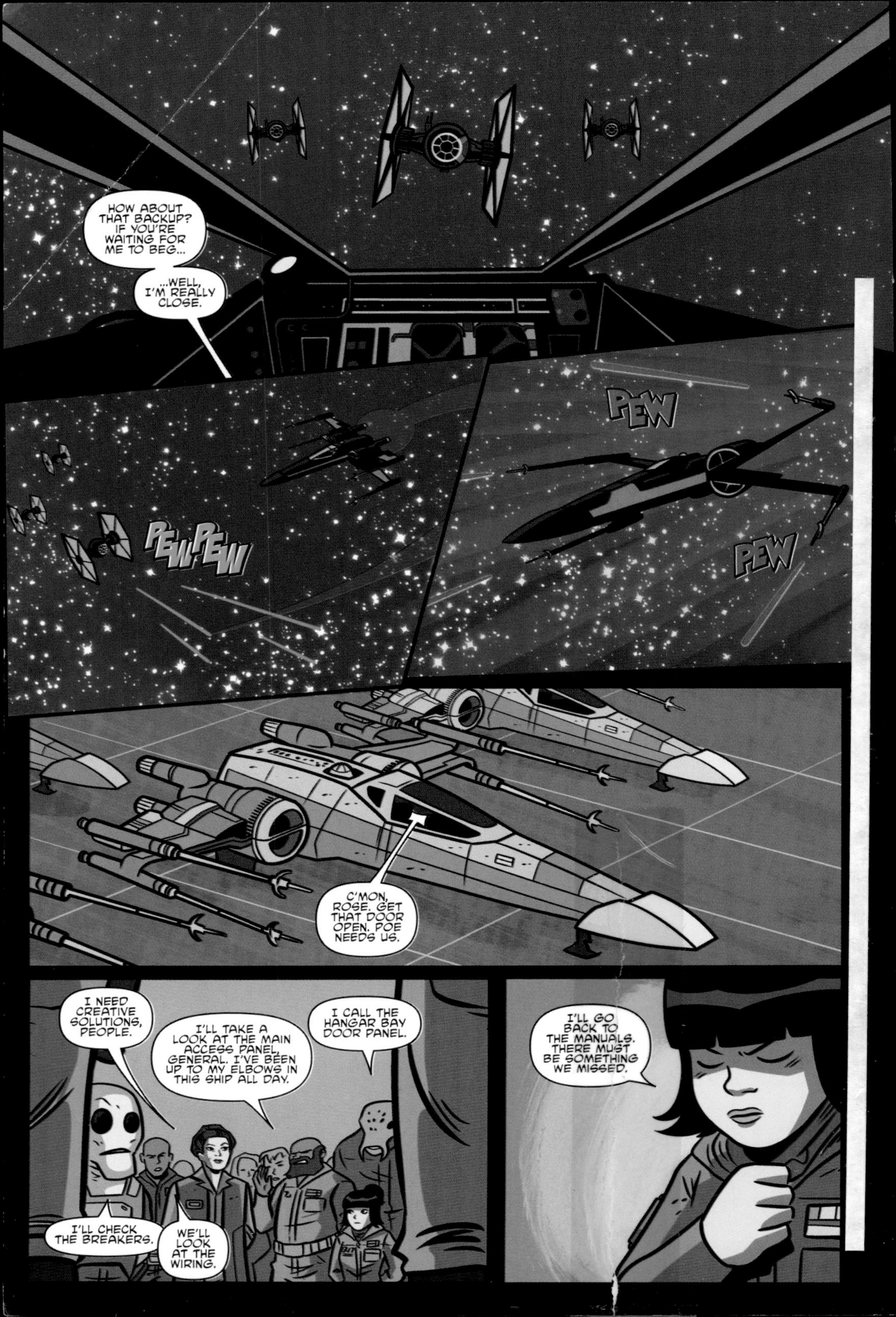
HOW ABOUT THAT BACKUP? IF YOU'RE WAITING FOR ME TO BEG...
...WELL, I'M REALLY CLOSE.
PEWPEW
PEW
PEW
C'MON, ROSE. GET THAT DOOR OPEN. POE NEEDS US.
I NEED CREATIVE SOLUTIONS, PEOPLE.
I'LL TAKE A LOOK AT THE MAIN ACCESS PANEL, GENERAL. I'VE BEEN UP TO MY ELBOWS IN THIS SHIP ALL DAY.
I CALL THE HANGAR BAY DOOR PANEL.
I'LL CHECK THE BREAKERS.
WE'LL LOOK AT THE WIRING.
I'LL GO BACK TO THE MANUALS. THERE MUST BE SOMETHING WE MISSED.

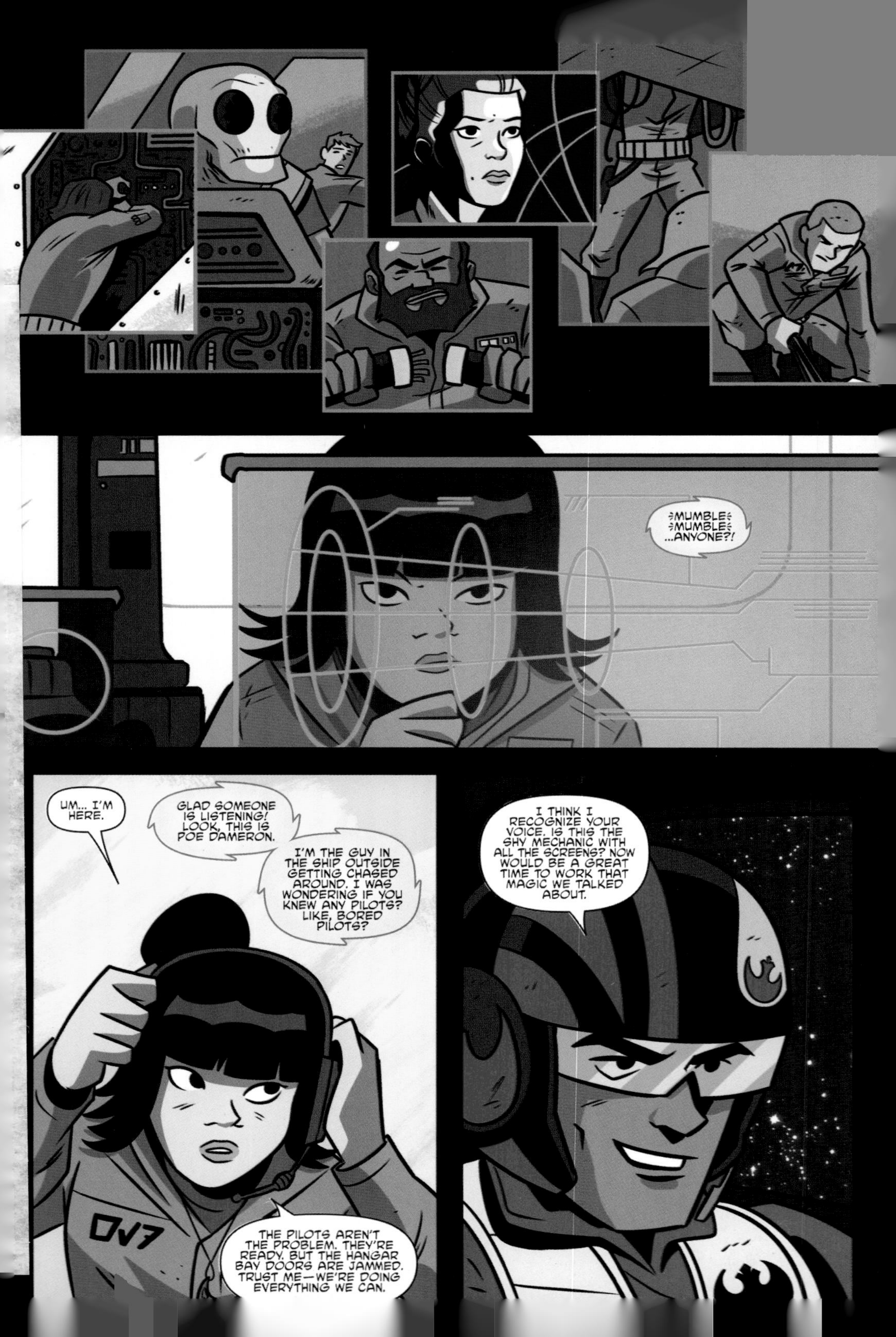

≈MUMBLE≈ ≈MUMBLE≈ ...ANYONE?!
UM... I'M HERE.
GLAD SOMEONE IS LISTENING! LOOK, THIS IS POE DAMERON.
I'M THE GUY IN THE SHIP OUTSIDE GETTING CHASED AROUND. I WAS WONDERING IF YOU KNEW ANY PILOTS? LIKE, BORED PILOTS?
THE PILOTS AREN'T THE PROBLEM. THEY'RE READY. BUT THE HANGAR BAY DOORS ARE JAMMED. TRUST ME—WE'RE DOING EVERYTHING WE CAN.
DV7
I THINK I RECOGNIZE YOUR VOICE. IS THIS THE SHY MECHANIC WITH ALL THE SCREENS? NOW WOULD BE A GREAT TIME TO WORK THAT MAGIC WE TALKED ABOUT.

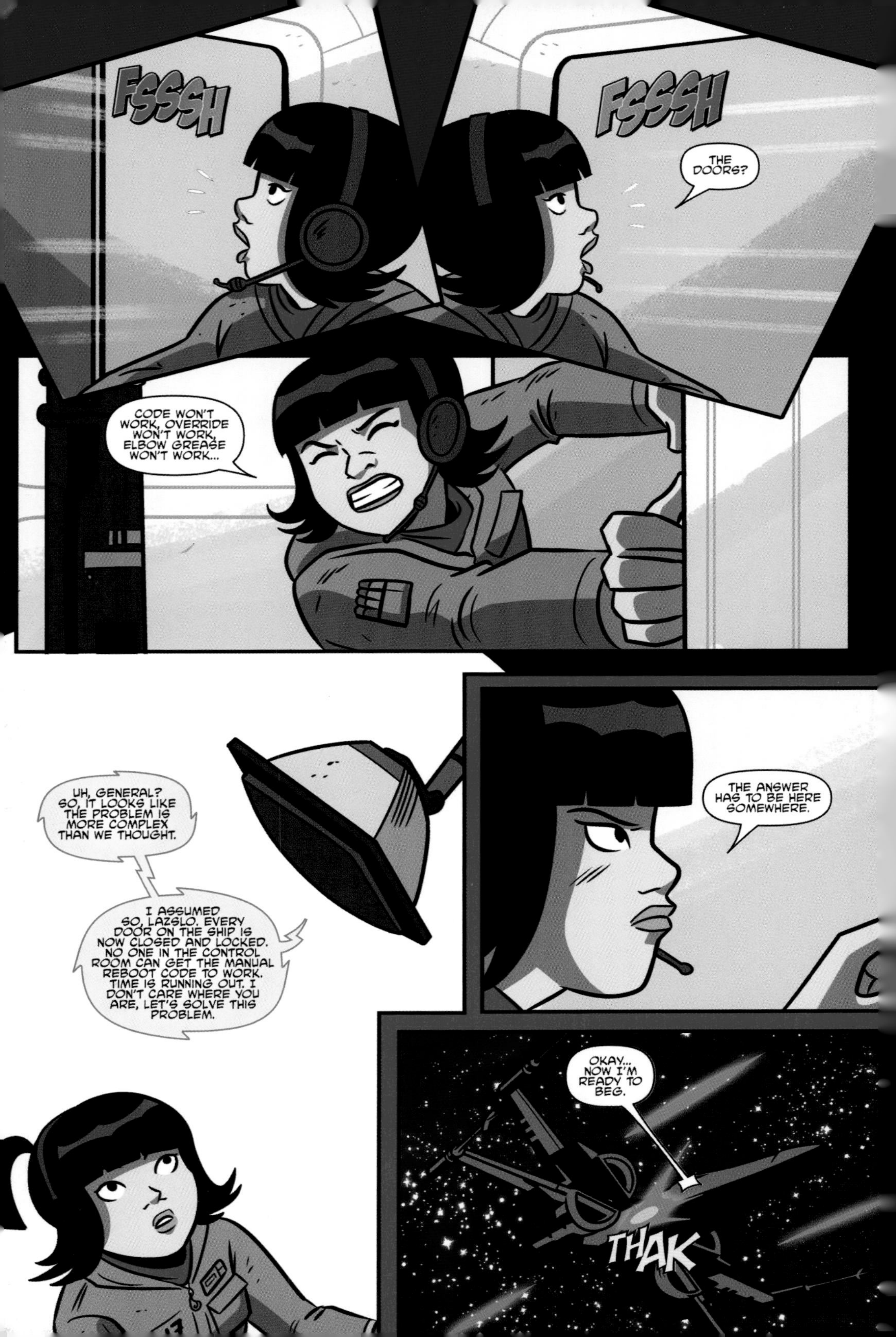
FSSSH
FSSSH
THE DOORS?
CODE WON'T WORK, OVERRIDE WON'T WORK, ELBOW GREASE WON'T WORK...
UH, GENERAL? SO, IT LOOKS LIKE THE PROBLEM IS MORE COMPLEX THAN WE THOUGHT.
I ASSUMED SO, LAZSLO. EVERY DOOR ON THE SHIP IS NOW CLOSED AND LOCKED. NO ONE IN THE CONTROL ROOM CAN GET THE MANUAL REBOOT CODE TO WORK. TIME IS RUNNING OUT. I DON'T CARE WHERE YOU ARE, LET'S SOLVE THIS PROBLEM.
THE ANSWER HAS TO BE HERE SOMEWHERE.
OKAY... NOW I'M READY TO BEG.
THAK

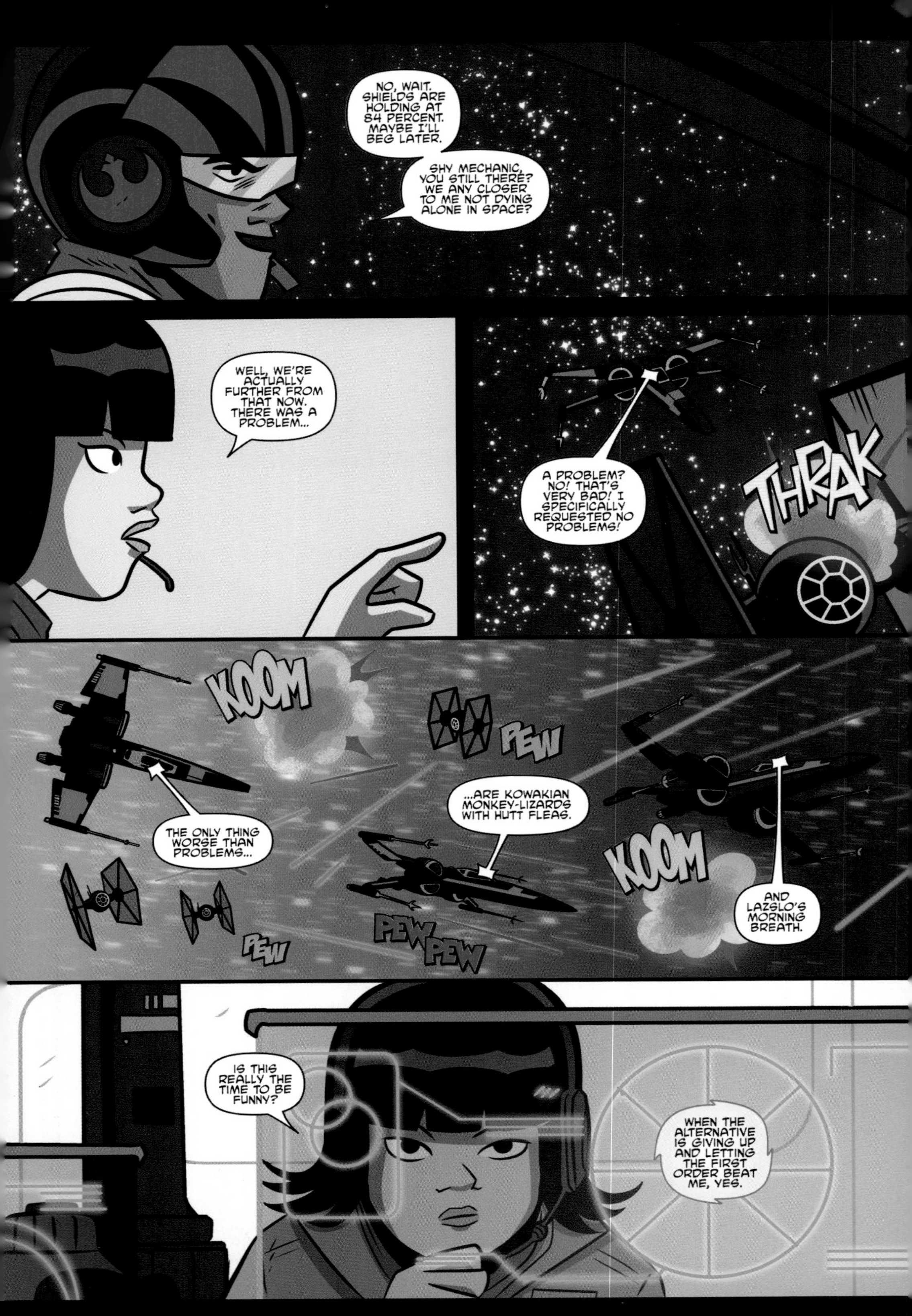

NO, WAIT. SHIELDS ARE HOLDING AT 84 PERCENT. MAYBE I'LL BEG LATER.
SHY MECHANIC, YOU STILL THERE? WE ANY CLOSER TO ME NOT DYING ALONE IN SPACE?
WELL, WE'RE ACTUALLY FURTHER FROM THAT NOW. THERE WAS A PROBLEM...
A PROBLEM? NO! THAT'S VERY BAD! I SPECIFICALLY REQUESTED NO PROBLEMS!
THRAK
KOOM
PEW
THE ONLY THING WORSE THAN PROBLEMS...
...ARE KOWAKIAN MONKEY-LIZARDS WITH HUTT FLEAS.
KOOM
AND LAZSLO'S MORNING BREATH.
PEW
PEW PEW
IS THIS REALLY THE TIME TO BE FUNNY?
WHEN THE ALTERNATIVE IS GIVING UP AND LETTING THE FIRST ORDER BEAT ME, YES.

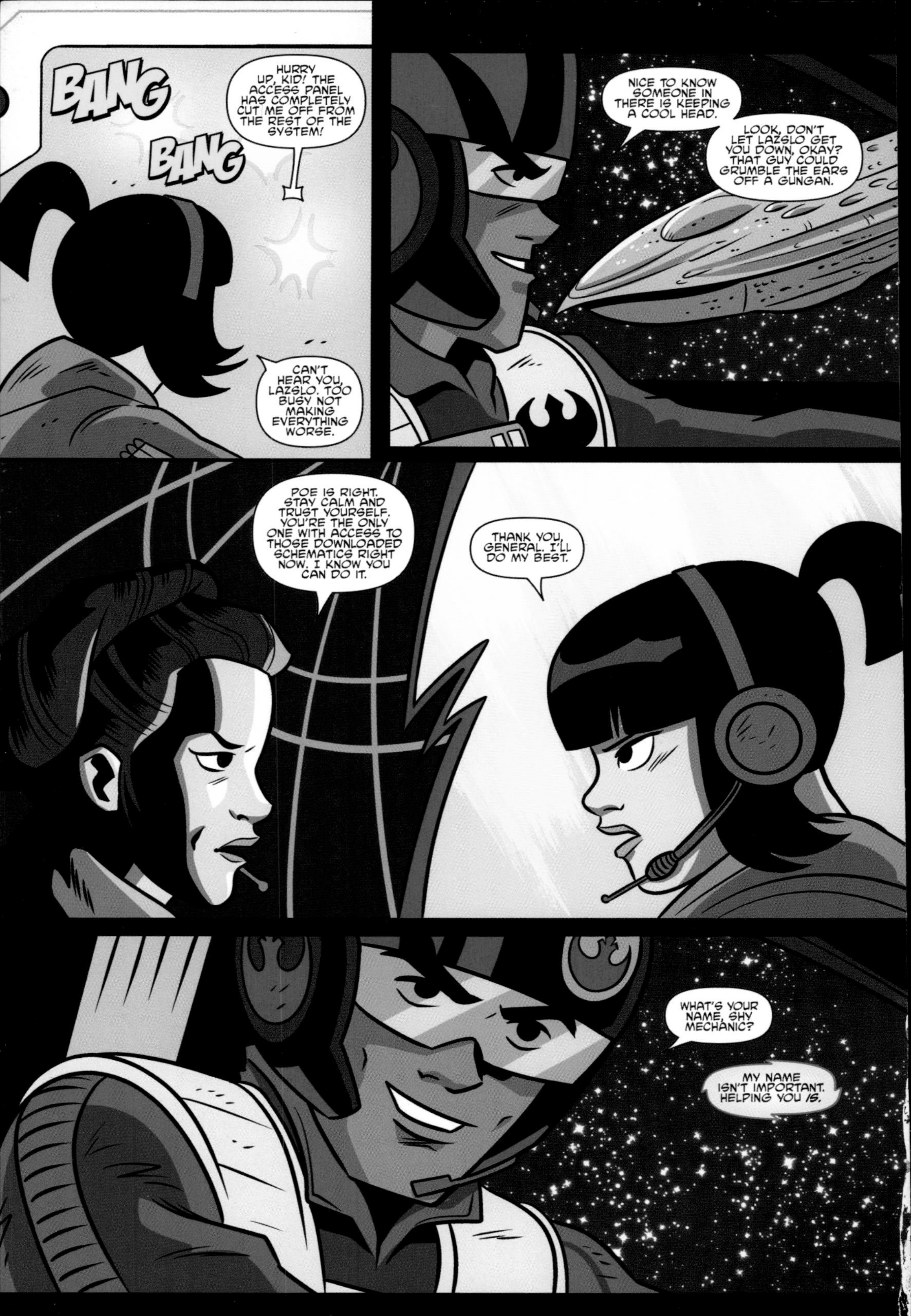
BANG
BANG
HURRY UP, KID! THE ACCESS PANEL HAS COMPLETELY CUT ME OFF FROM THE REST OF THE SYSTEM!
CAN'T HEAR YOU, LAZSLO. TOO BUSY NOT MAKING EVERYTHING WORSE.
NICE TO KNOW SOMEONE IN THERE IS KEEPING A COOL HEAD.
LOOK, DON'T LET LAZSLO GET YOU DOWN, OKAY? THAT GUY COULD GRUMBLE THE EARS OFF A GUNGAN.
POE IS RIGHT. STAY CALM AND TRUST YOURSELF. YOU'RE THE ONLY ONE WITH ACCESS TO THOSE DOWNLOADED SCHEMATICS RIGHT NOW. I KNOW YOU CAN DO IT.
THANK YOU, GENERAL. I'LL DO MY BEST.
WHAT'S YOUR NAME, SHY MECHANIC?
MY NAME ISN'T IMPORTANT. HELPING YOU *IS*.

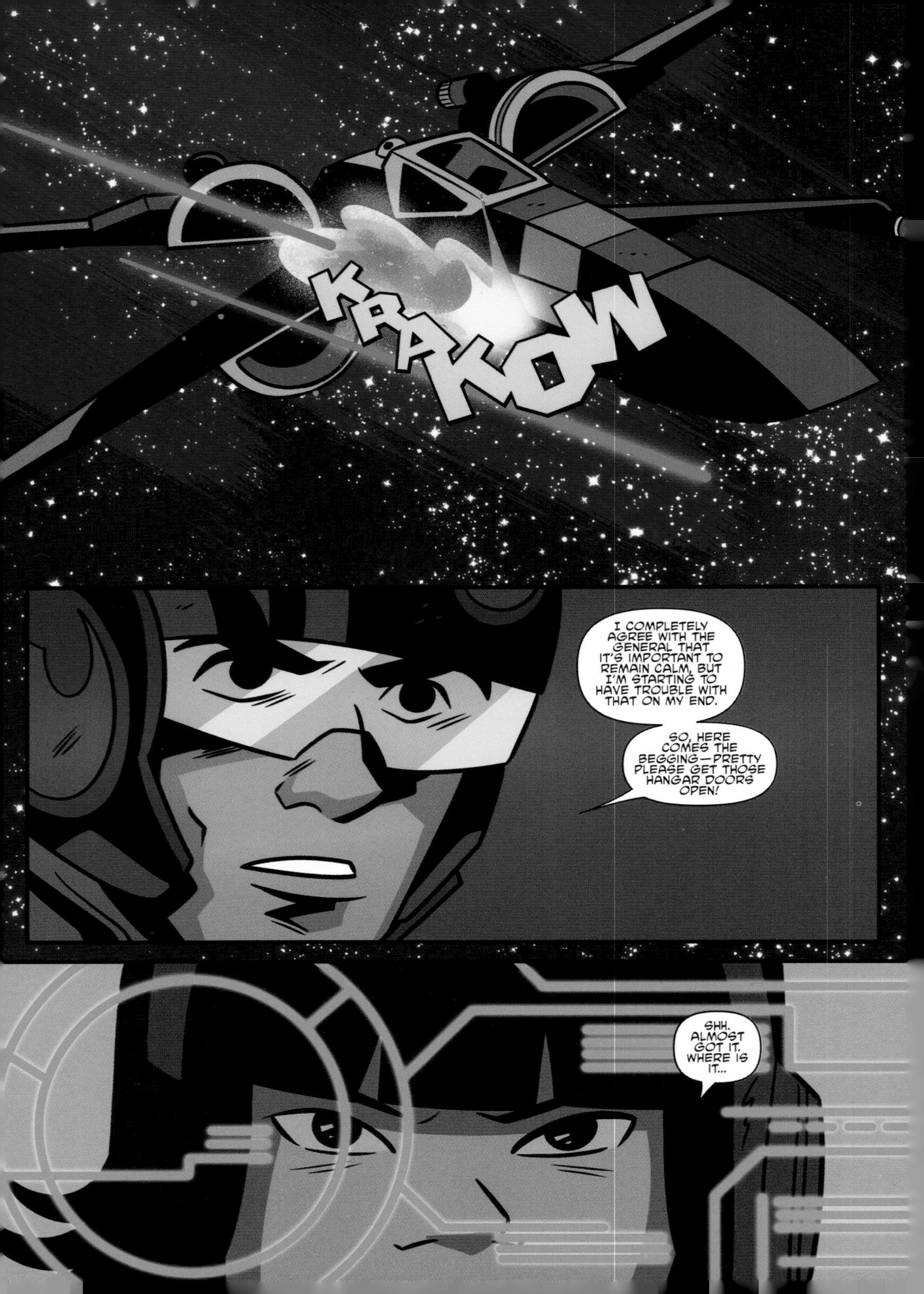
KRAKOW
I COMPLETELY AGREE WITH THE GENERAL THAT IT'S IMPORTANT TO REMAIN CALM, BUT I'M STARTING TO HAVE TROUBLE WITH THAT ON MY END.
SO, HERE COMES THE BEGGING—PRETTY PLEASE GET THOSE HANGAR DOORS OPEN!
SHH. ALMOST GOT IT. WHERE IS IT...

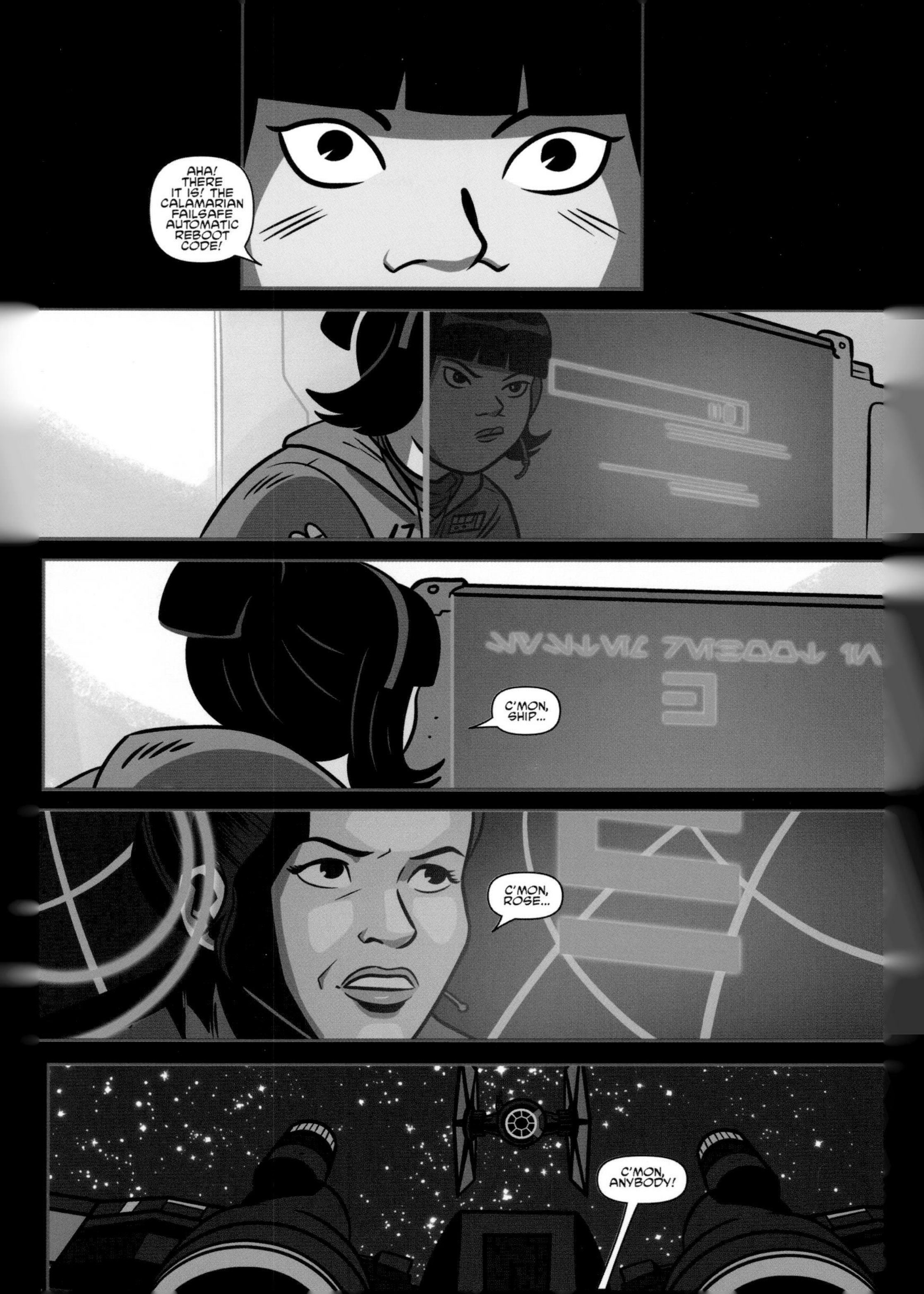
AHA! THERE IT IS! THE CALAMARIAN FAILSAFE AUTOMATIC REBOOT CODE!
C'MON, SHIP...
C'MON, ROSE...
C'MON, ANYBODY!

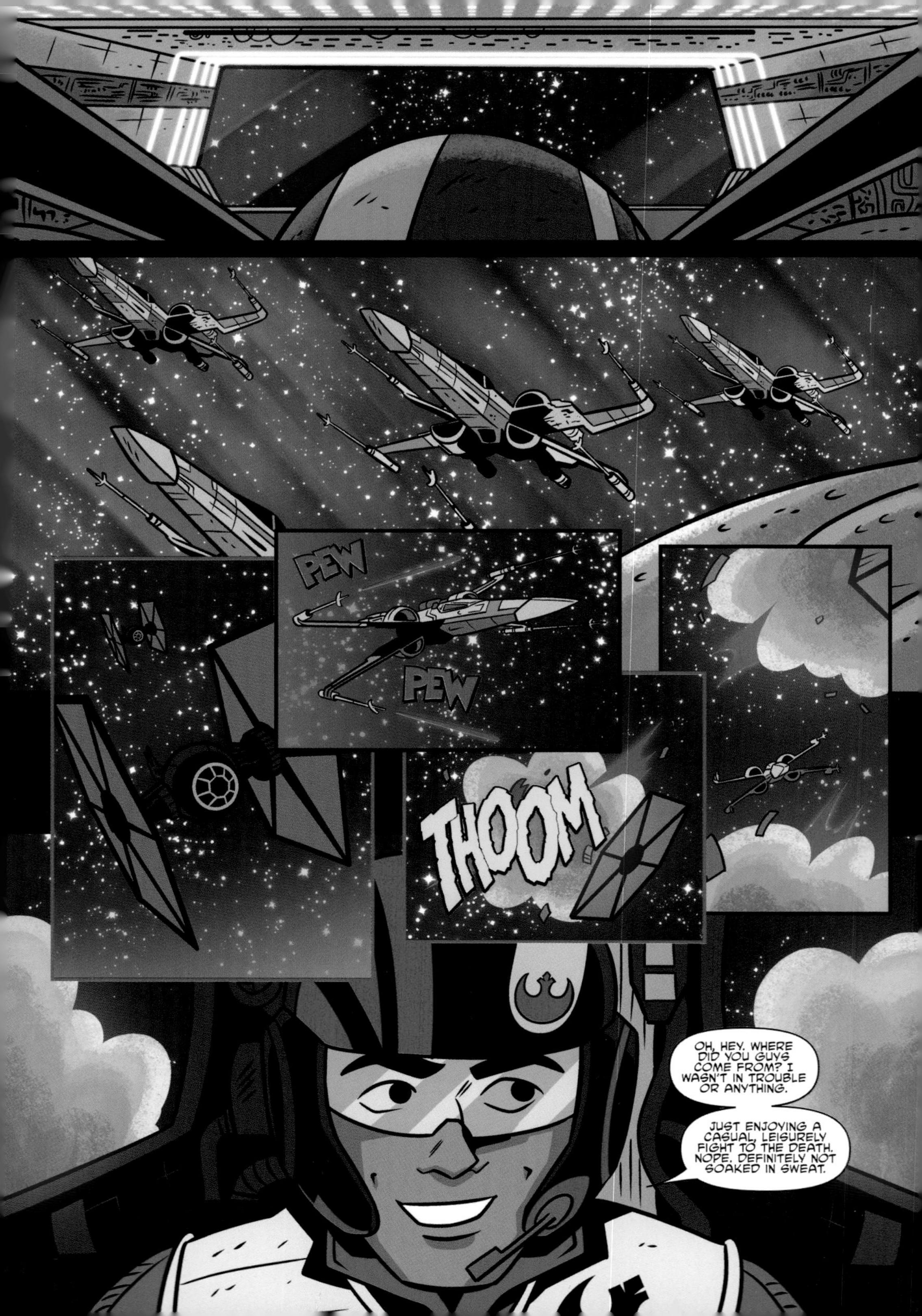
PEW
PEW
THOOM
OH, HEY. WHERE DID YOU GUYS COME FROM? I WASN'T IN TROUBLE OR ANYTHING.
JUST ENJOYING A CASUAL, LEISURELY FIGHT TO THE DEATH. NOPE. DEFINITELY NOT SOAKED IN SWEAT.

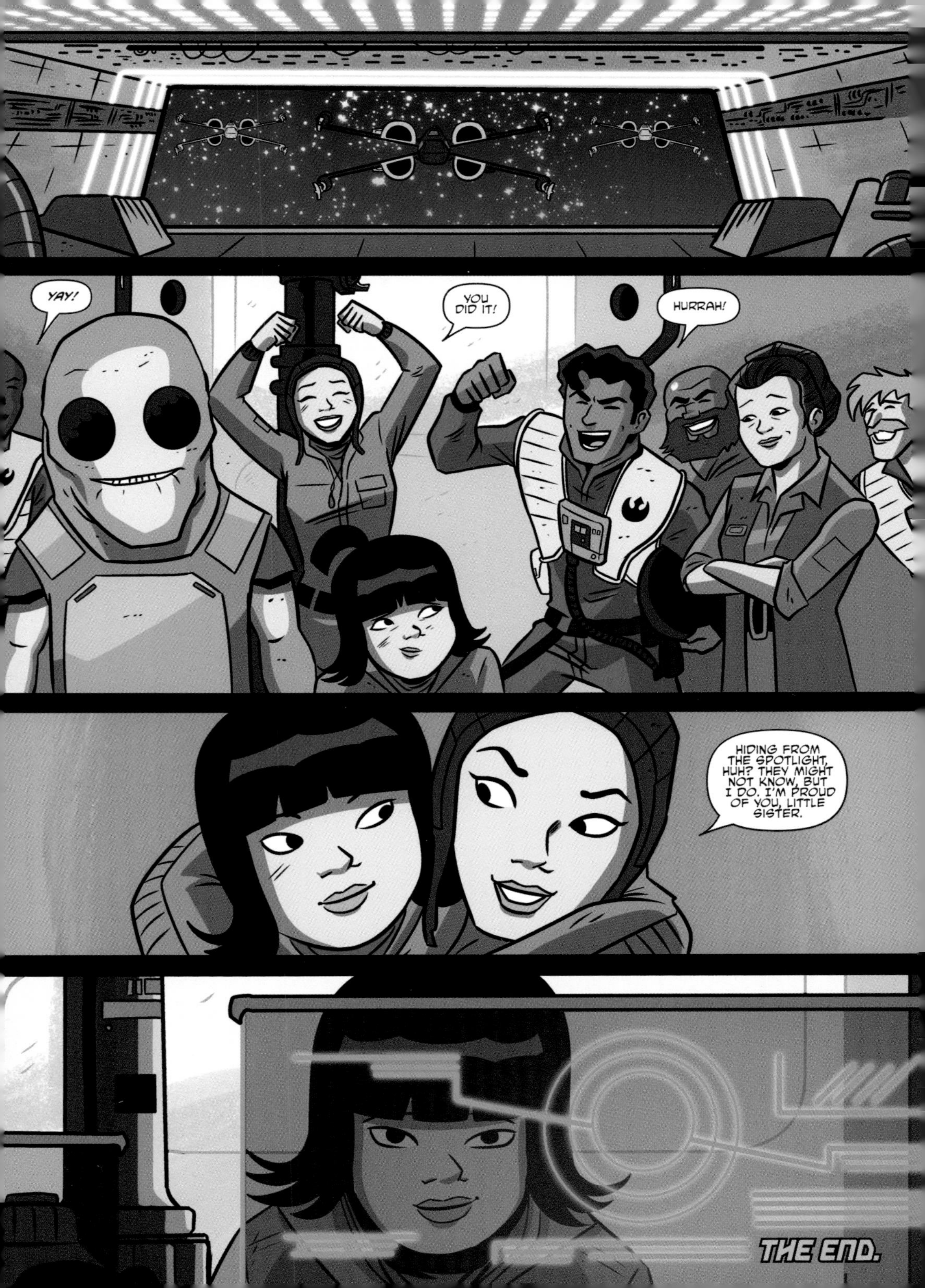
YAY!
YOU DID IT!
HURRAH!
HIDING FROM THE SPOTLIGHT, HUH? THEY MIGHT NOT KNOW, BUT I DO. I'M PROUD OF YOU, LITTLE SISTER.
THE END.

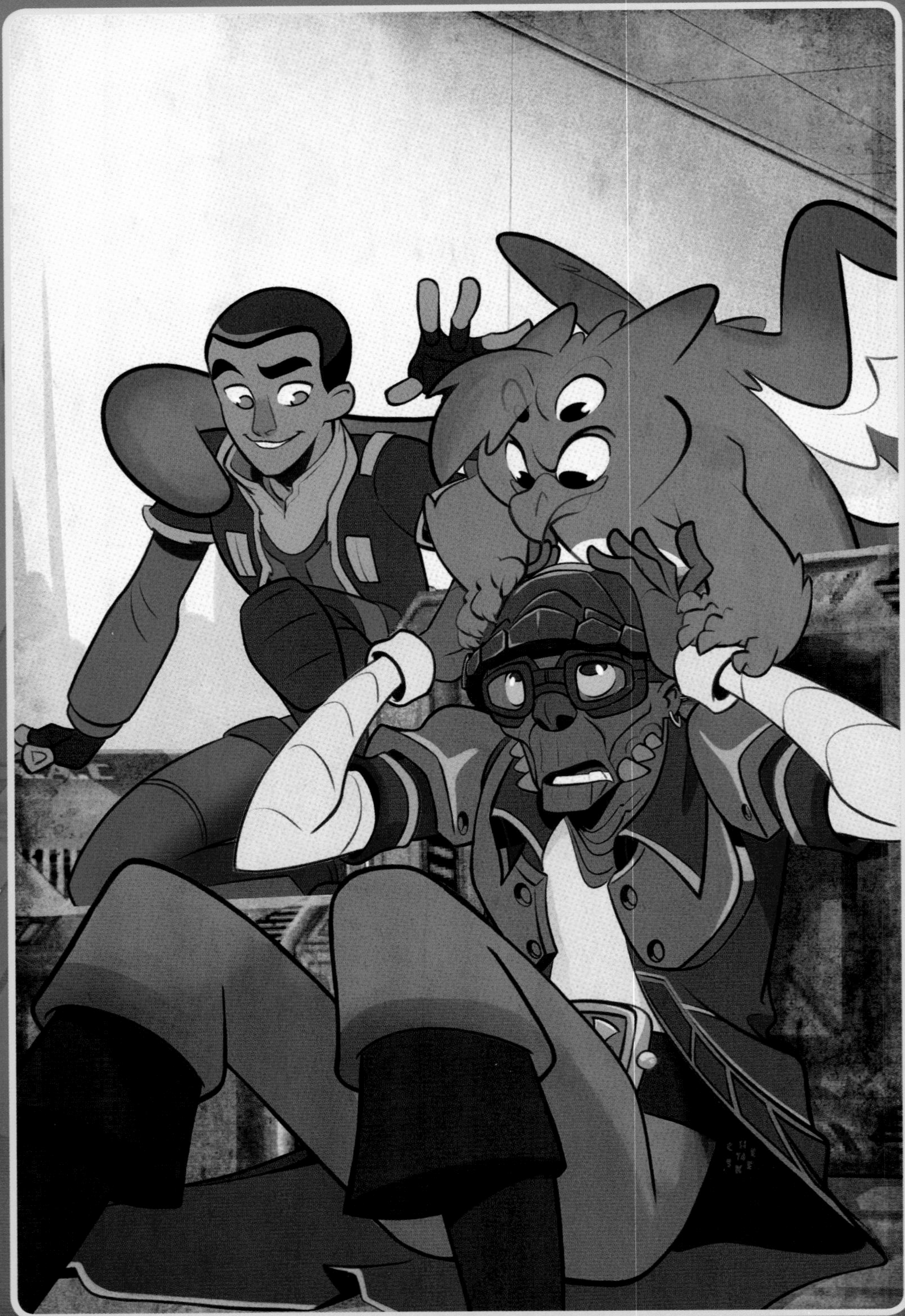

Art by Sean Galloway

STAR WARS ADVENTURES™

ENDANGERED

WRITER
SHOLLY FISCH
PENCILERS
SEAN GALLOWAY
AND JAMAL PEPPERS
INKERS
CASSEY KUO
AND GARY MARTIN
COLORIST
LUIS ANTONIO DELGADO
LETTERER
TOM B. LONG

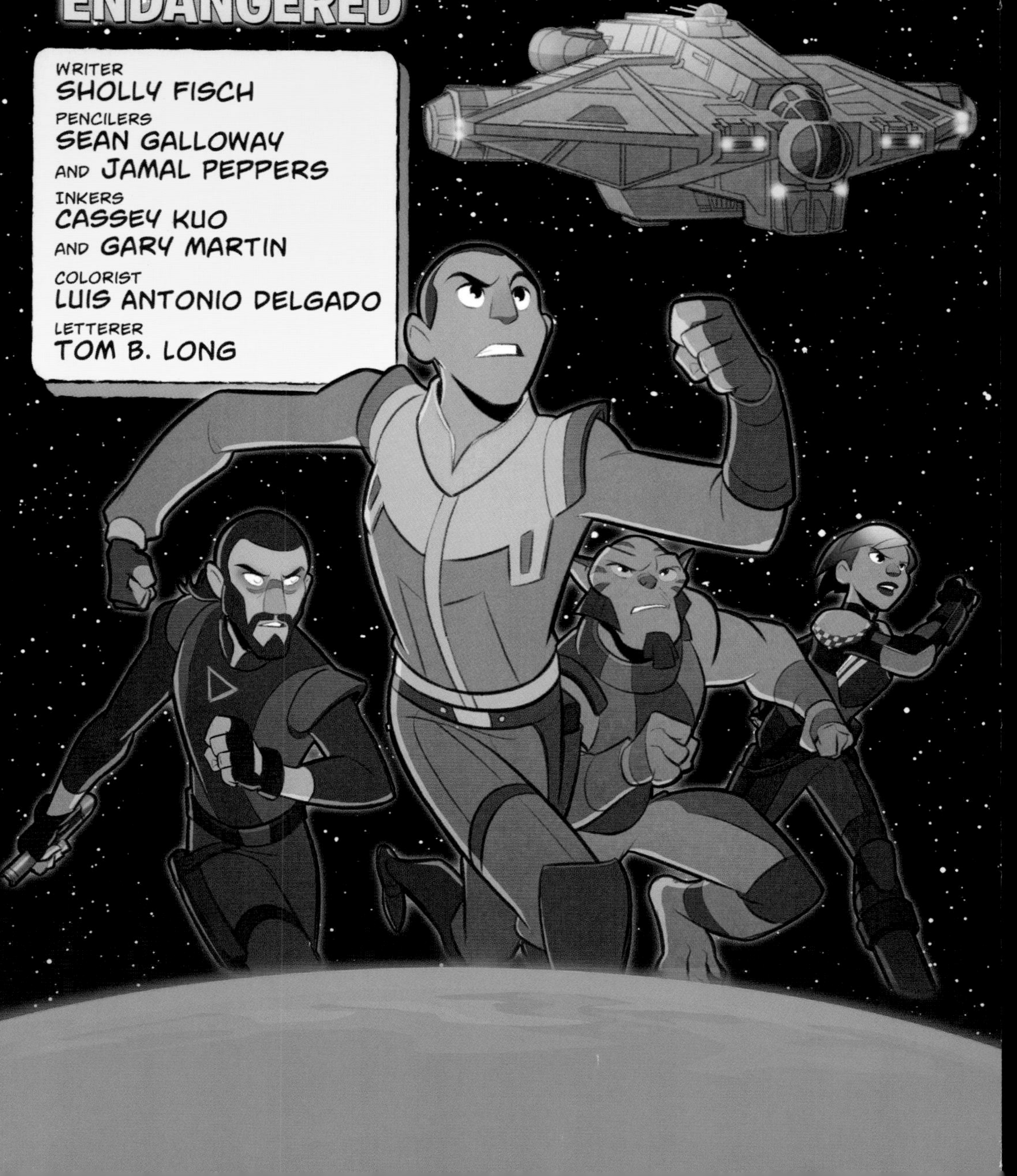

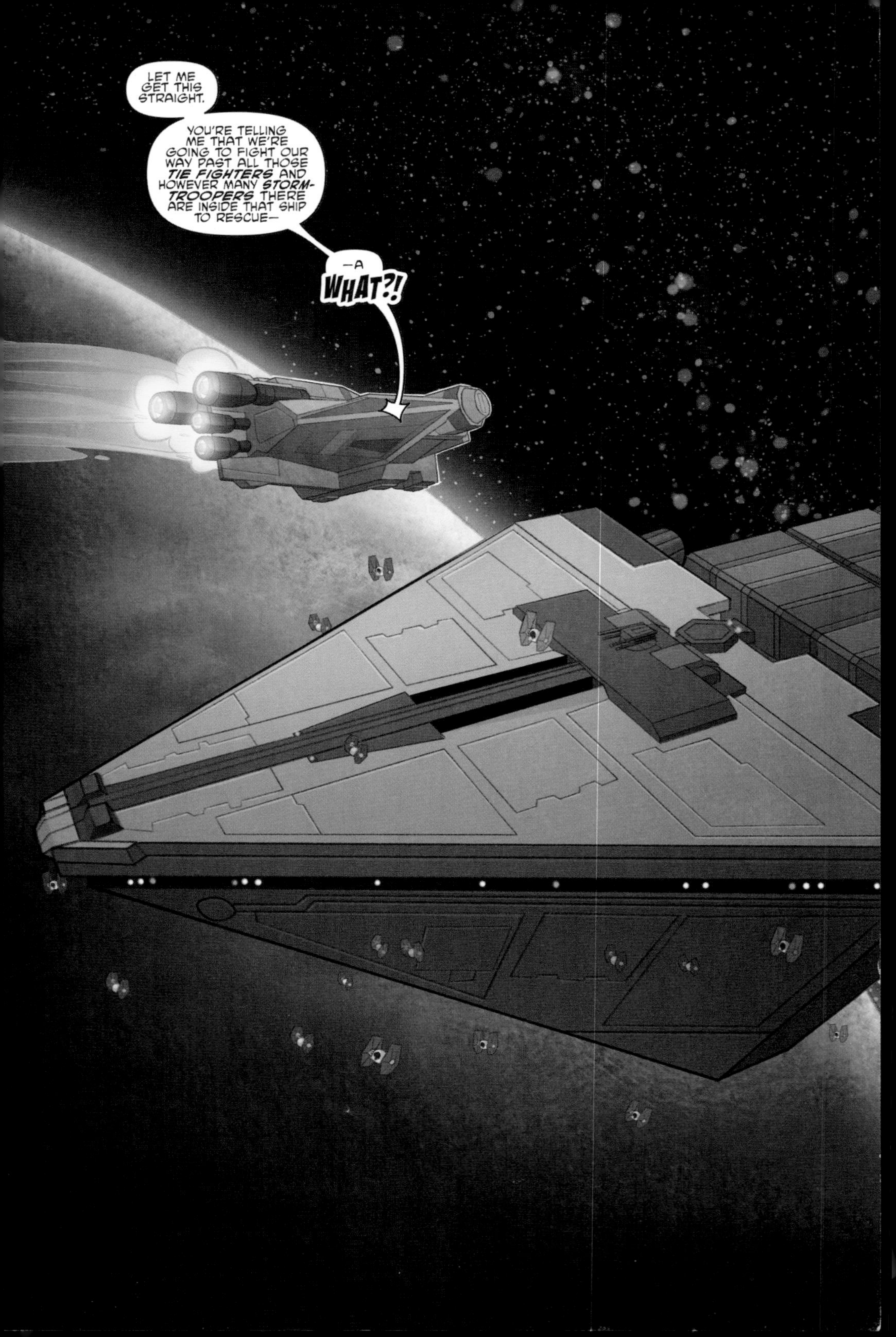
LET ME GET THIS STRAIGHT.
YOU'RE TELLING ME THAT WE'RE GOING TO FIGHT OUR WAY PAST ALL THOSE *TIE FIGHTERS* AND HOWEVER MANY *STORM-TROOPERS* THERE ARE INSIDE THAT SHIP TO RESCUE—
—A WHAT?!

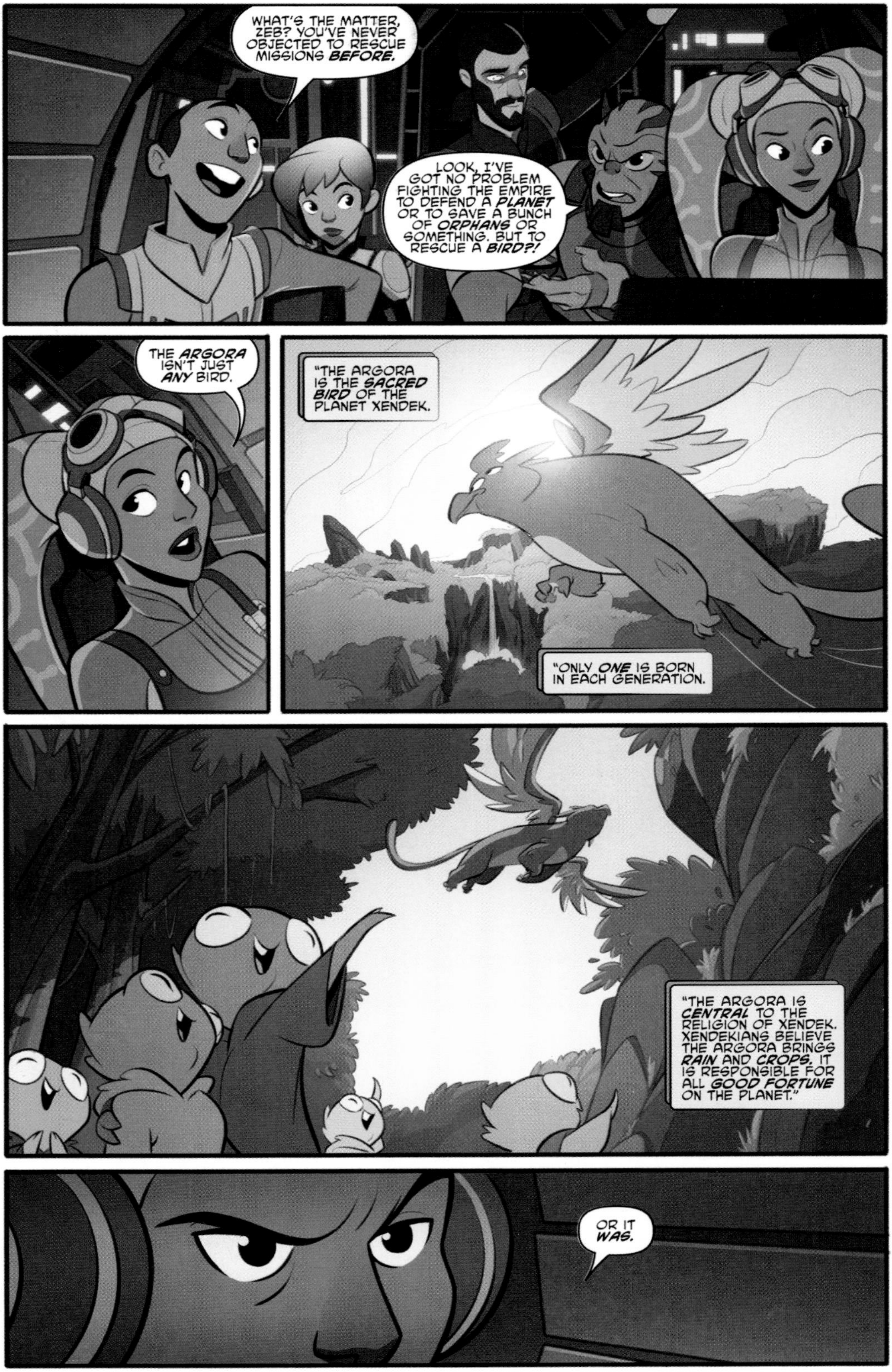
WHAT'S THE MATTER, ZEB? YOU'VE NEVER OBJECTED TO RESCUE MISSIONS *BEFORE.*
LOOK, I'VE GOT NO PROBLEM FIGHTING THE EMPIRE TO DEFEND A *PLANET* OR TO SAVE A BUNCH OF *ORPHANS* OR SOMETHING. BUT TO RESCUE A *BIRD?!*
THE *ARGORA* ISN'T JUST *ANY* BIRD.
"THE ARGORA IS THE *SACRED BIRD* OF THE PLANET XENDEK.
"ONLY *ONE* IS BORN IN EACH GENERATION.
"THE ARGORA IS *CENTRAL* TO THE RELIGION OF XENDEK. XENDEKIANS BELIEVE THE ARGORA BRINGS *RAIN* AND *CROPS.* IT IS RESPONSIBLE FOR ALL *GOOD FORTUNE* ON THE PLANET."
OR IT *WAS.*

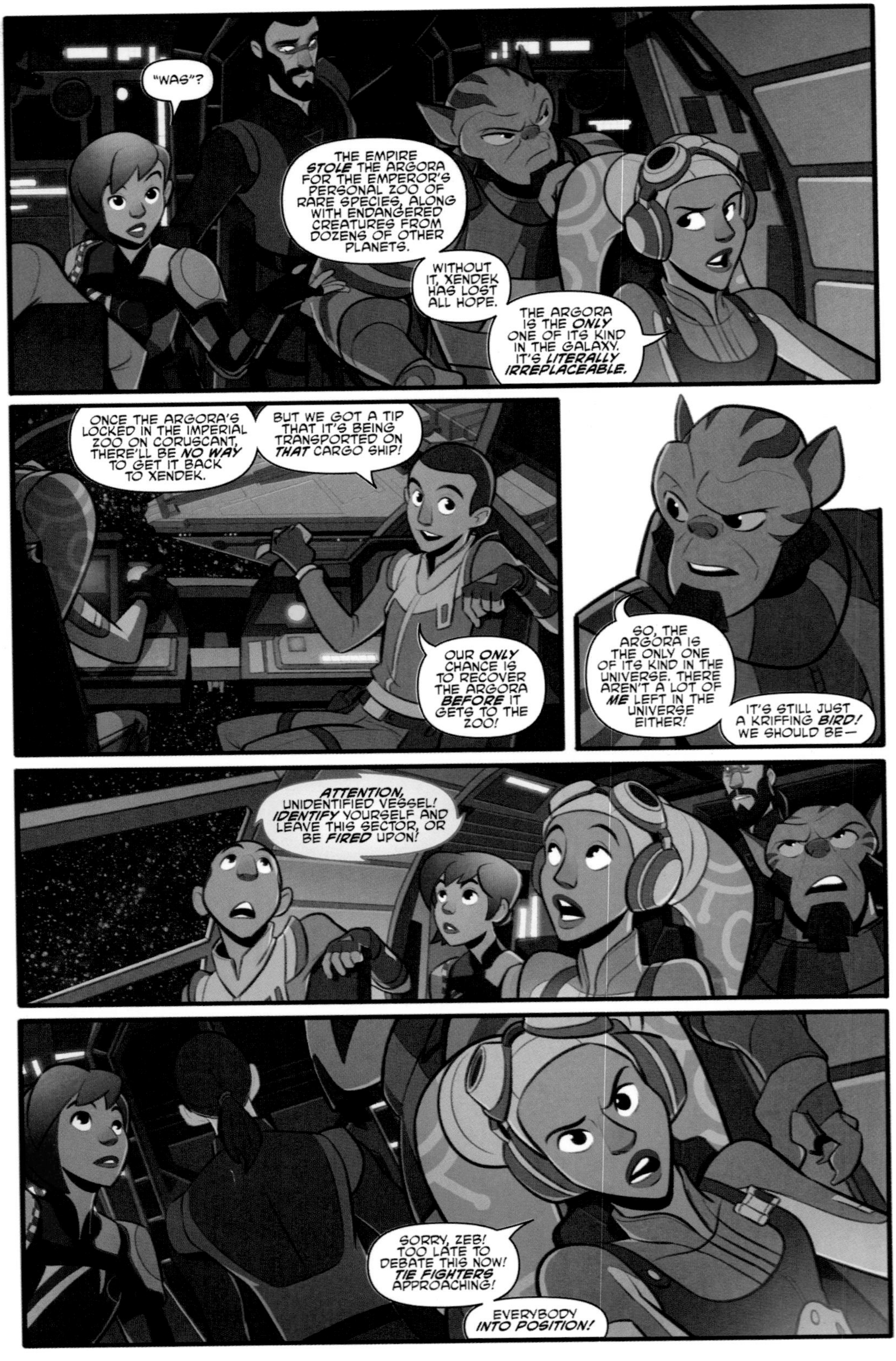

"WAS"?
THE EMPIRE STOLE THE ARGORA FOR THE EMPEROR'S PERSONAL ZOO OF RARE SPECIES, ALONG WITH ENDANGERED CREATURES FROM DOZENS OF OTHER PLANETS.
WITHOUT IT, XENDEK HAS LOST ALL HOPE.
THE ARGORA IS THE ONLY ONE OF ITS KIND IN THE GALAXY. IT'S LITERALLY IRREPLACEABLE.
ONCE THE ARGORA'S LOCKED IN THE IMPERIAL ZOO ON CORUSCANT, THERE'LL BE NO WAY TO GET IT BACK TO XENDEK.
BUT WE GOT A TIP THAT IT'S BEING TRANSPORTED ON THAT CARGO SHIP!
OUR ONLY CHANCE IS TO RECOVER THE ARGORA BEFORE IT GETS TO THE ZOO!
SO, THE ARGORA IS THE ONLY ONE OF ITS KIND IN THE UNIVERSE. THERE AREN'T A LOT OF ME LEFT IN THE UNIVERSE EITHER!
IT'S STILL JUST A KRIFFING BIRD! WE SHOULD BE—
ATTENTION, UNIDENTIFIED VESSEL! IDENTIFY YOURSELF AND LEAVE THIS SECTOR, OR BE FIRED UPON!
SORRY, ZEB! TOO LATE TO DEBATE THIS NOW! TIE FIGHTERS APPROACHING!
EVERYBODY INTO POSITION!

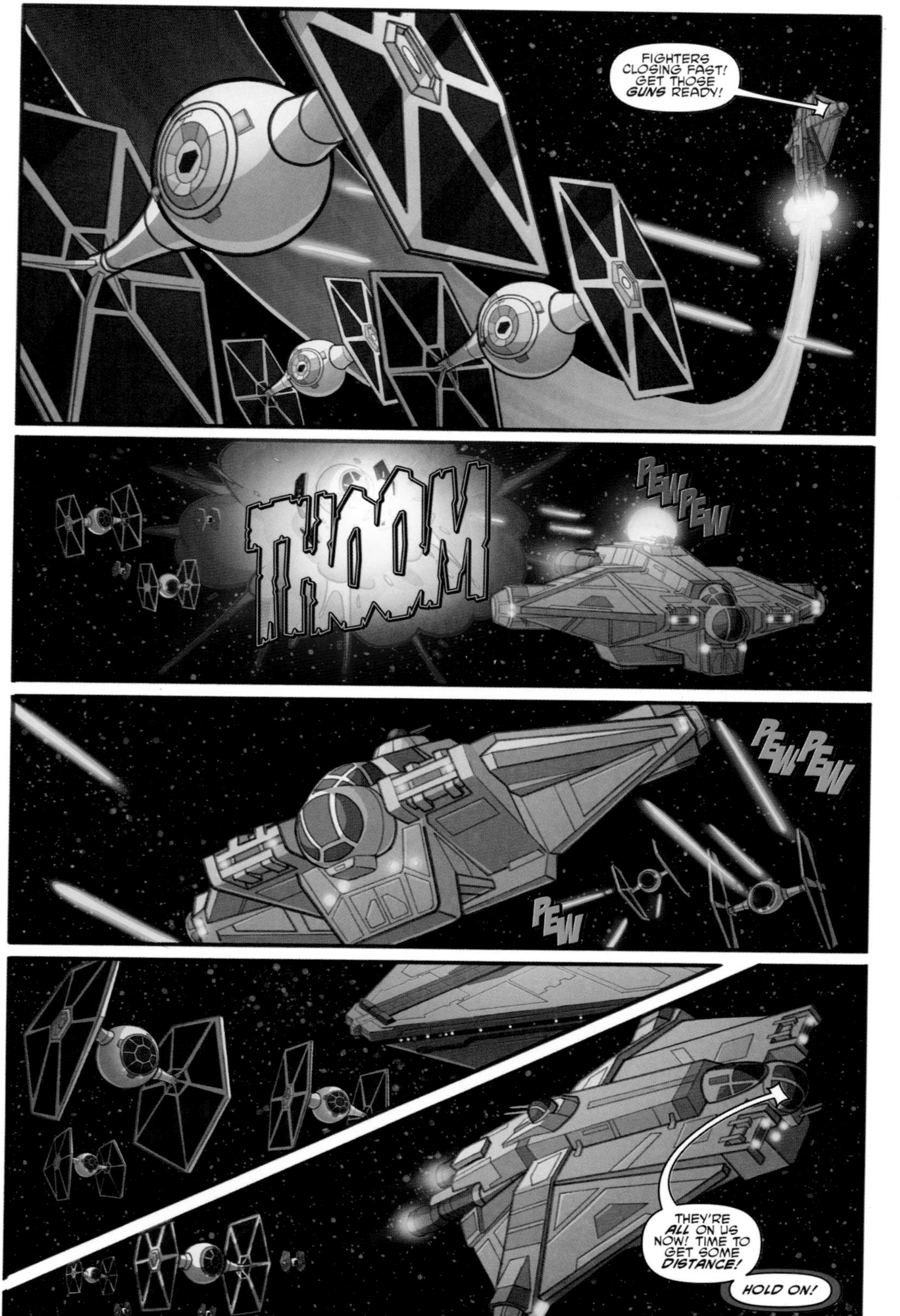

FIGHTERS CLOSING FAST! GET THOSE GUNS READY!
THOOM
PEW PEW
PEW PEW
PEW
THEY'RE ALL ON US NOW! TIME TO GET SOME DISTANCE!
HOLD ON!

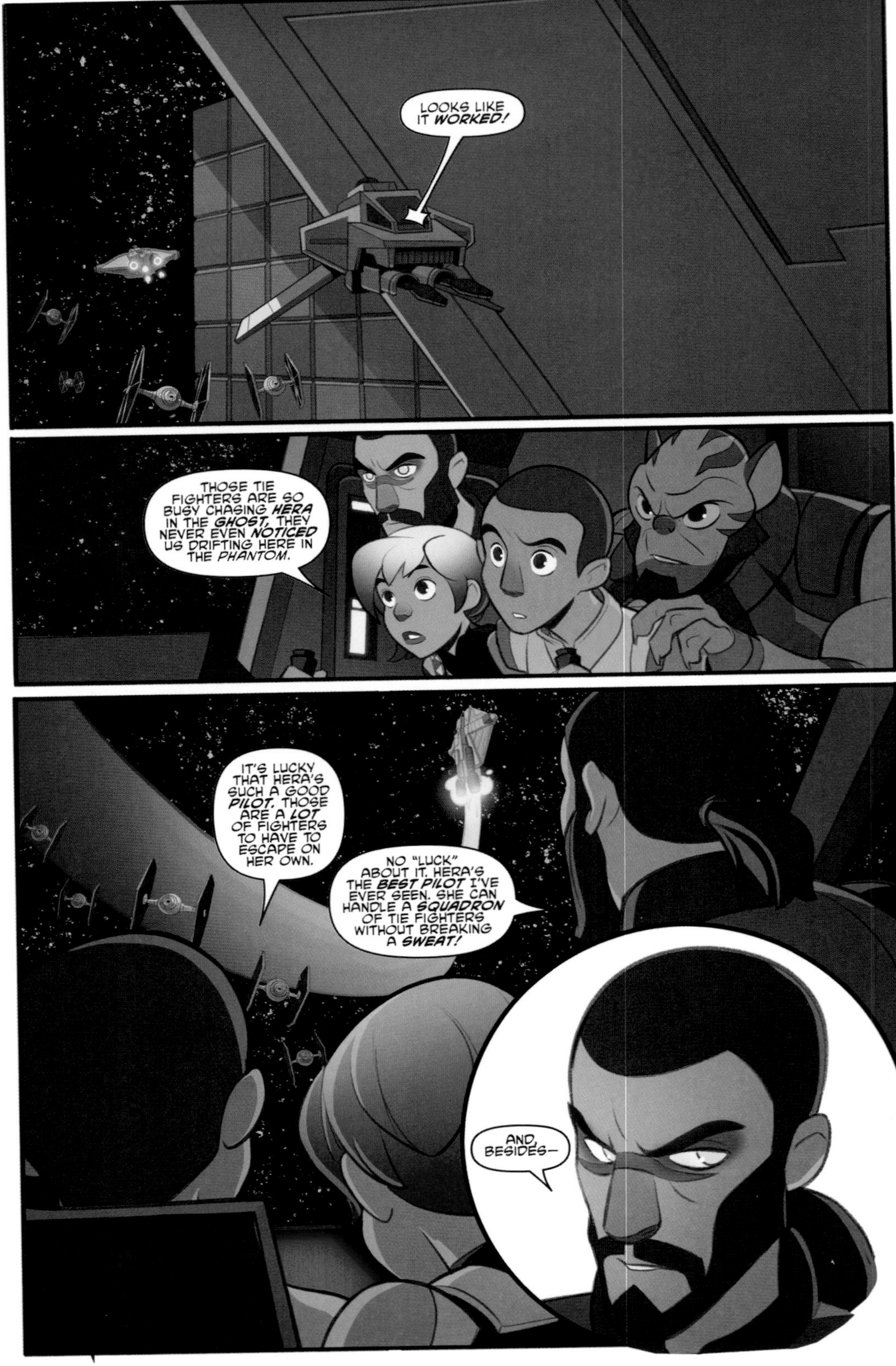
LOOKS LIKE IT WORKED!
THOSE TIE FIGHTERS ARE SO BUSY CHASING HERA IN THE GHOST, THEY NEVER EVEN NOTICED US DRIFTING HERE IN THE PHANTOM.
IT'S LUCKY THAT HERA'S SUCH A GOOD PILOT. THOSE ARE A LOT OF FIGHTERS TO HAVE TO ESCAPE ON HER OWN.
NO "LUCK" ABOUT IT. HERA'S THE BEST PILOT I'VE EVER SEEN. SHE CAN HANDLE A SQUADRON OF TIE FIGHTERS WITHOUT BREAKING A SWEAT!
AND, BESIDES—

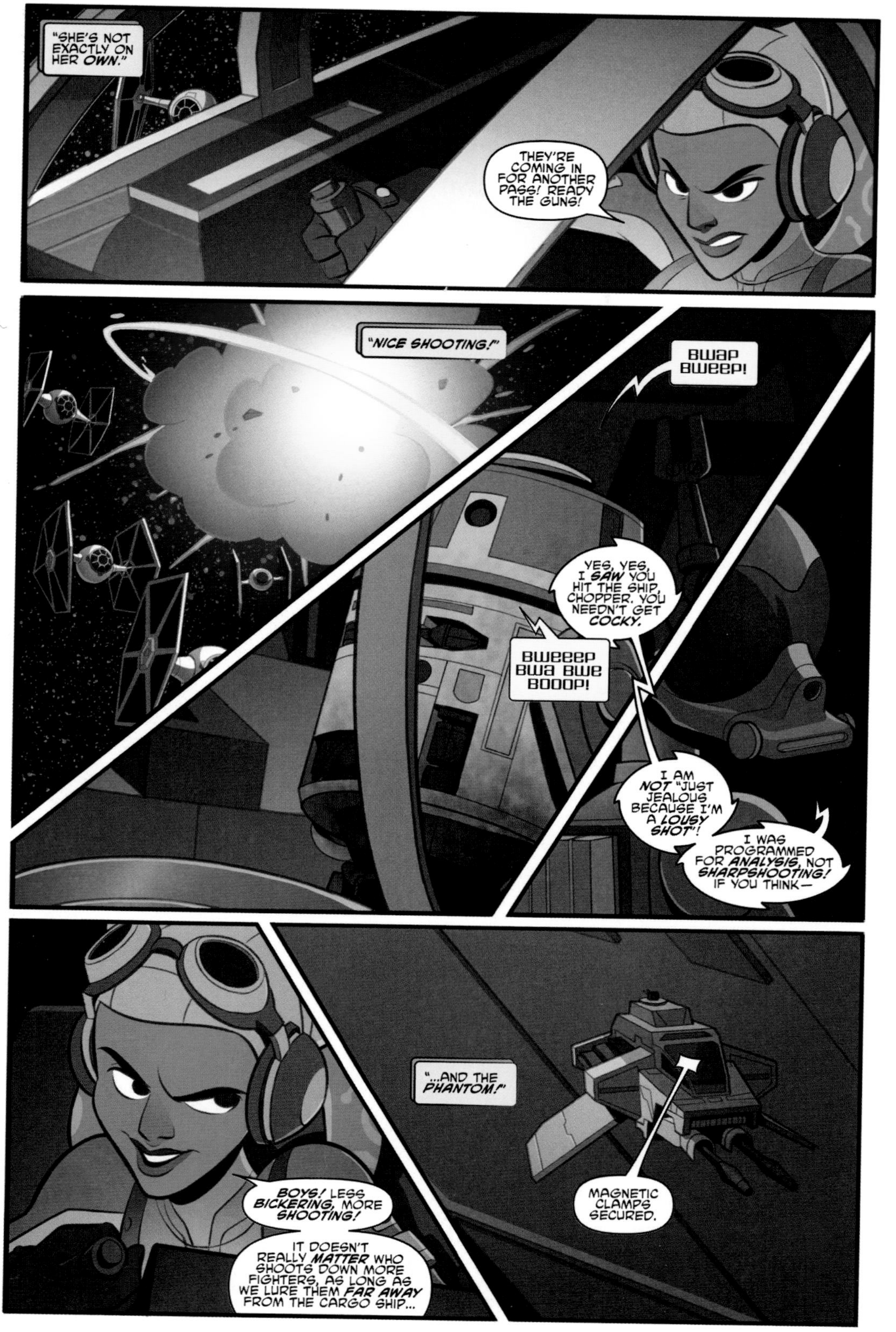
"SHE'S NOT EXACTLY ON HER *OWN.*"
THEY'RE COMING IN FOR ANOTHER PASS! READY THE GUNS!
"NICE SHOOTING!"
BWAP BWEEP!
YES, YES, I *SAW* YOU HIT THE SHIP, CHOPPER. YOU NEEDN'T GET *COCKY.*
BWEEEP BWA BWE BOOOP!
I AM *NOT* "JUST JEALOUS BECAUSE I'M A *LOUSY SHOT*"!
I WAS PROGRAMMED FOR *ANALYSIS,* NOT *SHARPSHOOTING!* IF YOU THINK—
BOYS! LESS *BICKERING,* MORE *SHOOTING!*
IT DOESN'T REALLY *MATTER* WHO SHOOTS DOWN MORE FIGHTERS, AS LONG AS WE LURE THEM *FAR AWAY* FROM THE CARGO SHIP...
"...AND THE *PHANTOM!*"
MAGNETIC CLAMPS SECURED.

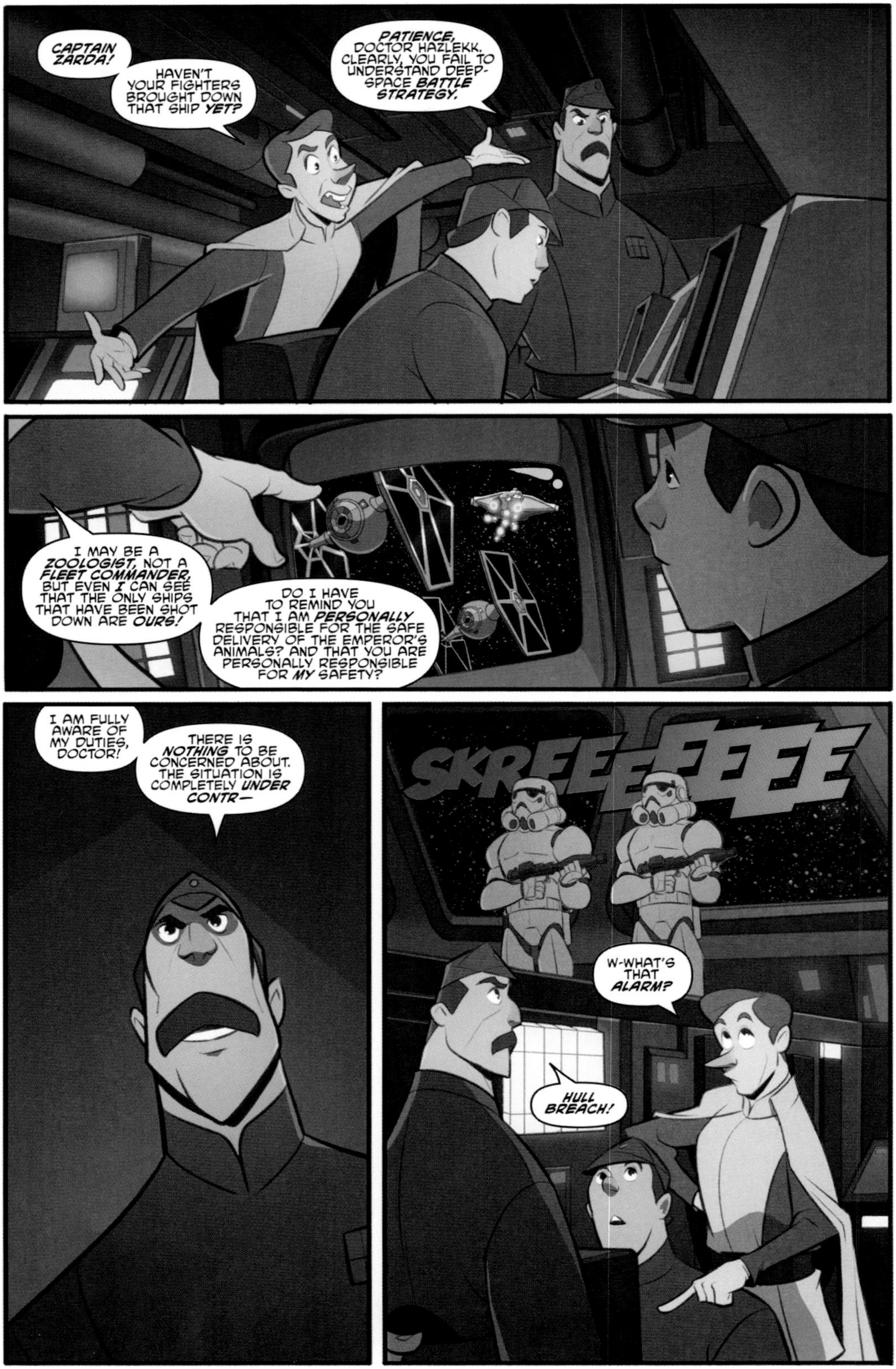
CAPTAIN ZARDA!
HAVEN'T YOUR FIGHTERS BROUGHT DOWN THAT SHIP YET?
PATIENCE, DOCTOR HAZLEKK. CLEARLY, YOU FAIL TO UNDERSTAND DEEP-SPACE BATTLE STRATEGY.
I MAY BE A ZOOLOGIST, NOT A FLEET COMMANDER, BUT EVEN I CAN SEE THAT THE ONLY SHIPS THAT HAVE BEEN SHOT DOWN ARE OURS!
DO I HAVE TO REMIND YOU THAT I AM PERSONALLY RESPONSIBLE FOR THE SAFE DELIVERY OF THE EMPEROR'S ANIMALS? AND THAT YOU ARE PERSONALLY RESPONSIBLE FOR MY SAFETY?
I AM FULLY AWARE OF MY DUTIES, DOCTOR!
THERE IS NOTHING TO BE CONCERNED ABOUT. THE SITUATION IS COMPLETELY UNDER CONTR—
SKREEEEEEEE
W-WHAT'S THAT ALARM?
HULL BREACH!

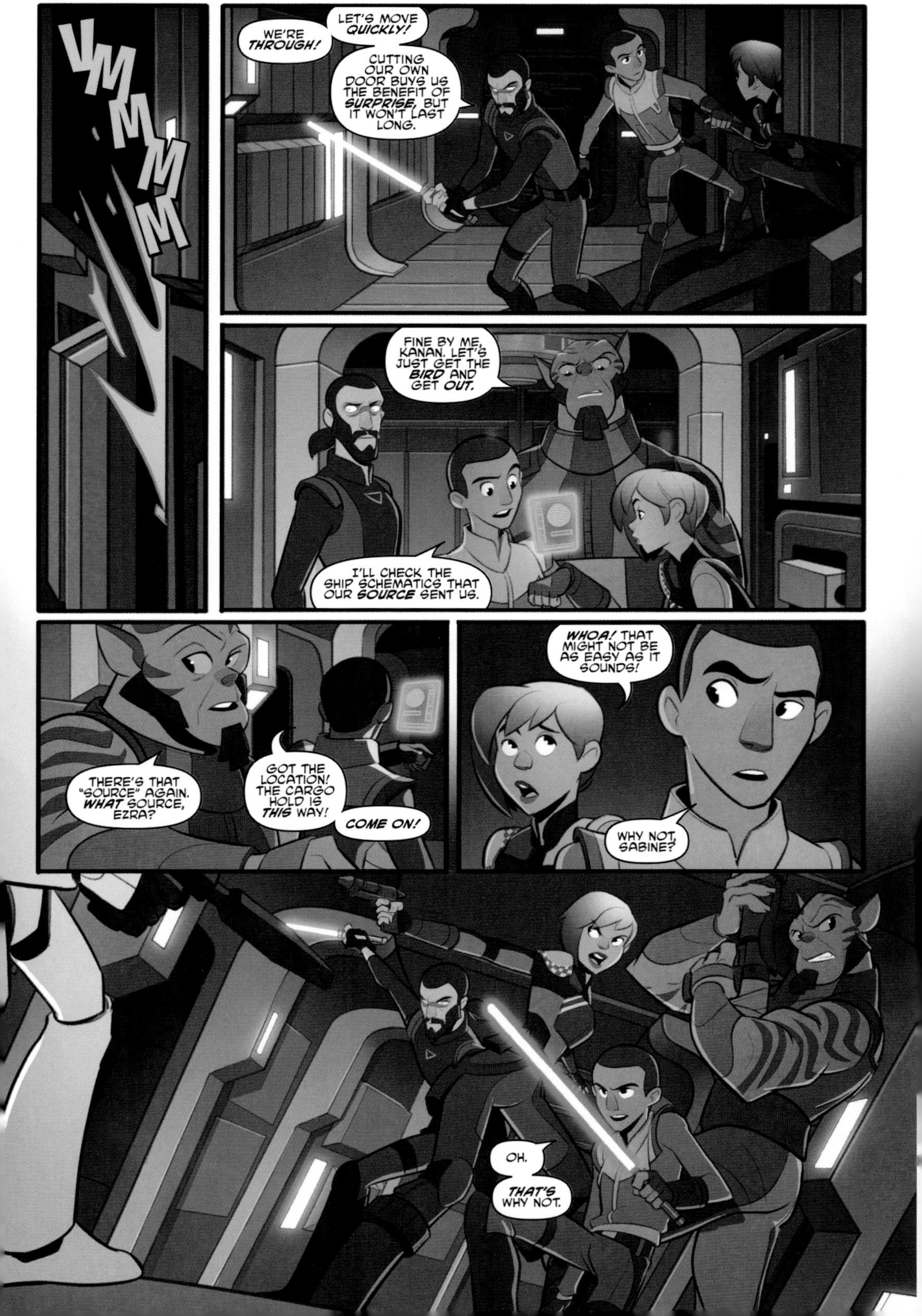
VMMMMM
WE'RE *THROUGH!*
LET'S MOVE *QUICKLY!*
CUTTING OUR OWN DOOR BUYS US THE BENEFIT OF *SURPRISE*, BUT IT WON'T LAST LONG.
FINE BY ME, KANAN. LET'S JUST GET THE *BIRD* AND GET *OUT.*
I'LL CHECK THE SHIP SCHEMATICS THAT OUR *SOURCE* SENT US.
THERE'S THAT "SOURCE" AGAIN. *WHAT* SOURCE, EZRA?
GOT THE LOCATION! THE CARGO HOLD IS *THIS* WAY!
COME ON!
WHOA! THAT MIGHT NOT BE AS EASY AS IT SOUNDS!
WHY NOT, SABINE?
OH.
THAT'S WHY NOT.

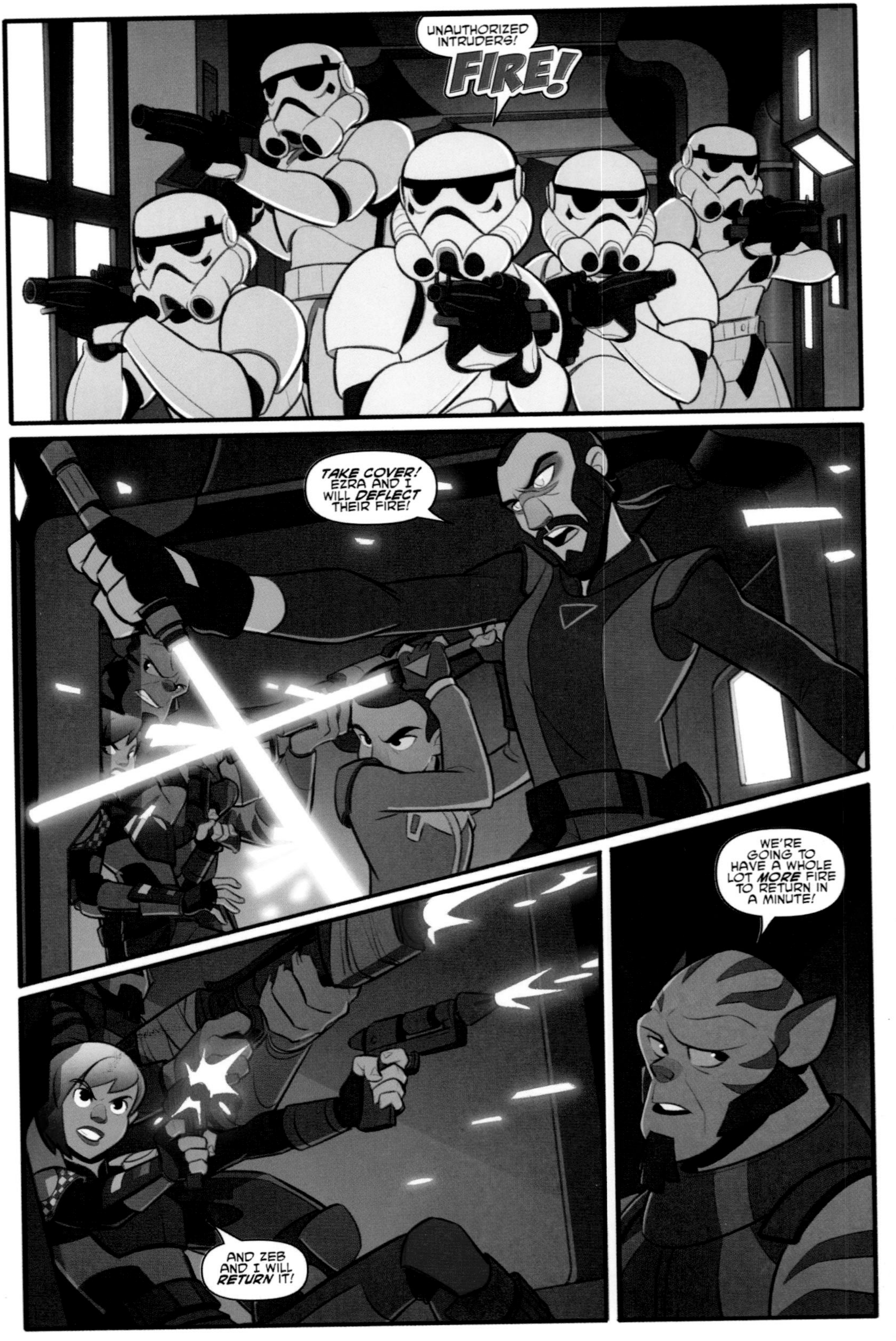
UNAUTHORIZED INTRUDERS! FIRE!
TAKE COVER! EZRA AND I WILL DEFLECT THEIR FIRE!
AND ZEB AND I WILL RETURN IT!
WE'RE GOING TO HAVE A WHOLE LOT MORE FIRE TO RETURN IN A MINUTE!

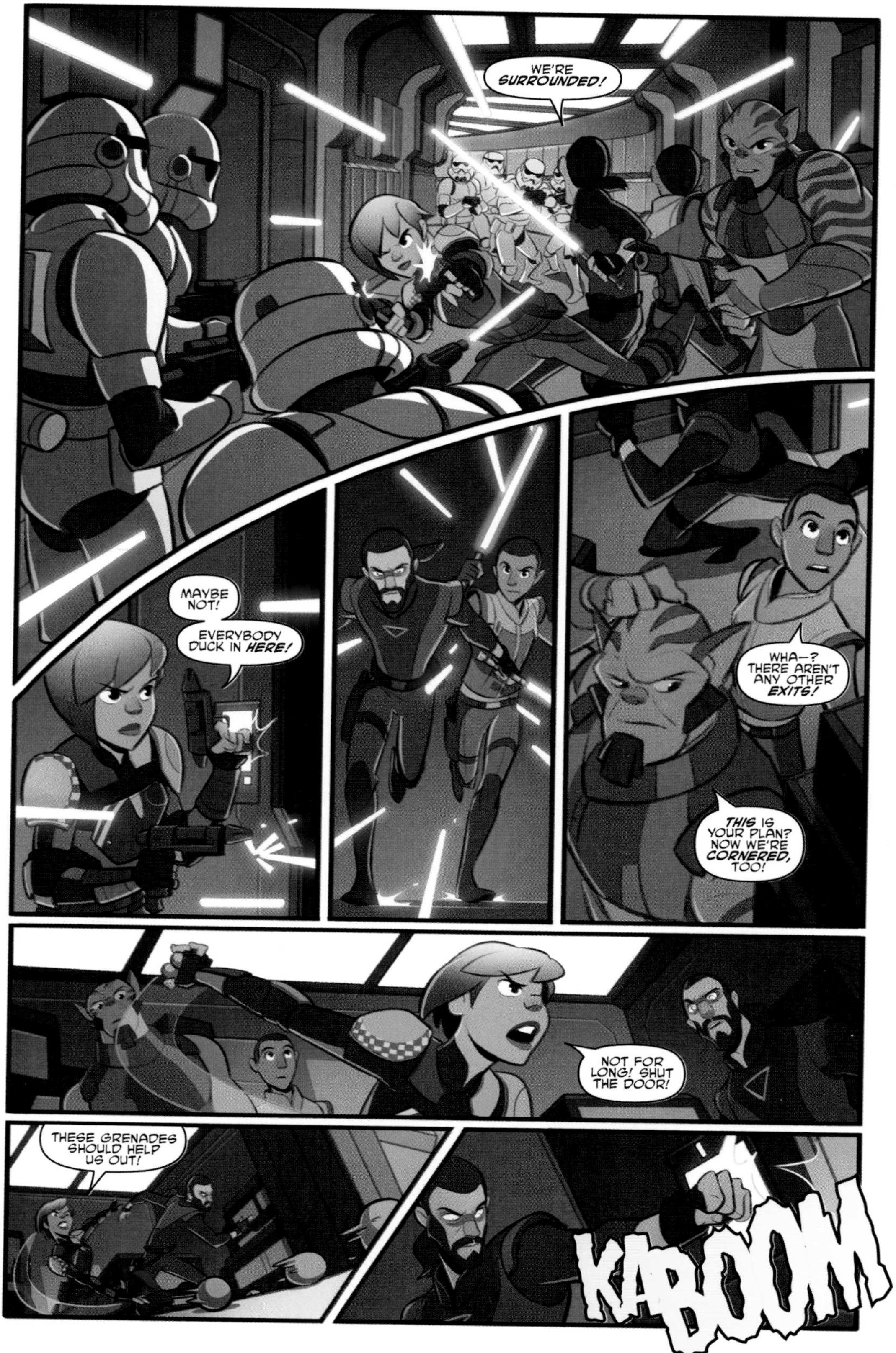
WE'RE *SURROUNDED!*
MAYBE NOT!
EVERYBODY DUCK IN *HERE!*
WHA--? THERE AREN'T ANY OTHER *EXITS!*
THIS IS YOUR PLAN? NOW WE'RE *CORNERED,* TOO!
NOT FOR LONG! SHUT THE DOOR!
THESE GRENADES SHOULD HELP US OUT!
KABOOM

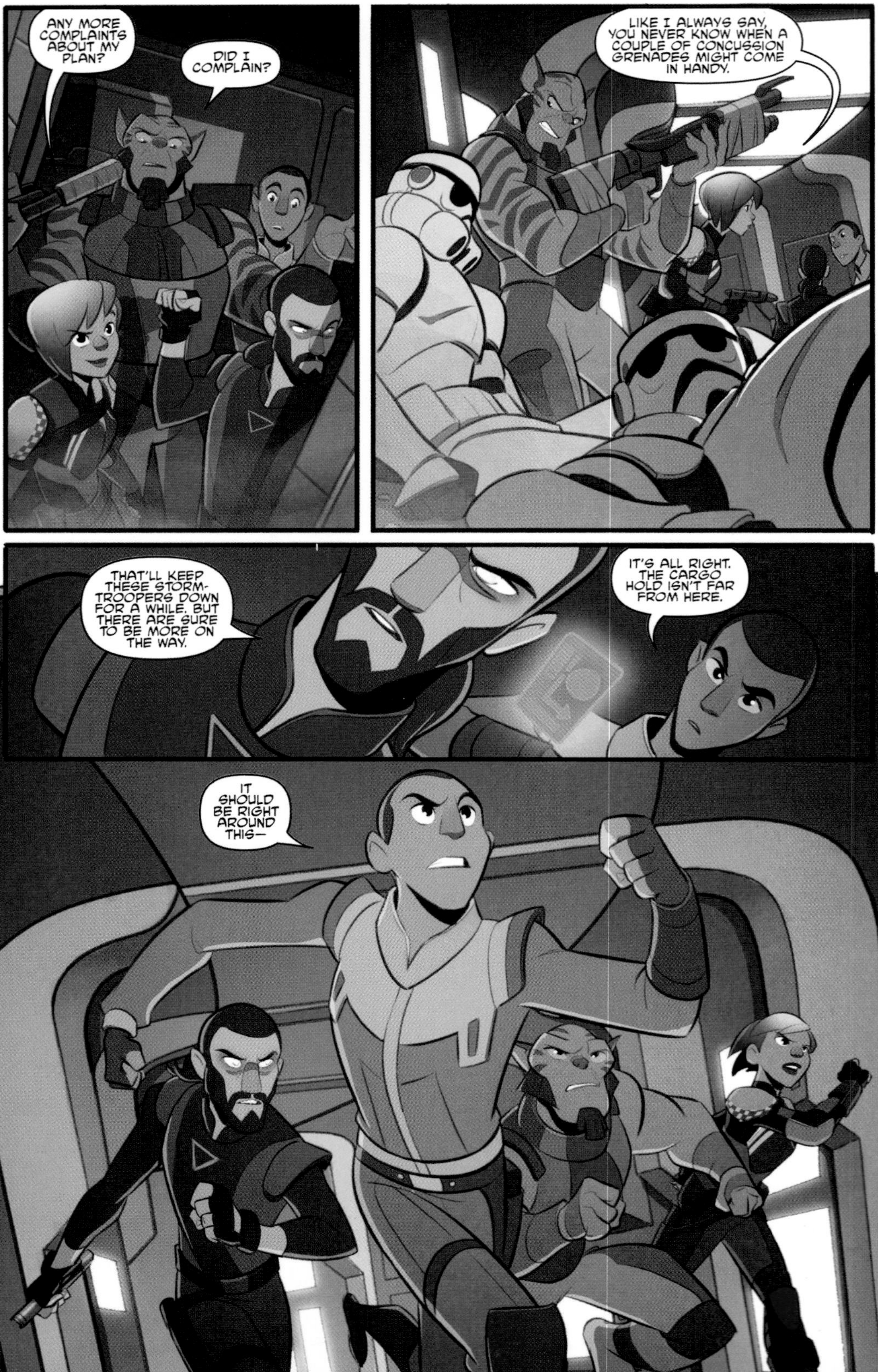
ANY MORE COMPLAINTS ABOUT MY PLAN?
DID I COMPLAIN?
LIKE I ALWAYS SAY, YOU NEVER KNOW WHEN A COUPLE OF CONCUSSION GRENADES MIGHT COME IN HANDY.
THAT'LL KEEP THESE STORM-TROOPERS DOWN FOR A WHILE. BUT THERE ARE SURE TO BE MORE ON THE WAY.
IT'S ALL RIGHT. THE CARGO HOLD ISN'T FAR FROM HERE.
IT SHOULD BE RIGHT AROUND THIS—

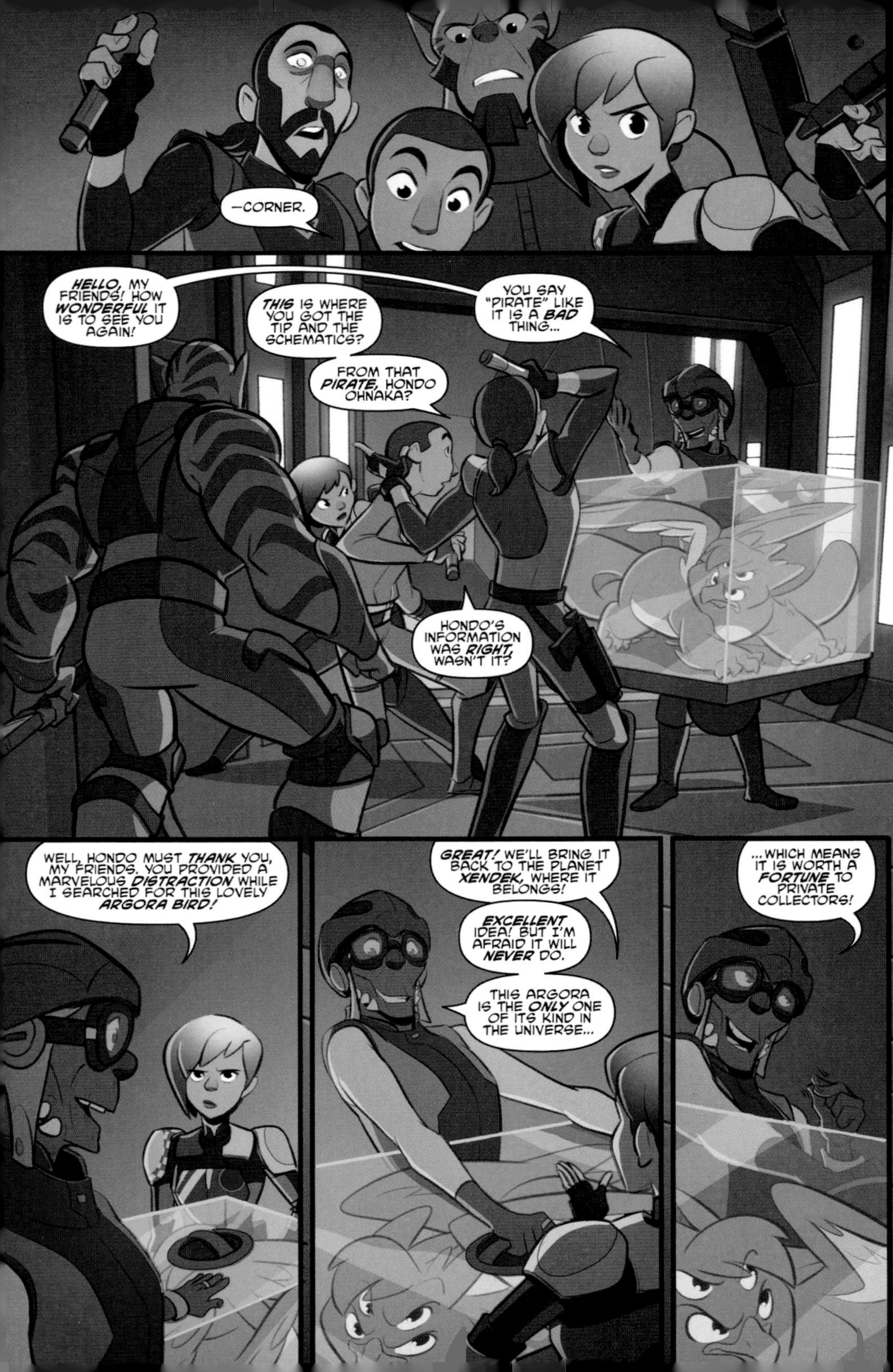

—CORNER.
THIS IS WHERE YOU GOT THE TIP AND THE SCHEMATICS?
FROM THAT PIRATE, HONDO OHNAKA?
HELLO, MY FRIENDS! HOW WONDERFUL IT IS TO SEE YOU AGAIN!
YOU SAY "PIRATE" LIKE IT IS A BAD THING...
HONDO'S INFORMATION WAS RIGHT, WASN'T IT?
WELL, HONDO MUST THANK YOU, MY FRIENDS. YOU PROVIDED A MARVELOUS DISTRACTION WHILE I SEARCHED FOR THIS LOVELY ARGORA BIRD!
GREAT! WE'LL BRING IT BACK TO THE PLANET XENDEK, WHERE IT BELONGS!
EXCELLENT IDEA! BUT I'M AFRAID IT WILL NEVER DO.
THIS ARGORA IS THE ONLY ONE OF ITS KIND IN THE UNIVERSE...
...WHICH MEANS IT IS WORTH A FORTUNE TO PRIVATE COLLECTORS!

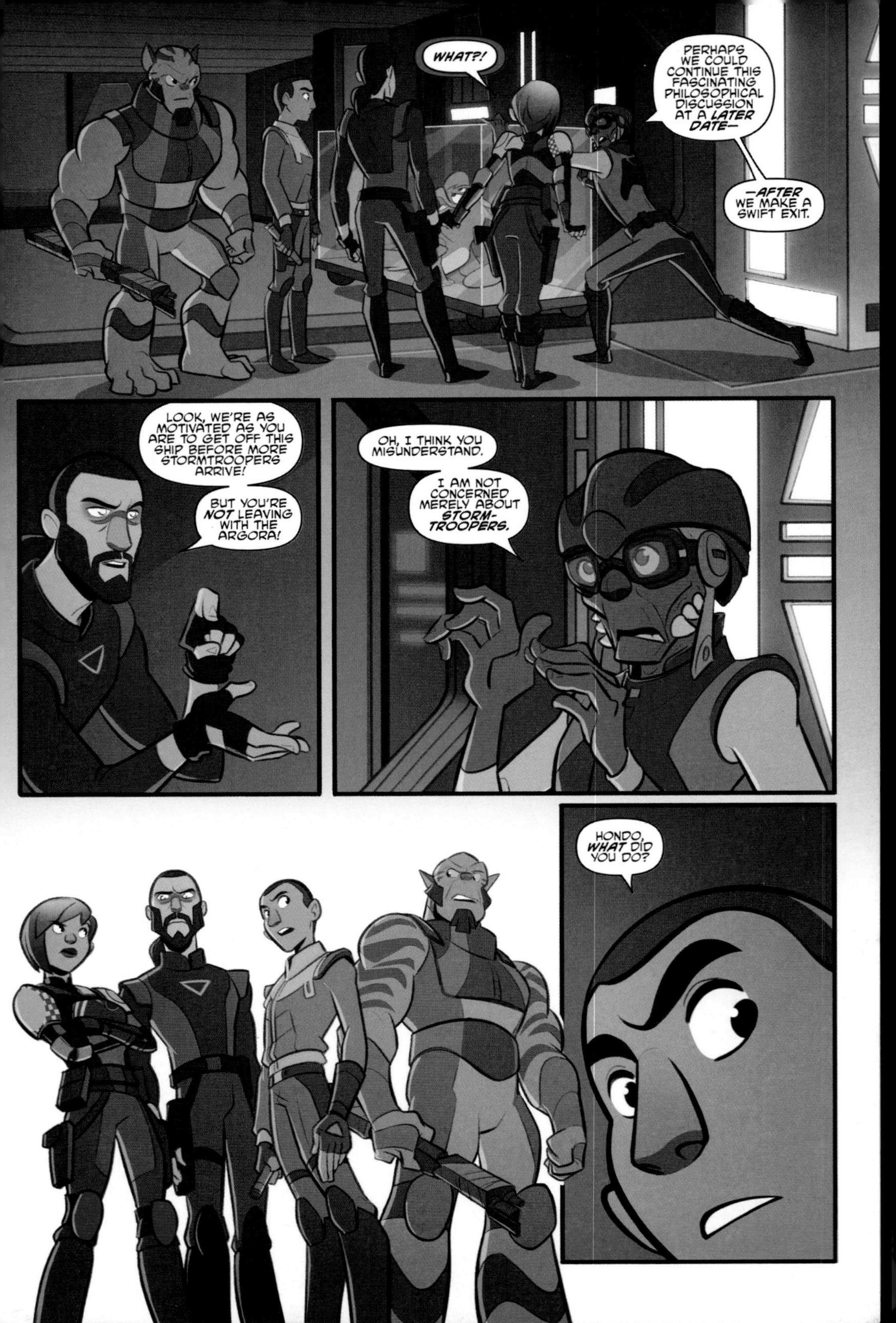
WHAT?!
PERHAPS WE COULD CONTINUE THIS FASCINATING PHILOSOPHICAL DISCUSSION AT A LATER DATE—
—AFTER WE MAKE A SWIFT EXIT.
LOOK, WE'RE AS MOTIVATED AS YOU ARE TO GET OFF THIS SHIP BEFORE MORE STORMTROOPERS ARRIVE!
BUT YOU'RE NOT LEAVING WITH THE ARGORA!
OH, I THINK YOU MISUNDERSTAND.
I AM NOT CONCERNED MERELY ABOUT STORM-TROOPERS.
HONDO, WHAT DID YOU DO?

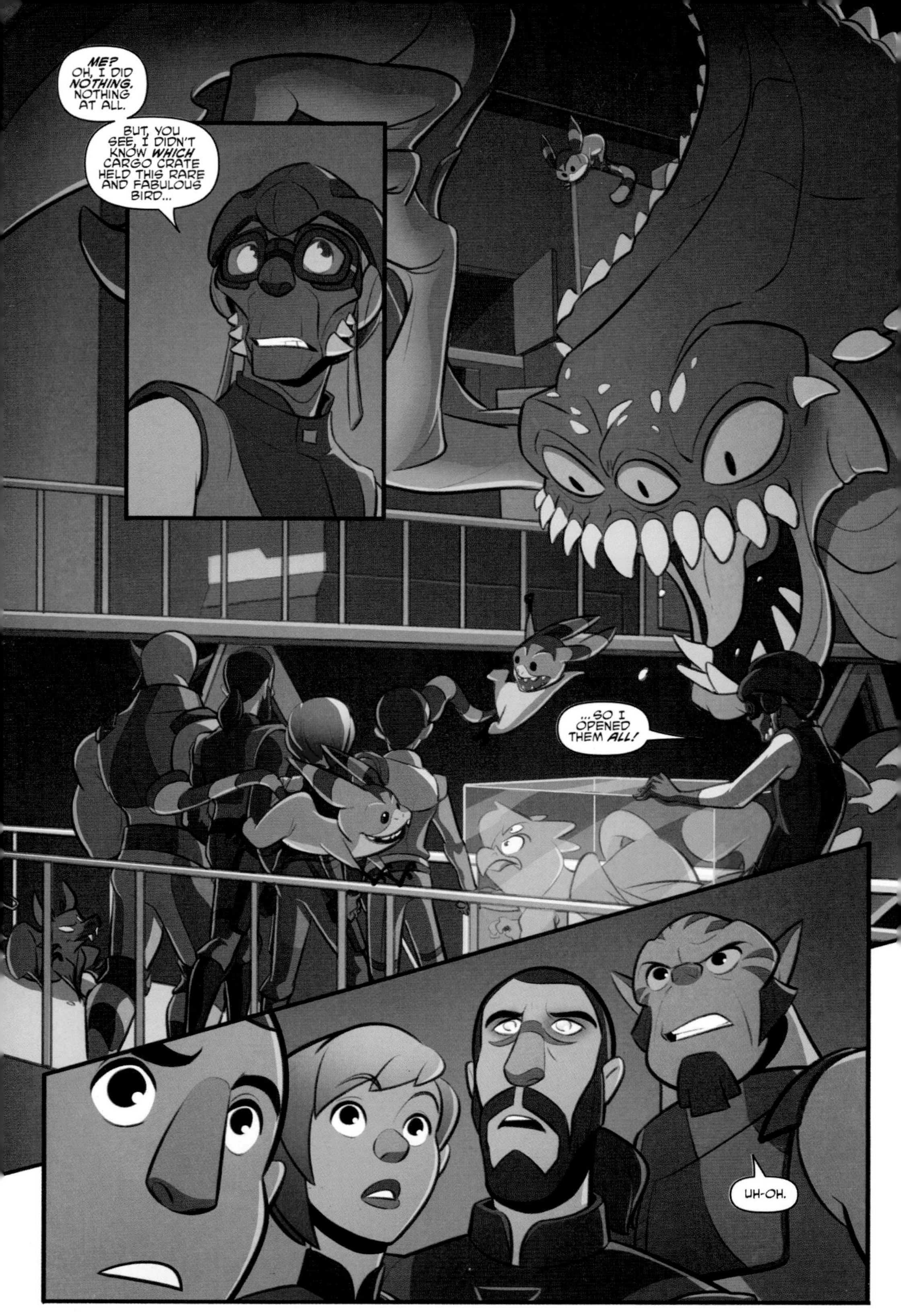
ME? OH, I DID NOTHING, NOTHING AT ALL.
BUT, YOU SEE, I DIDN'T KNOW WHICH CARGO CRATE HELD THIS RARE AND FABULOUS BIRD...
...SO I OPENED THEM ALL!
UH-OH.

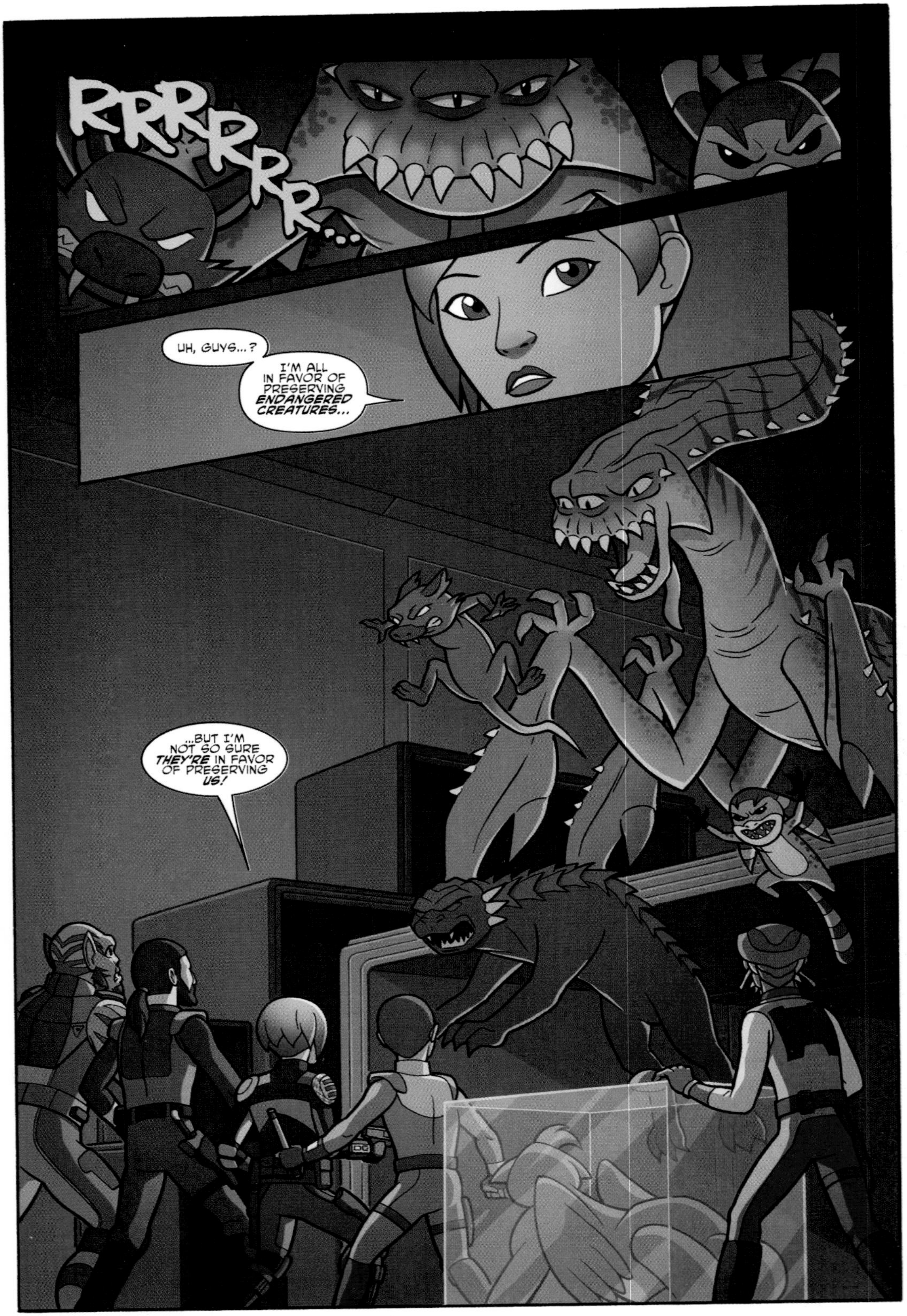
RRRRRRR...
UH, GUYS...?
I'M ALL IN FAVOR OF PRESERVING ENDANGERED CREATURES...
...BUT I'M NOT SO SURE THEY'RE IN FAVOR OF PRESERVING US!

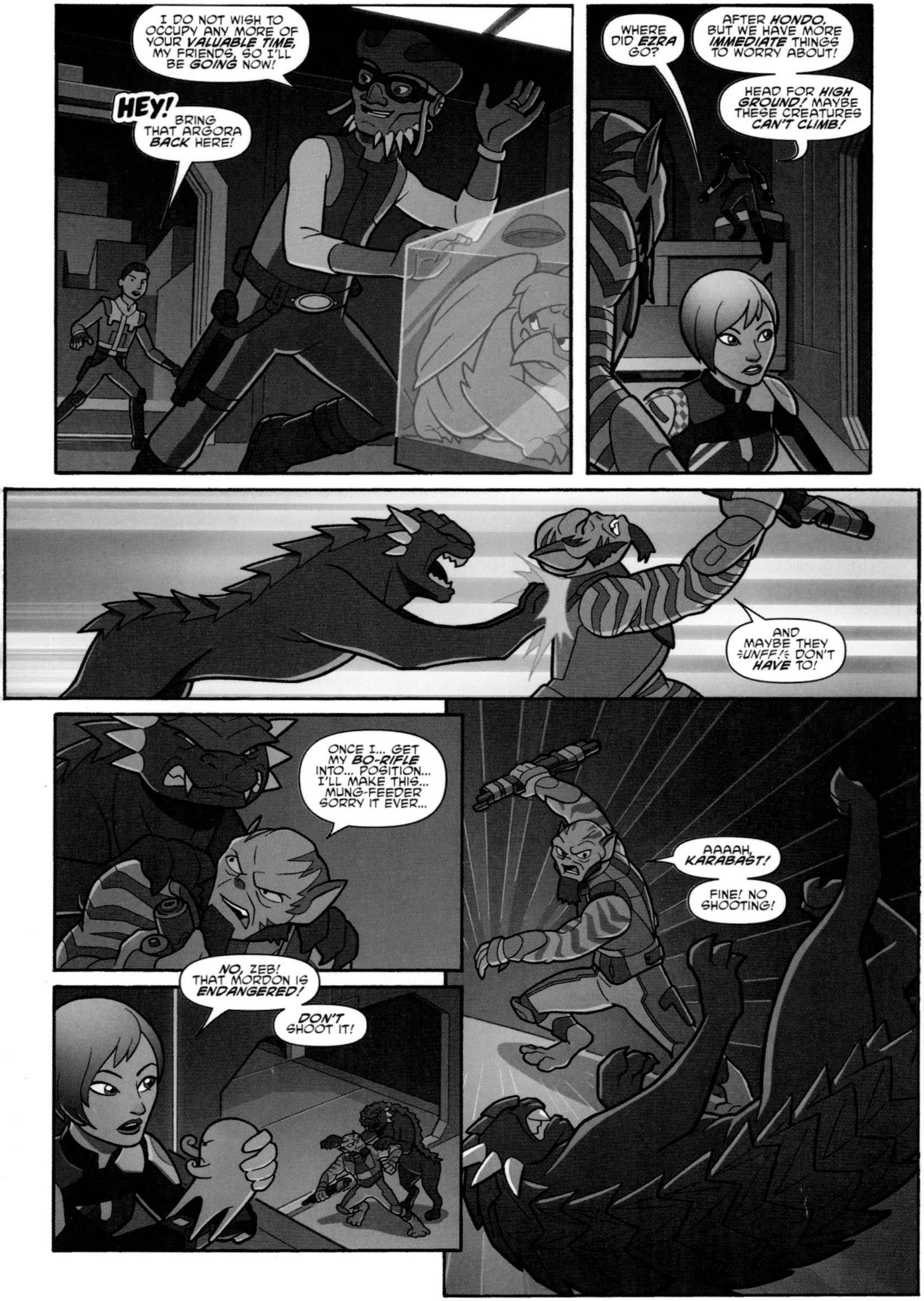
I DO NOT WISH TO OCCUPY ANY MORE OF YOUR VALUABLE TIME, MY FRIENDS, SO I'LL BE GOING NOW!
HEY! BRING THAT ARGORA BACK HERE!
WHERE DID EZRA GO?
AFTER HONDO, BUT WE HAVE MORE IMMEDIATE THINGS TO WORRY ABOUT!
HEAD FOR HIGH GROUND! MAYBE THESE CREATURES CAN'T CLIMB!
AND MAYBE THEY =UNFF!= DON'T HAVE TO!
ONCE I... GET MY BO-RIFLE INTO... POSITION... I'LL MAKE THIS... MUNG-FEEDER SORRY IT EVER...
NO, ZEB! THAT MORDON IS ENDANGERED!
DON'T SHOOT IT!
AAAAH, KARABAST!
FINE! NO SHOOTING!

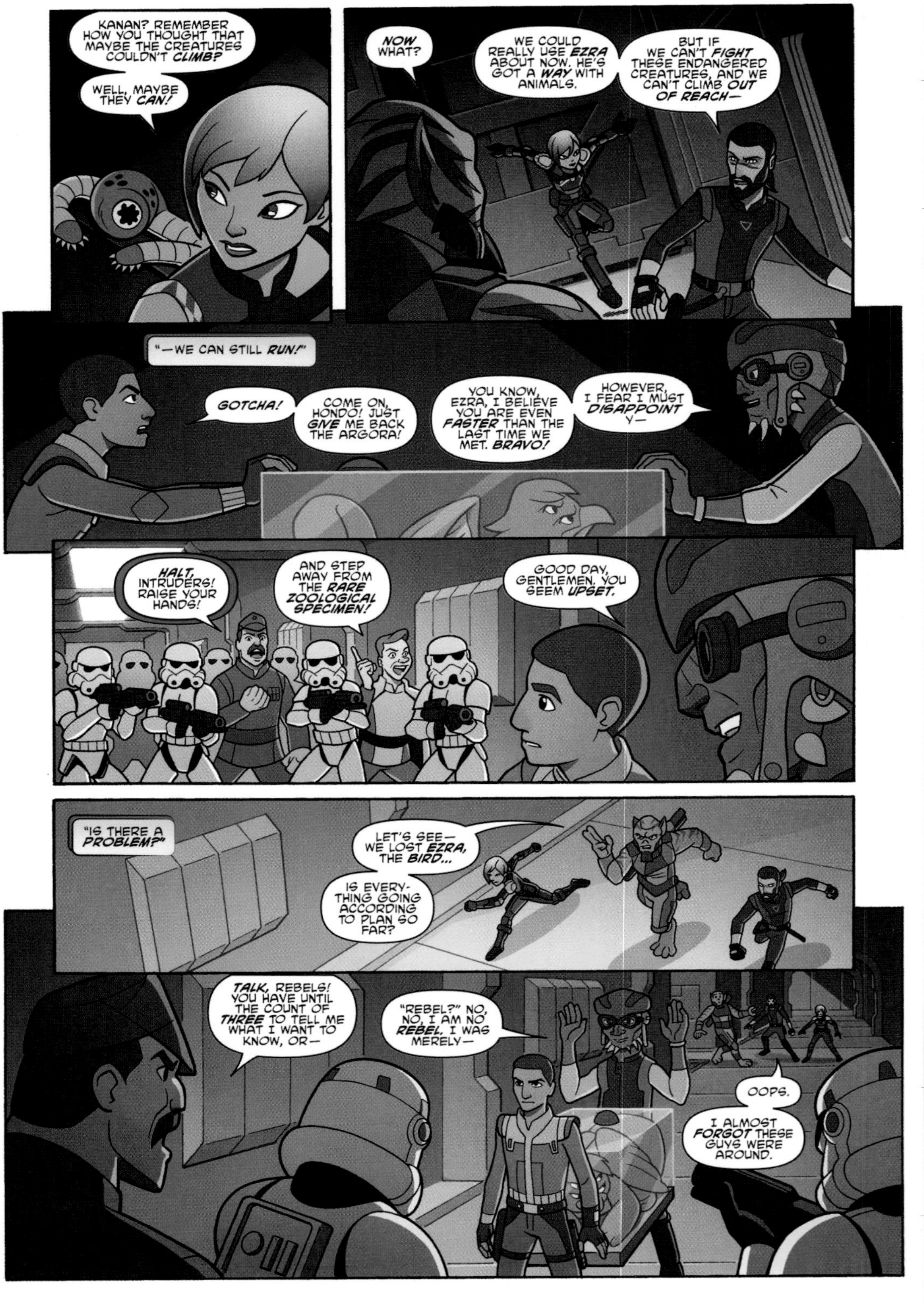

KANAN? REMEMBER HOW YOU THOUGHT THAT MAYBE THE CREATURES COULDN'T *CLIMB?*
WELL, MAYBE THEY *CAN!*
NOW WHAT?
WE COULD REALLY USE *EZRA* ABOUT NOW. HE'S GOT A *WAY* WITH ANIMALS.
BUT IF WE CAN'T *FIGHT* THESE ENDANGERED CREATURES, AND WE CAN'T CLIMB *OUT OF REACH—*
"—WE CAN STILL *RUN!"*
GOTCHA!
COME ON, HONDO! JUST *GIVE* ME BACK THE ARGORA!
YOU KNOW, EZRA, I BELIEVE YOU ARE EVEN *FASTER* THAN THE LAST TIME WE MET. *BRAVO!*
HOWEVER, I FEAR I MUST *DISAPPOINT* Y—
HALT, INTRUDERS! RAISE YOUR HANDS!
AND STEP AWAY FROM THE *RARE ZOOLOGICAL SPECIMEN!*
GOOD DAY, GENTLEMEN. YOU SEEM *UPSET.*
"IS THERE A *PROBLEM?"*
LET'S SEE— WE LOST *EZRA*, THE *BIRD...*
IS EVERY-THING GOING ACCORDING TO PLAN SO FAR?
TALK, REBELS! YOU HAVE UNTIL THE COUNT OF *THREE* TO TELL ME WHAT I WANT TO KNOW, OR—
"REBEL?" NO, NO, I AM NO *REBEL*. I WAS MERELY—
OOPS.
I ALMOST *FORGOT* THESE GUYS WERE AROUND.

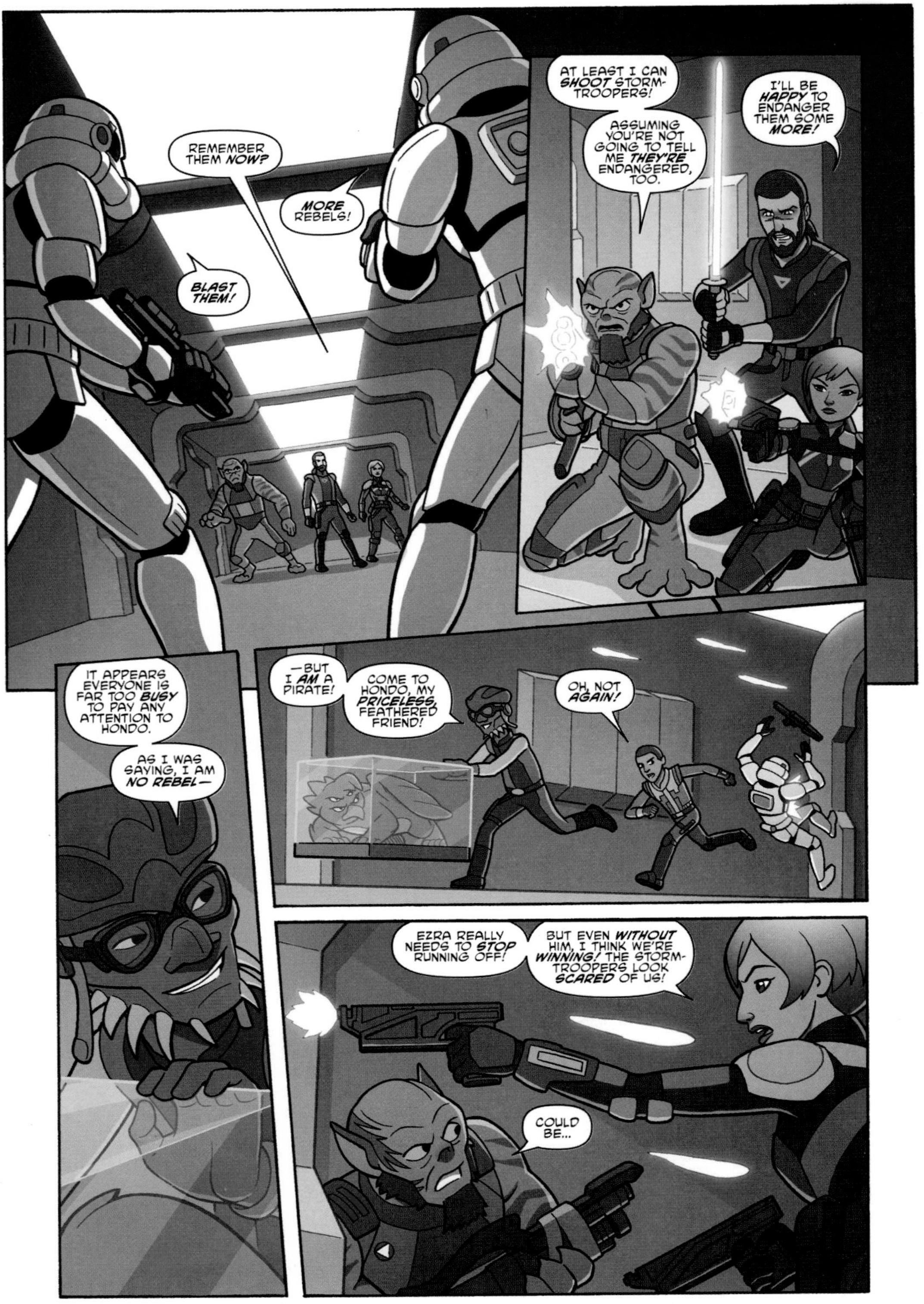
REMEMBER THEM NOW?
MORE REBELS!
BLAST THEM!
AT LEAST I CAN SHOOT STORM-TROOPERS!
ASSUMING YOU'RE NOT GOING TO TELL ME THEY'RE ENDANGERED, TOO.
I'LL BE HAPPY TO ENDANGER THEM SOME MORE!
IT APPEARS EVERYONE IS FAR TOO BUSY TO PAY ANY ATTENTION TO HONDO.
AS I WAS SAYING, I AM NO REBEL—
—BUT I AM A PIRATE!
COME TO HONDO, MY PRICELESS, FEATHERED FRIEND!
OH, NOT AGAIN!
EZRA REALLY NEEDS TO STOP RUNNING OFF!
BUT EVEN WITHOUT HIM, I THINK WE'RE WINNING! THE STORM-TROOPERS LOOK SCARED OF US!
COULD BE...

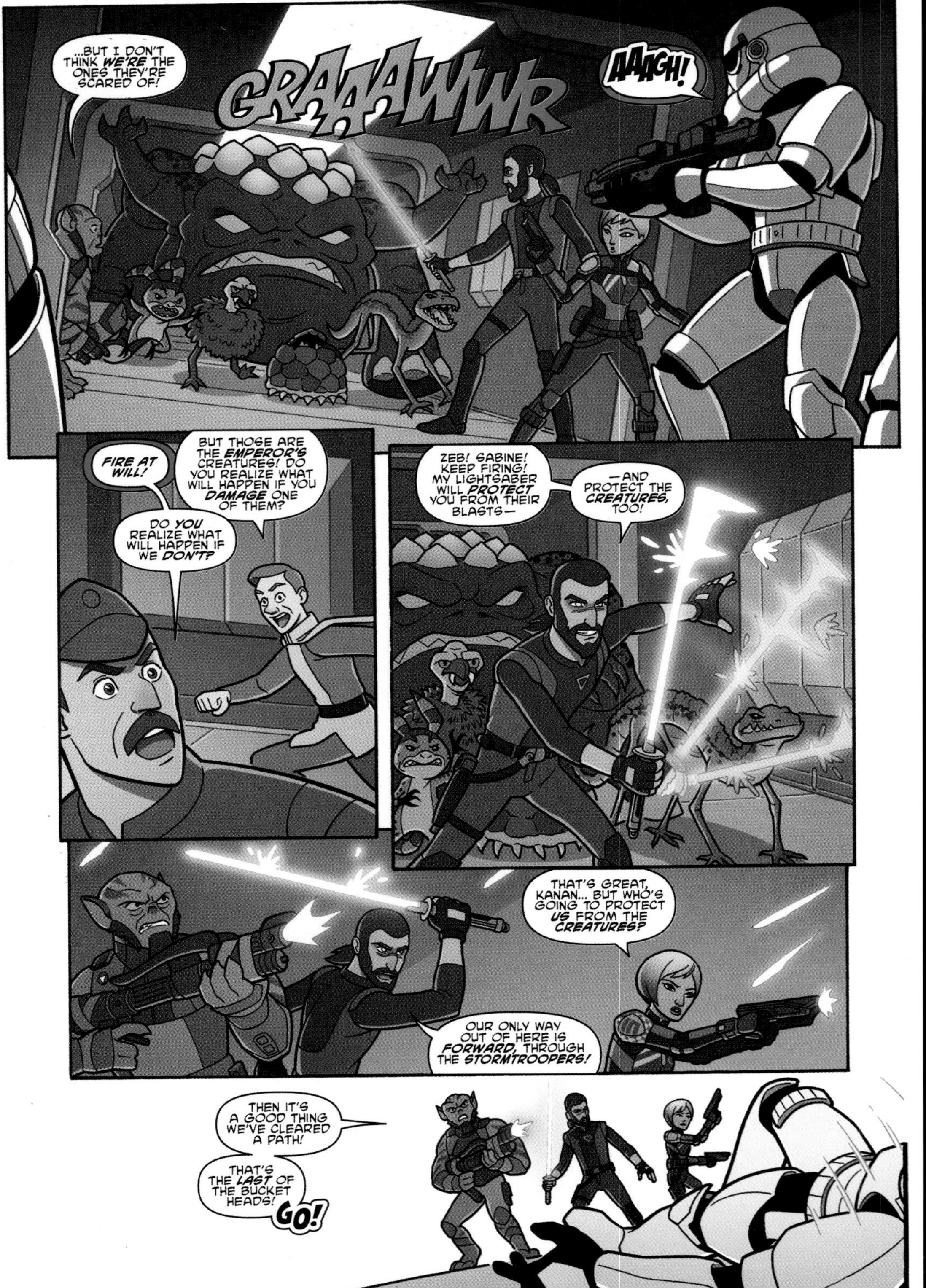
...BUT I DON'T THINK *WE'RE* THE ONES THEY'RE SCARED OF!
GRAAAWWR
AAAGH!
FIRE AT WILL!
BUT THOSE ARE THE *EMPEROR'S* CREATURES! DO YOU REALIZE WHAT WILL HAPPEN IF YOU *DAMAGE* ONE OF THEM?
DO *YOU* REALIZE WHAT WILL HAPPEN IF WE *DON'T?*
ZEB! SABINE! KEEP FIRING! MY LIGHTSABER WILL *PROTECT* YOU FROM THEIR BLASTS—
—AND PROTECT THE *CREATURES,* TOO!
THAT'S GREAT, KANAN... BUT WHO'S GOING TO PROTECT *US* FROM THE *CREATURES?*
OUR ONLY WAY OUT OF HERE IS *FORWARD,* THROUGH THE *STORMTROOPERS!*
THEN IT'S A GOOD THING WE'VE CLEARED A PATH!
THAT'S THE *LAST* OF THE BUCKET HEADS! GO!

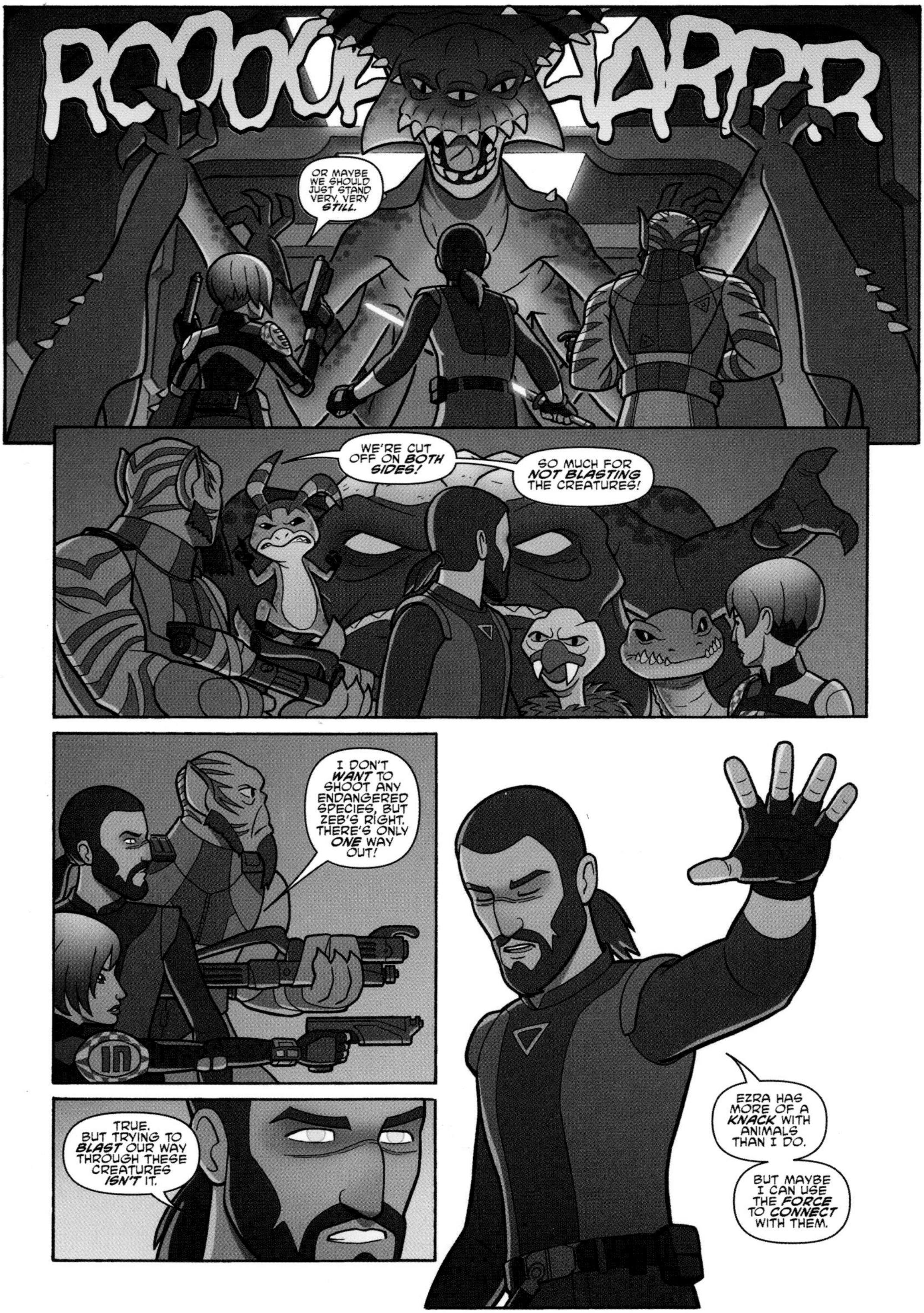
OR MAYBE WE SHOULD JUST STAND VERY, VERY STILL.
WE'RE CUT OFF ON BOTH SIDES!
SO MUCH FOR NOT BLASTING THE CREATURES!
I DON'T WANT TO SHOOT ANY ENDANGERED SPECIES, BUT ZEB'S RIGHT. THERE'S ONLY ONE WAY OUT!
TRUE. BUT TRYING TO BLAST OUR WAY THROUGH THESE CREATURES ISN'T IT.
EZRA HAS MORE OF A KNACK WITH ANIMALS THAN I DO.
BUT MAYBE I CAN USE THE FORCE TO CONNECT WITH THEM.

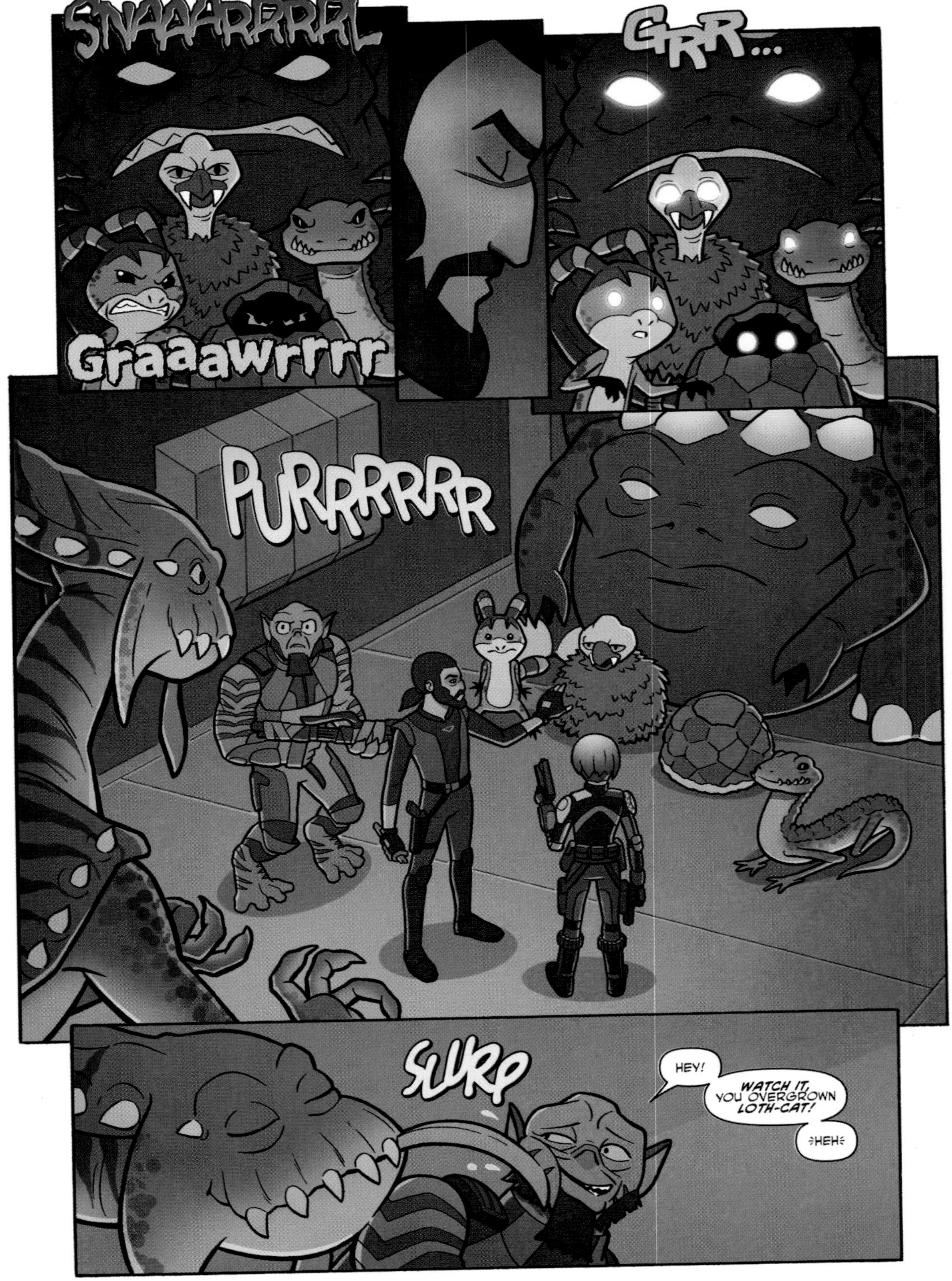
SNAAARRRRL
Graaawrrrr
GRR...
PURRRRRR
SLURP
HEY!
WATCH IT, YOU OVERGROWN LOTH-CAT!
HEH

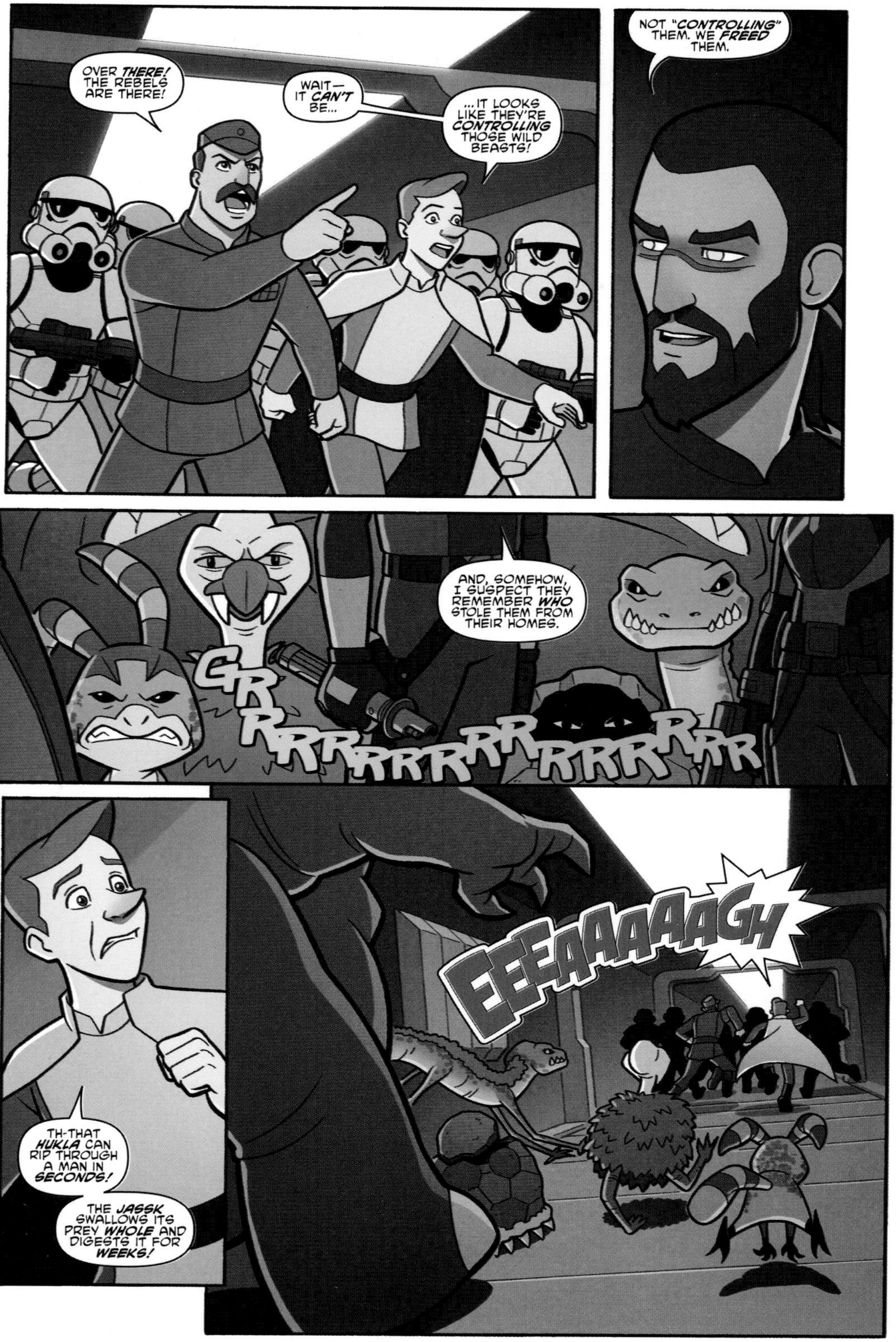

OVER THERE! THE REBELS ARE THERE!
WAIT— IT CAN'T BE...
...IT LOOKS LIKE THEY'RE CONTROLLING THOSE WILD BEASTS!
NOT "CONTROLLING" THEM. WE FREED THEM.
AND, SOMEHOW, I SUSPECT THEY REMEMBER WHO STOLE THEM FROM THEIR HOMES.
GRRRRRRRRRRRRRRRRRRR
TH-THAT HUKLA CAN RIP THROUGH A MAN IN SECONDS!
THE JASSK SWALLOWS ITS PREY WHOLE AND DIGESTS IT FOR WEEKS!
EEEAAAAAAGH

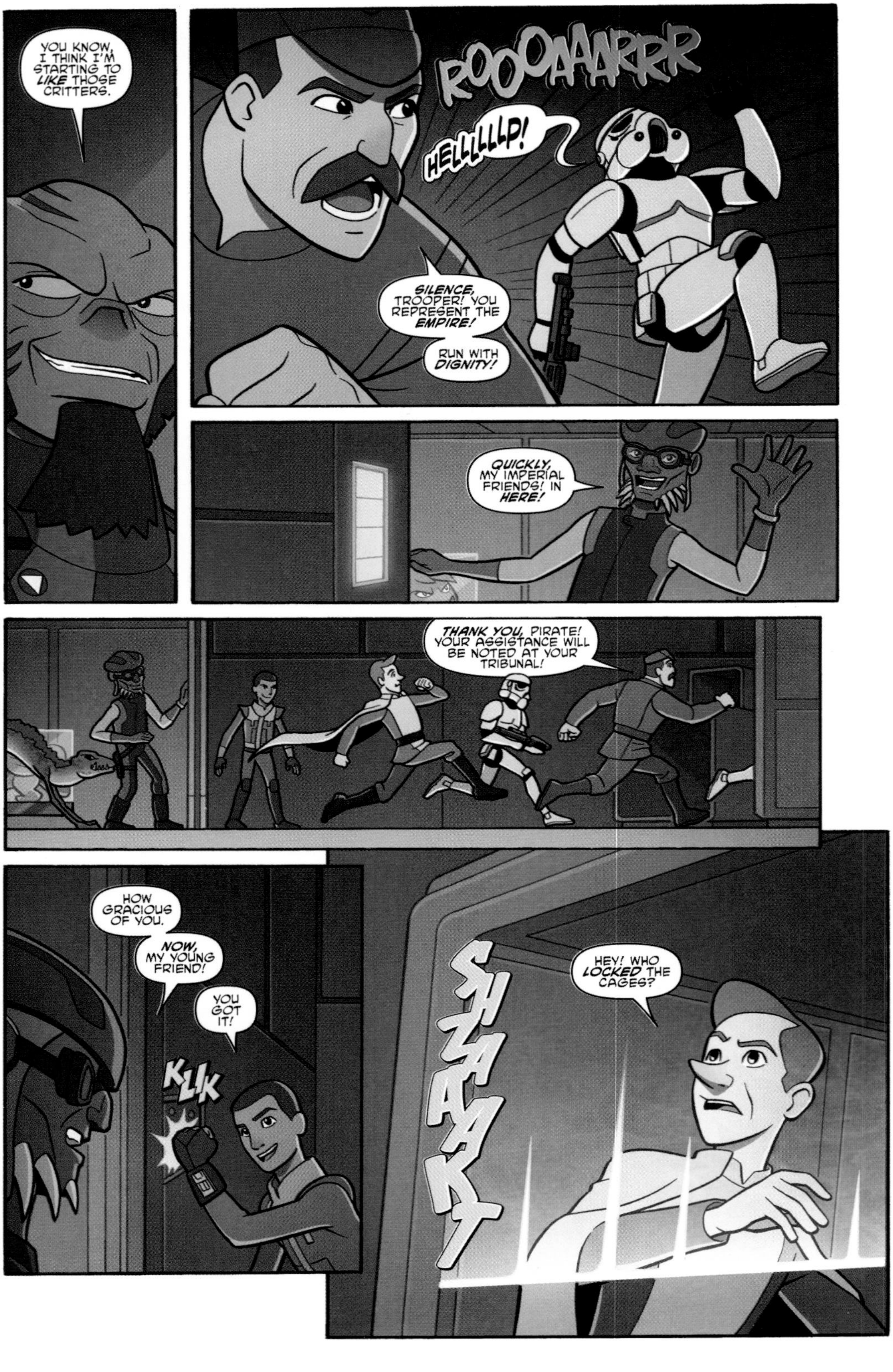

YOU KNOW, I THINK I'M STARTING TO LIKE THOSE CRITTERS.
ROOOAAARRR
HELLLLLLP!
SILENCE, TROOPER! YOU REPRESENT THE EMPIRE!
RUN WITH DIGNITY!
QUICKLY, MY IMPERIAL FRIENDS! IN HERE!
THANK YOU, PIRATE! YOUR ASSISTANCE WILL BE NOTED AT YOUR TRIBUNAL!
HOW GRACIOUS OF YOU.
NOW, MY YOUNG FRIEND!
YOU GOT IT!
KLIK
SHAAAKT
HEY! WHO LOCKED THE CAGES?

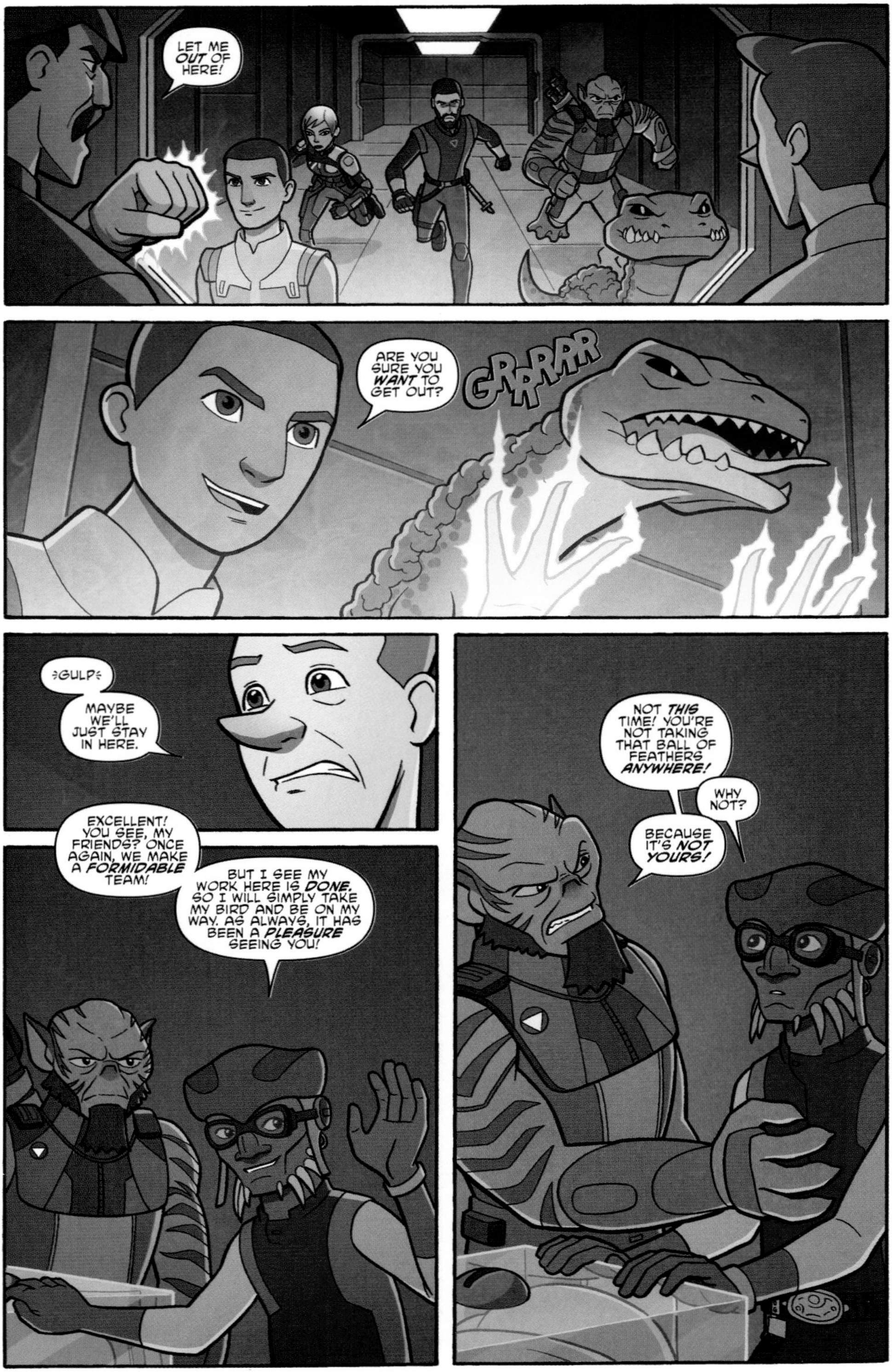
LET ME OUT OF HERE!
ARE YOU SURE YOU WANT TO GET OUT?
GRRRRR
GULP
MAYBE WE'LL JUST STAY IN HERE.
EXCELLENT! YOU SEE, MY FRIENDS? ONCE AGAIN, WE MAKE A FORMIDABLE TEAM!
BUT I SEE MY WORK HERE IS DONE, SO I WILL SIMPLY TAKE MY BIRD AND BE ON MY WAY. AS ALWAYS, IT HAS BEEN A PLEASURE SEEING YOU!
NOT THIS TIME! YOU'RE NOT TAKING THAT BALL OF FEATHERS ANYWHERE!
WHY NOT?
BECAUSE IT'S NOT YOURS!

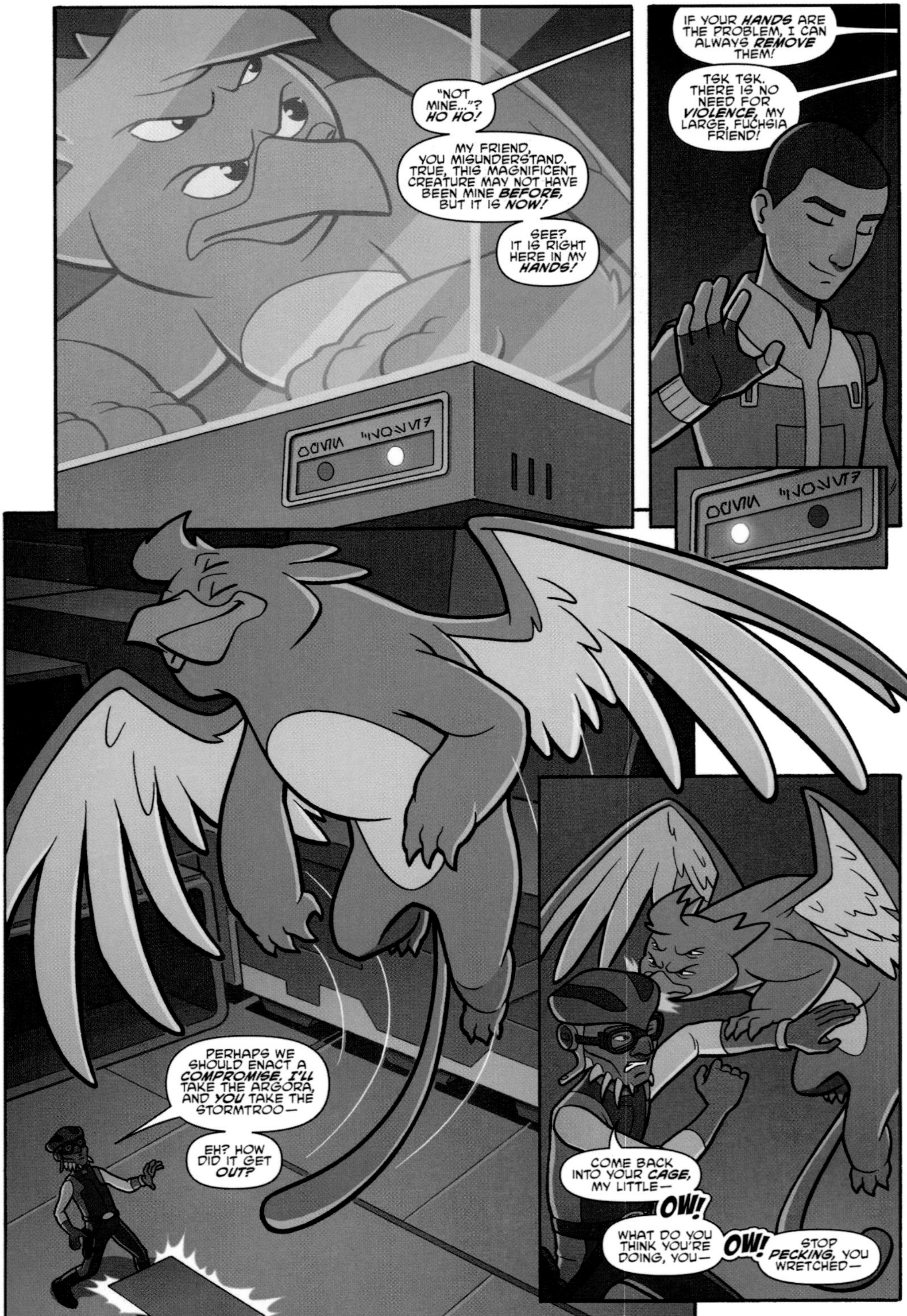
"NOT MINE..."? HO HO!
MY FRIEND, YOU MISUNDERSTAND. TRUE, THIS MAGNIFICENT CREATURE MAY NOT HAVE BEEN MINE BEFORE, BUT IT IS NOW!
SEE? IT IS RIGHT HERE IN MY HANDS!
IF YOUR HANDS ARE THE PROBLEM, I CAN ALWAYS REMOVE THEM!
TSK TSK. THERE IS NO NEED FOR VIOLENCE, MY LARGE, FUCHSIA FRIEND!
PERHAPS WE SHOULD ENACT A COMPROMISE. I'LL TAKE THE ARGORA, AND YOU TAKE THE STORMTROO—
EH? HOW DID IT GET OUT?
COME BACK INTO YOUR CAGE, MY LITTLE—
OW!
WHAT DO YOU THINK YOU'RE DOING, YOU—
OW!
STOP PECKING, YOU WRETCHED—

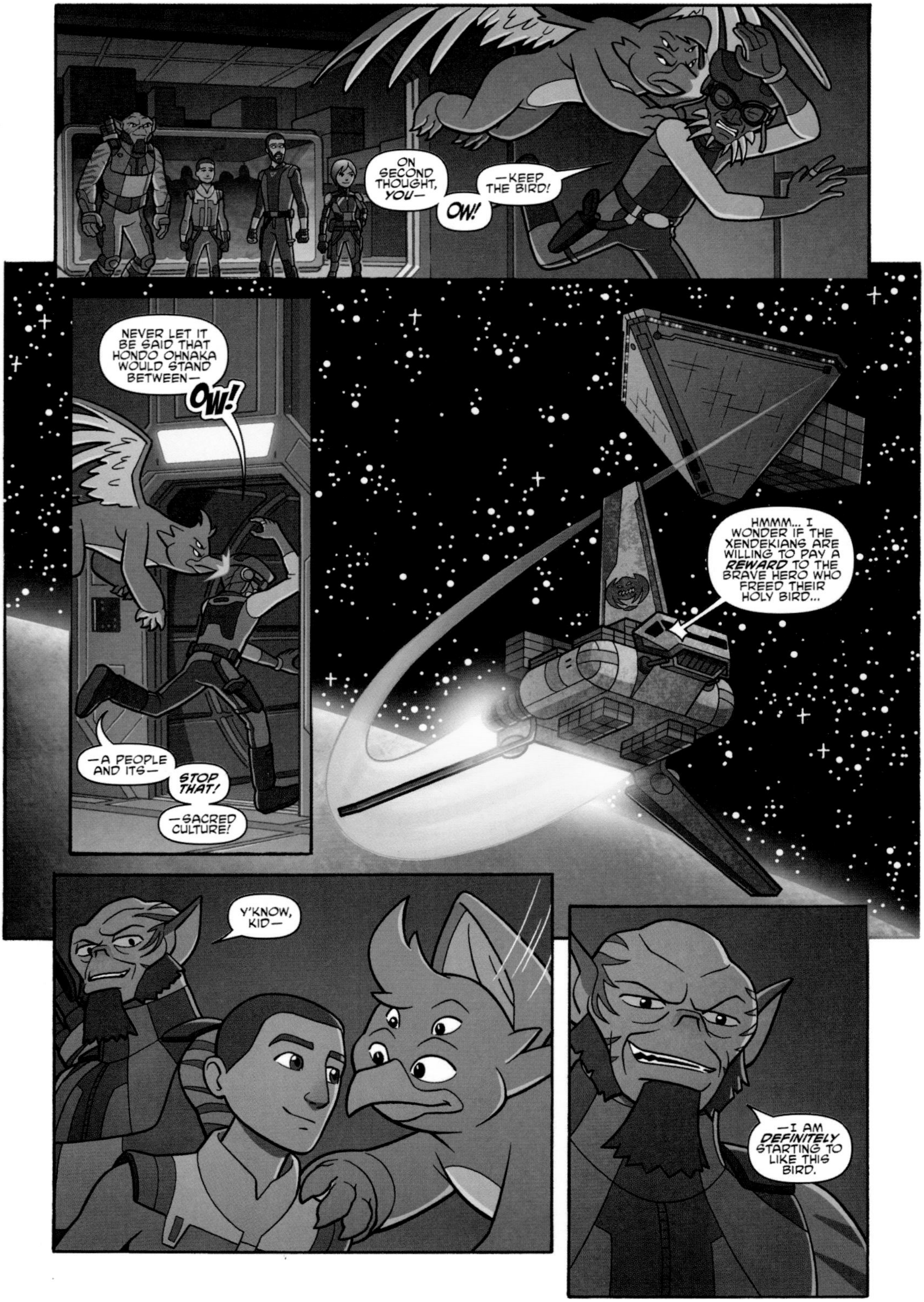
ON SECOND THOUGHT, YOU—
OW!
—KEEP THE BIRD!
NEVER LET IT BE SAID THAT HONDO OHNAKA WOULD STAND BETWEEN—
OW!
—A PEOPLE AND ITS—
STOP THAT!
—SACRED CULTURE!
HMMM... I WONDER IF THE XENDEKIANS ARE WILLING TO PAY A REWARD TO THE BRAVE HERO WHO FREED THEIR HOLY BIRD...
Y'KNOW, KID—
—I AM DEFINITELY STARTING TO LIKE THIS BIRD.

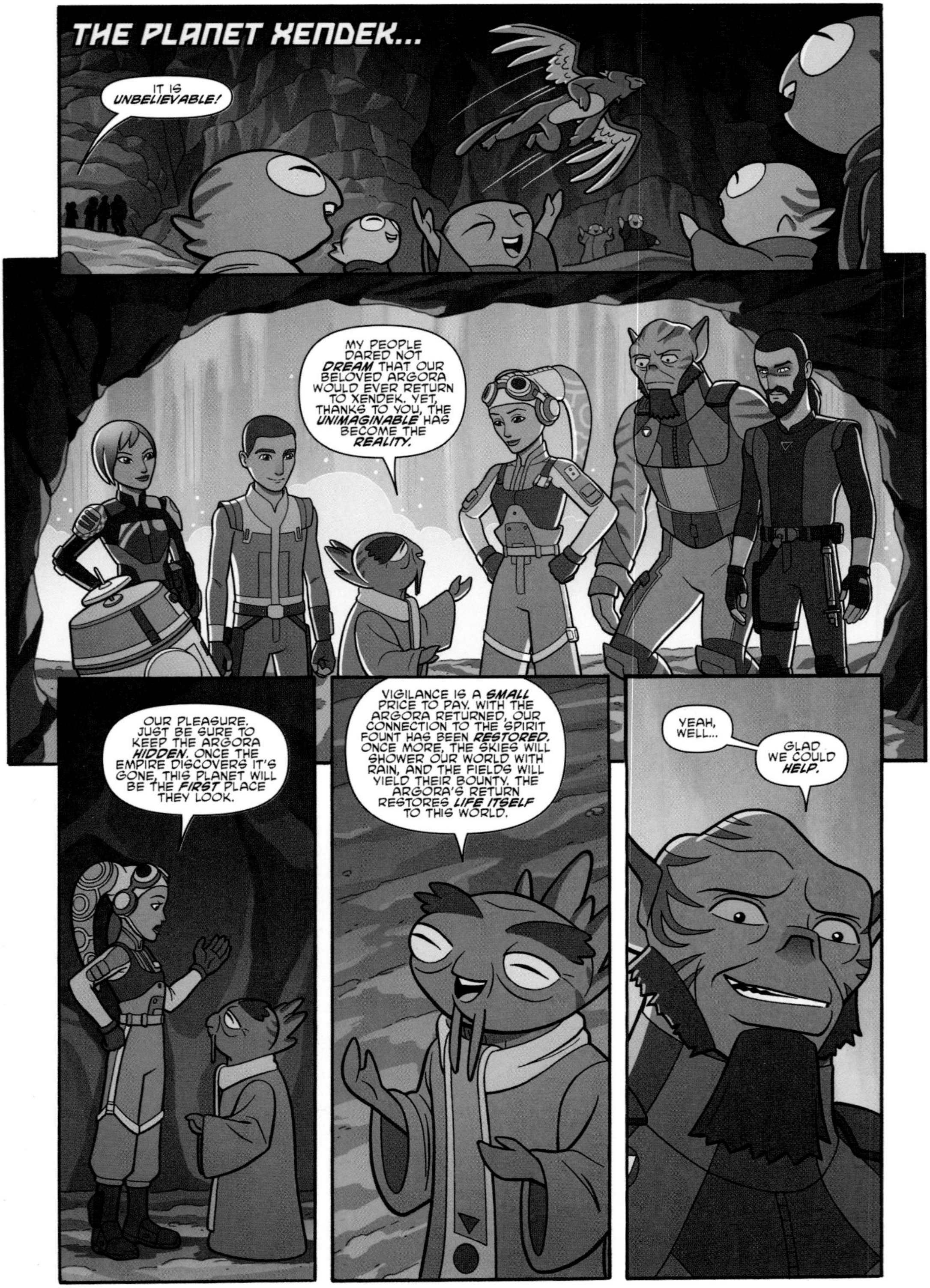
THE PLANET XENDEK...
IT IS UNBELIEVABLE!
MY PEOPLE DARED NOT DREAM THAT OUR BELOVED ARGORA WOULD EVER RETURN TO XENDEK. YET, THANKS TO YOU, THE UNIMAGINABLE HAS BECOME THE REALITY.
OUR PLEASURE. JUST BE SURE TO KEEP THE ARGORA HIDDEN. ONCE THE EMPIRE DISCOVERS IT'S GONE, THIS PLANET WILL BE THE FIRST PLACE THEY LOOK.
VIGILANCE IS A SMALL PRICE TO PAY. WITH THE ARGORA RETURNED, OUR CONNECTION TO THE SPIRIT FOUNT HAS BEEN RESTORED. ONCE MORE, THE SKIES WILL SHOWER OUR WORLD WITH RAIN, AND THE FIELDS WILL YIELD THEIR BOUNTY. THE ARGORA'S RETURN RESTORES LIFE ITSELF TO THIS WORLD.
YEAH, WELL...
GLAD WE COULD HELP.

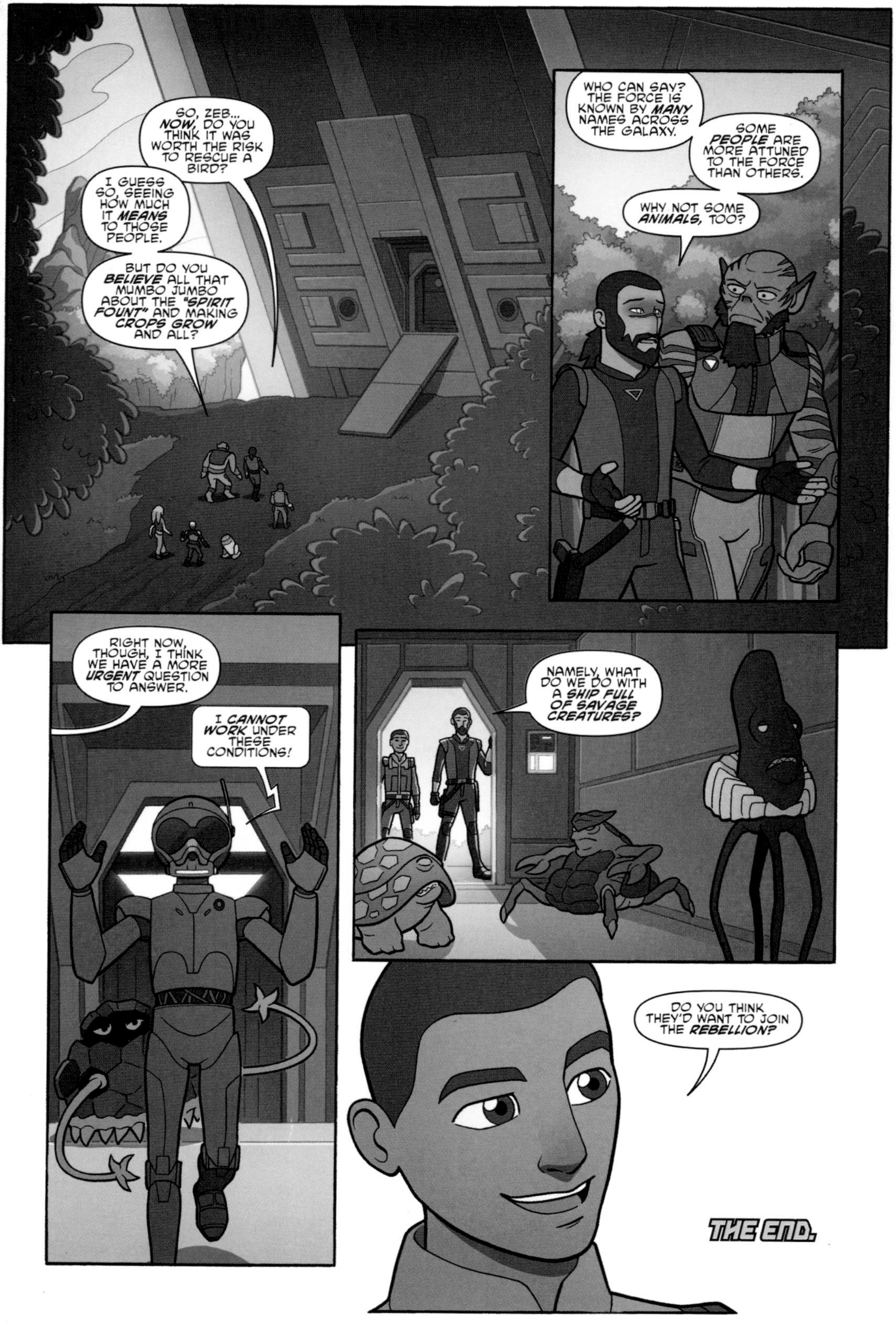

SO, ZEB... NOW, DO YOU THINK IT WAS WORTH THE RISK TO RESCUE A BIRD?
I GUESS SO, SEEING HOW MUCH IT MEANS TO THOSE PEOPLE.
BUT DO YOU BELIEVE ALL THAT MUMBO JUMBO ABOUT THE "SPIRIT FOUNT" AND MAKING CROPS GROW AND ALL?
WHO CAN SAY? THE FORCE IS KNOWN BY MANY NAMES ACROSS THE GALAXY.
SOME PEOPLE ARE MORE ATTUNED TO THE FORCE THAN OTHERS.
WHY NOT SOME ANIMALS, TOO?
RIGHT NOW, THOUGH, I THINK WE HAVE A MORE URGENT QUESTION TO ANSWER.
I CANNOT WORK UNDER THESE CONDITIONS!
NAMELY, WHAT DO WE DO WITH A SHIP FULL OF SAVAGE CREATURES?
DO YOU THINK THEY'D WANT TO JOIN THE REBELLION?
THE END.

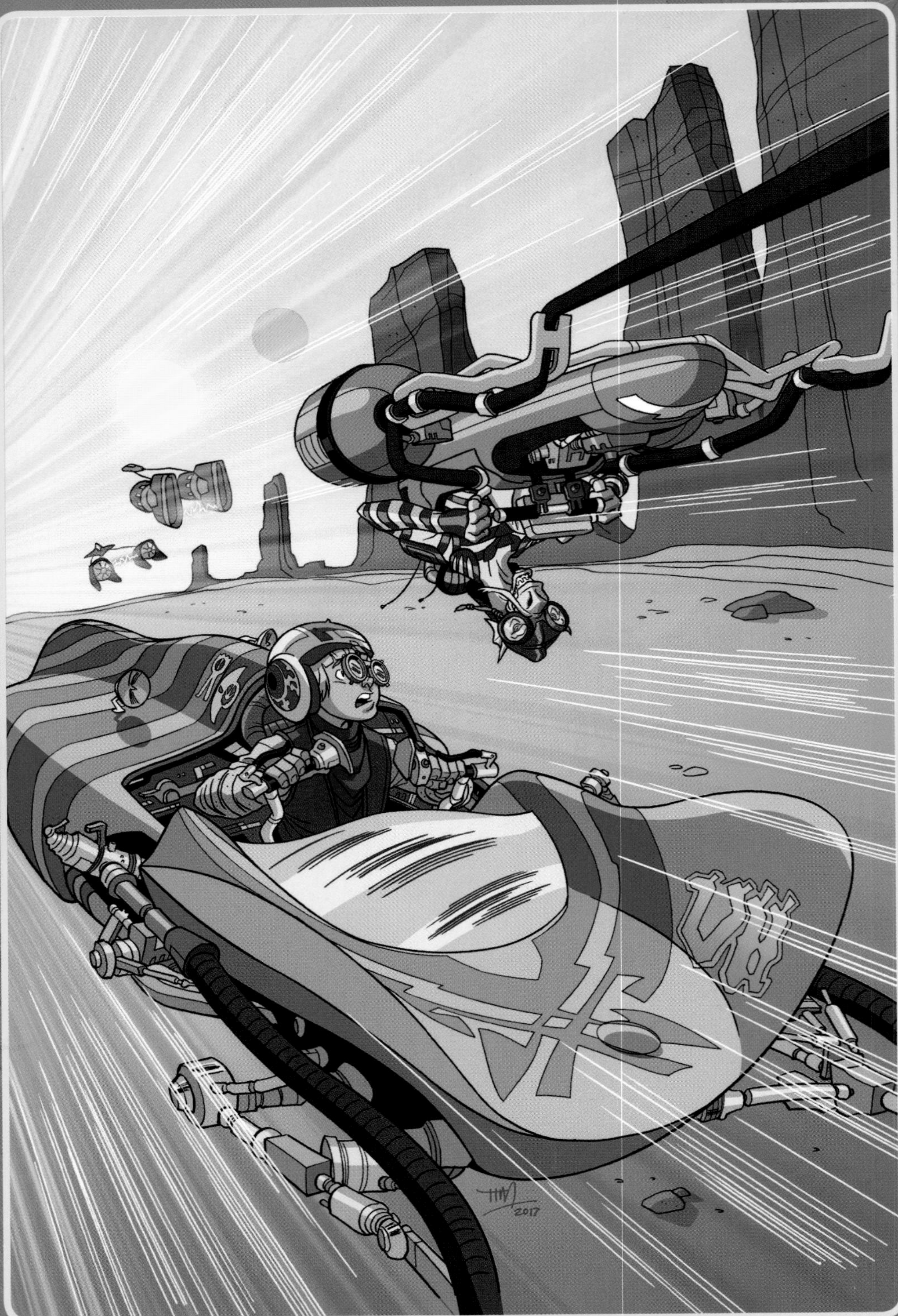

Art by Tim Levins

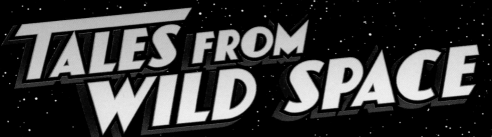

TALES FROM WILD SPACE

Podracer's Rescue

WRITER
SHAUN MANNING
ARTIST
CHAD THOMAS
COLORIST
CHARLIE KIRCHOFF
LETTERER
TOM B. LONG

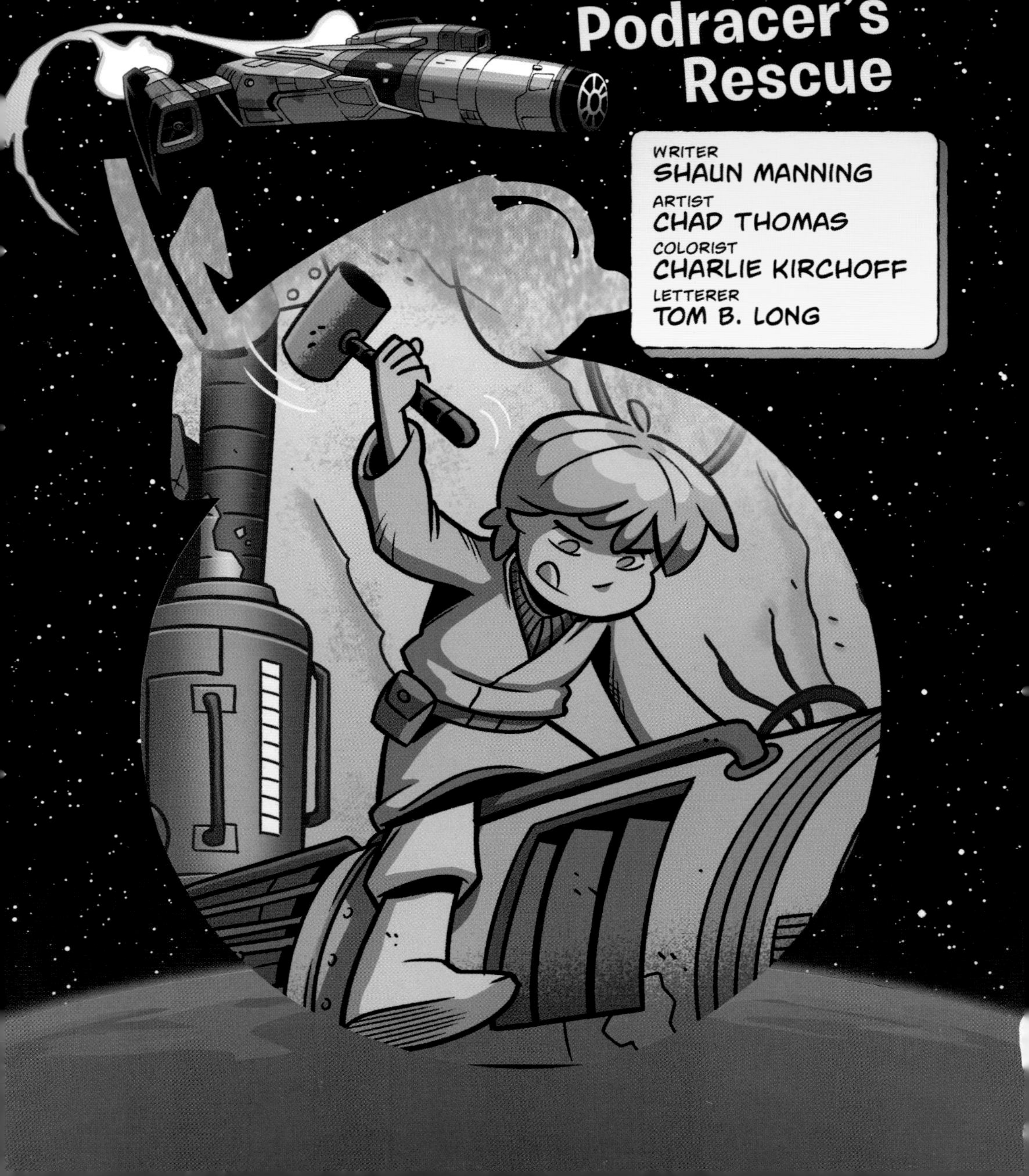

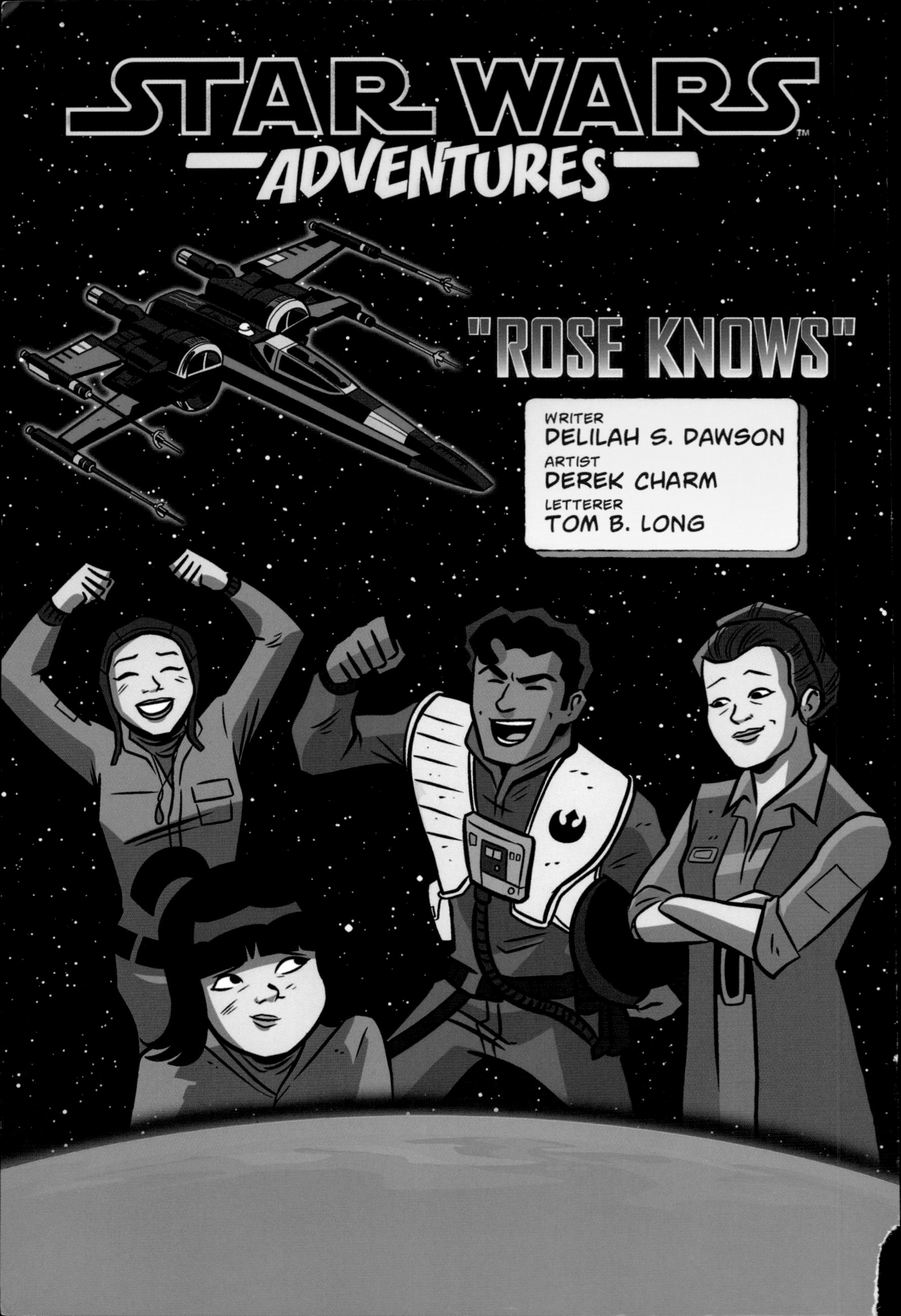

STAR WARS ADVENTURES
"ROSE KNOWS"
WRITER
DELILAH S. DAWSON
ARTIST
DEREK CHARM
LETTERER
TOM B. LONG

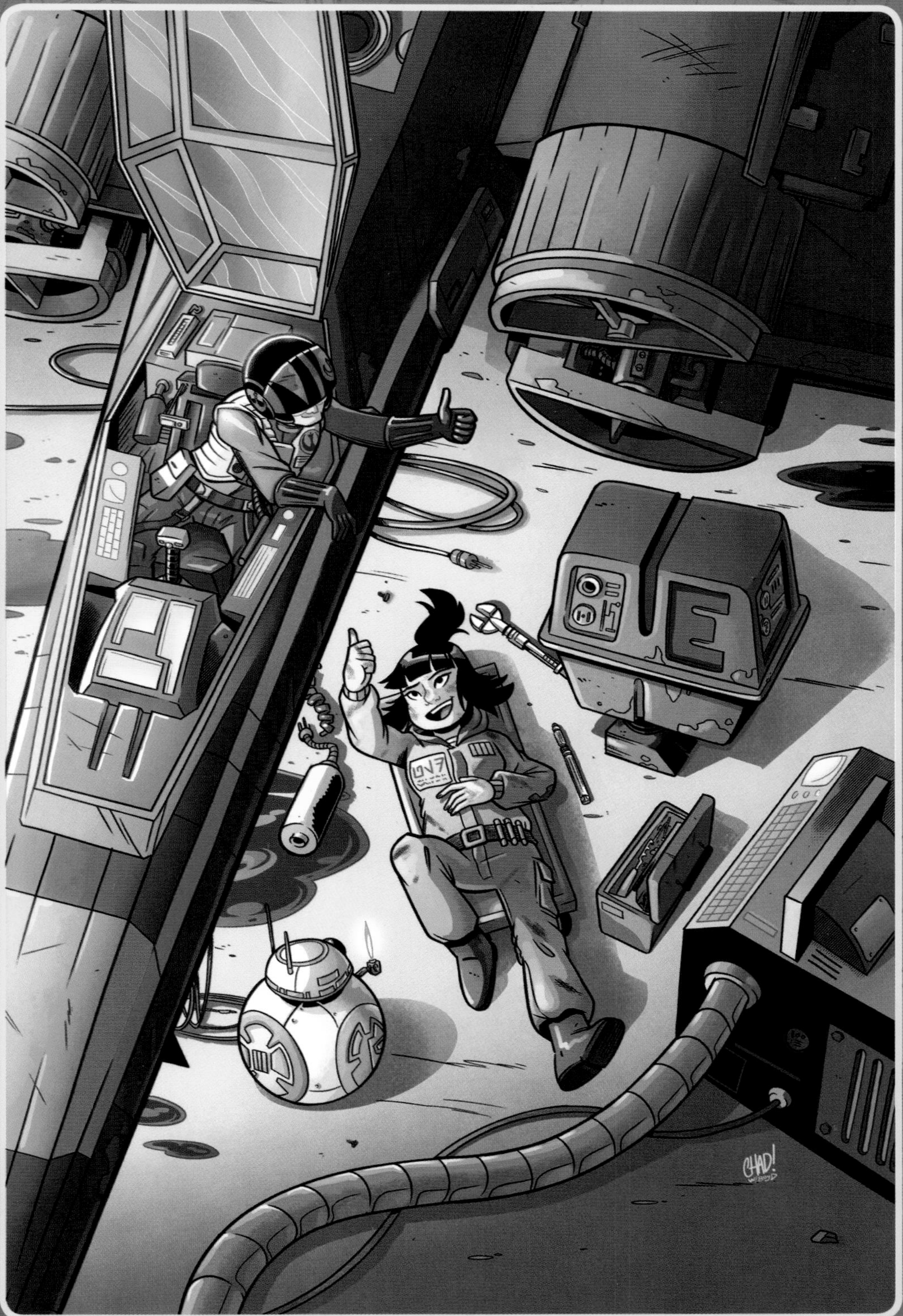

Art by Chad Thomas, Colors by Jordan Boyd

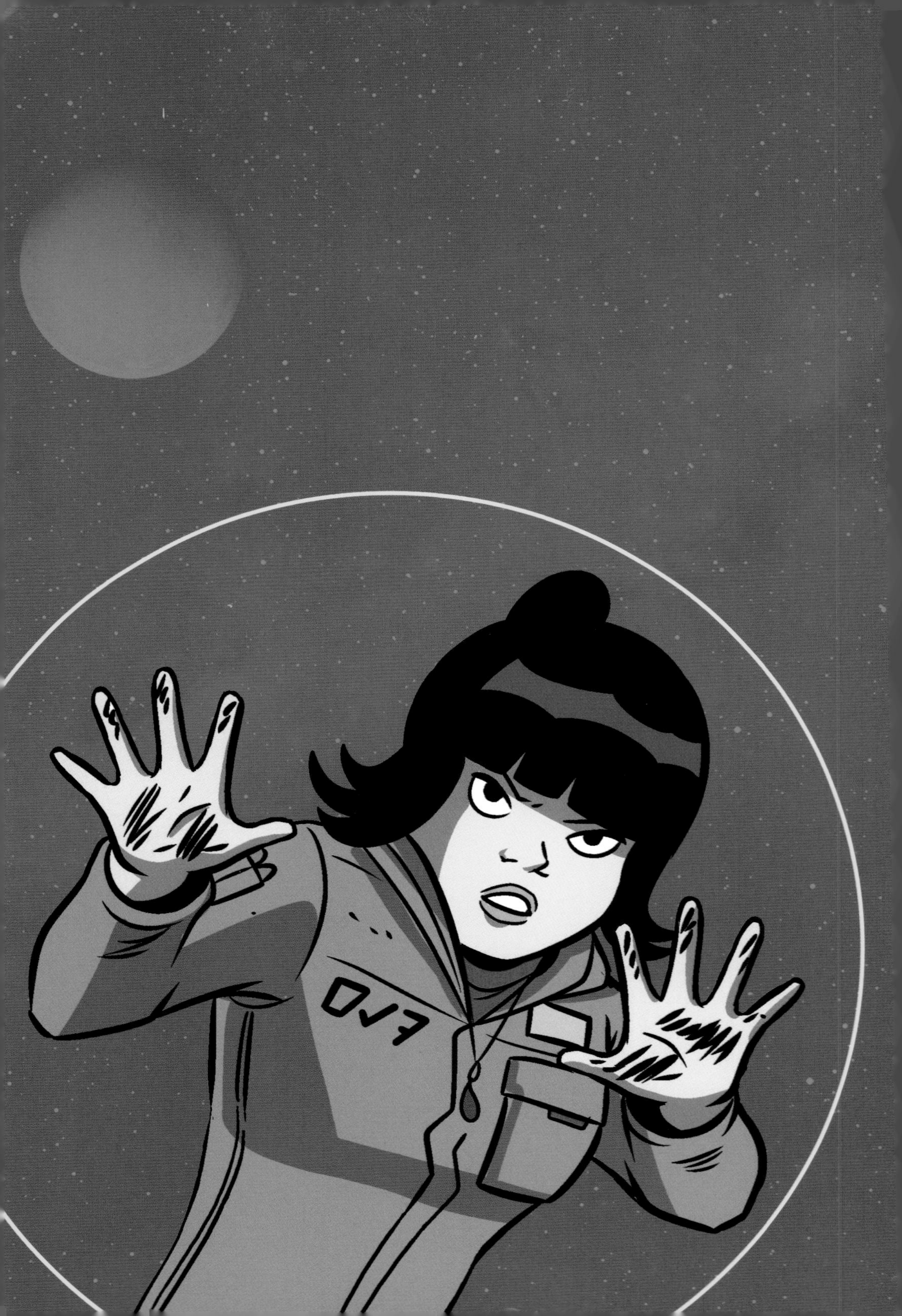

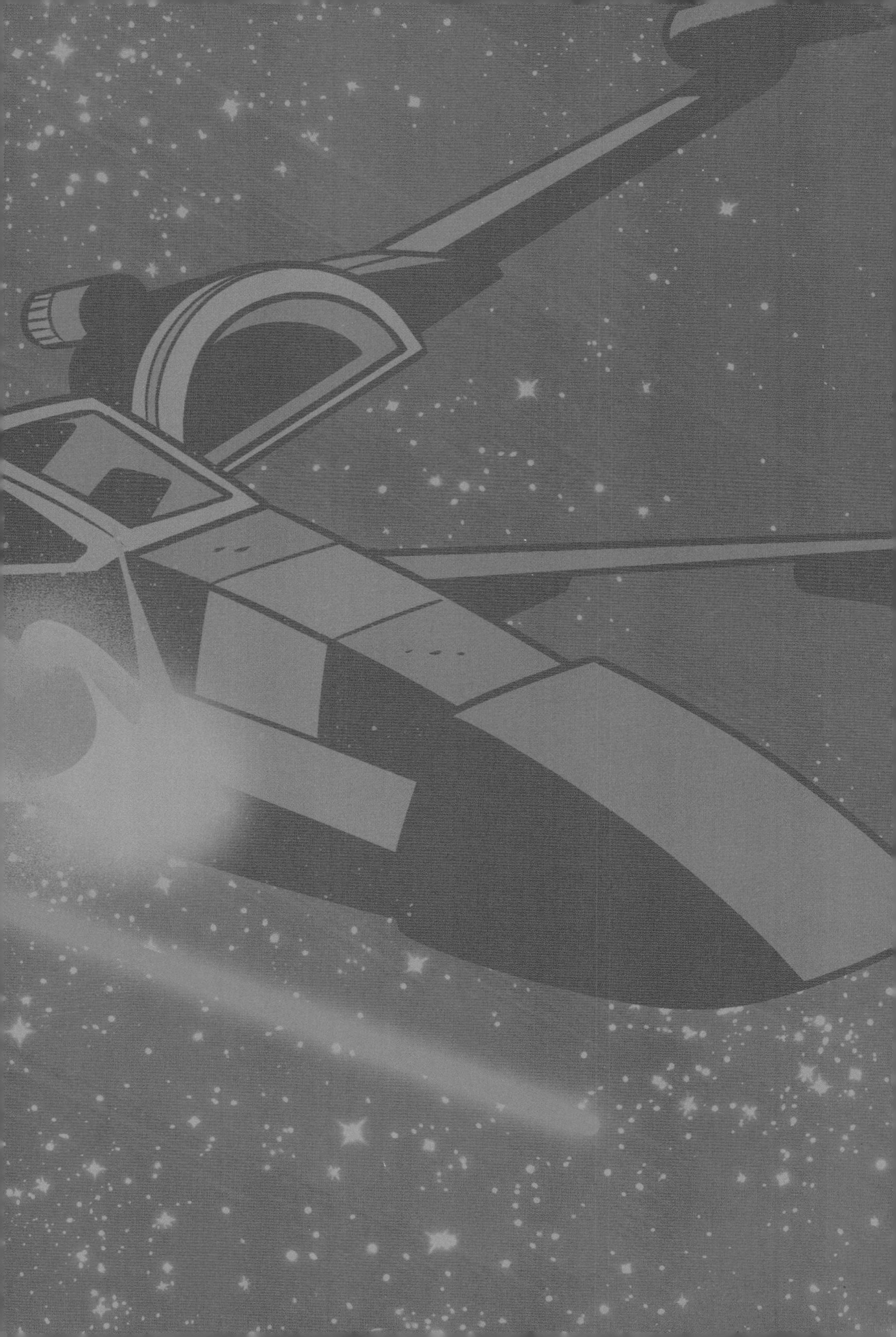

More STAR WARS from IDW

Star Wars Adventures, Vol. 1–2

Star Wars: Forces of Destiny

Star Wars: The Force Awakens Graphic Novel Adaptation

Star Wars: Rogue One Graphic Novel Adaptation

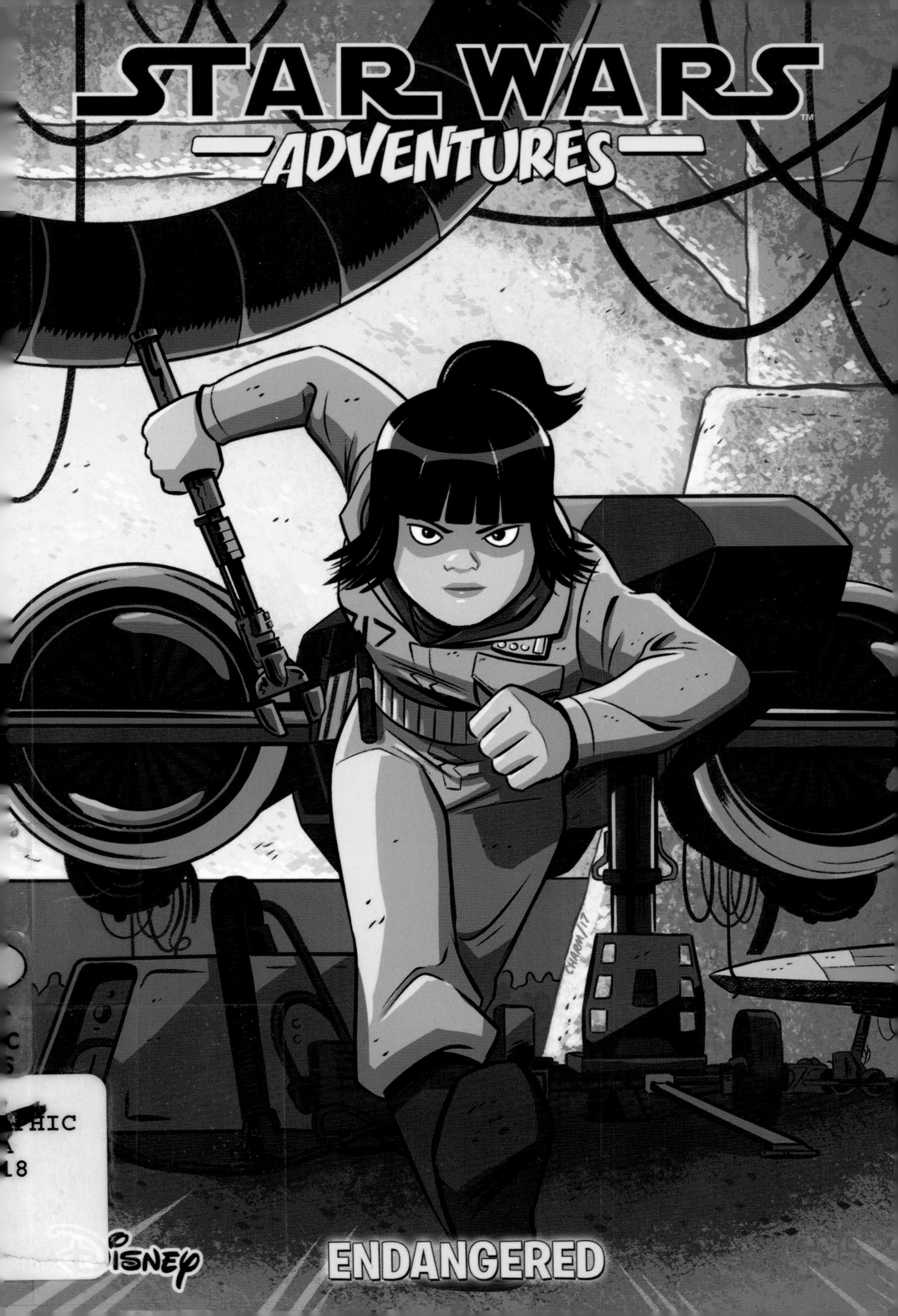
STAR WARS
ADVENTURES
CHARM/17
DISNEY
ENDANGERED

Facebook: **facebook.com/idwpublishing**
Twitter: **@idwpublishing**
YouTube: **youtube.com/idwpublishing**
Tumblr: **tumblr.idwpublishing.com**
Instagram: **instagram.com/idwpublishing**

ISBN: 978-1-68405-249-3   21 20 19 18   1 2 3 4

COVER ARTIST
DEREK CHARM

SERIES ASSISTANT EDITOR
PETER ADRIAN BEHRAVESH

SERIES EDITORS
BOBBY CURNOW
and DENTON J. TIPTON

COLLECTION EDITORS
JUSTIN EISINGER
and ALONZO SIMON

COLLECTION DESIGNER
CLYDE GRAPA

PUBLISHER
GREG GOLDSTEIN

Originally published as STAR WARS ADVENTURES issues #6–8.

Greg Goldstein, President & Publisher
Robbie Robbins, EVP & Sr. Art Director
Matthew Ruzicka, CPA, Chief Financial Officer
David Hedgecock, Associate Publisher
Lorelei Bunjes, VP of Digital Services
Eric Moss, Sr. Director, Licensing & Business Development

Ted Adams, Founder & CEO of IDW Media Holdings

Lucasfilm Credits:
Assistant Editor: Nick Martino
Senior Editor: Frank Parisi
Creative Director: Michael Siglain
Story Group: James Waugh, Leland Chee,
Pablo Hidalgo, Matt Martin

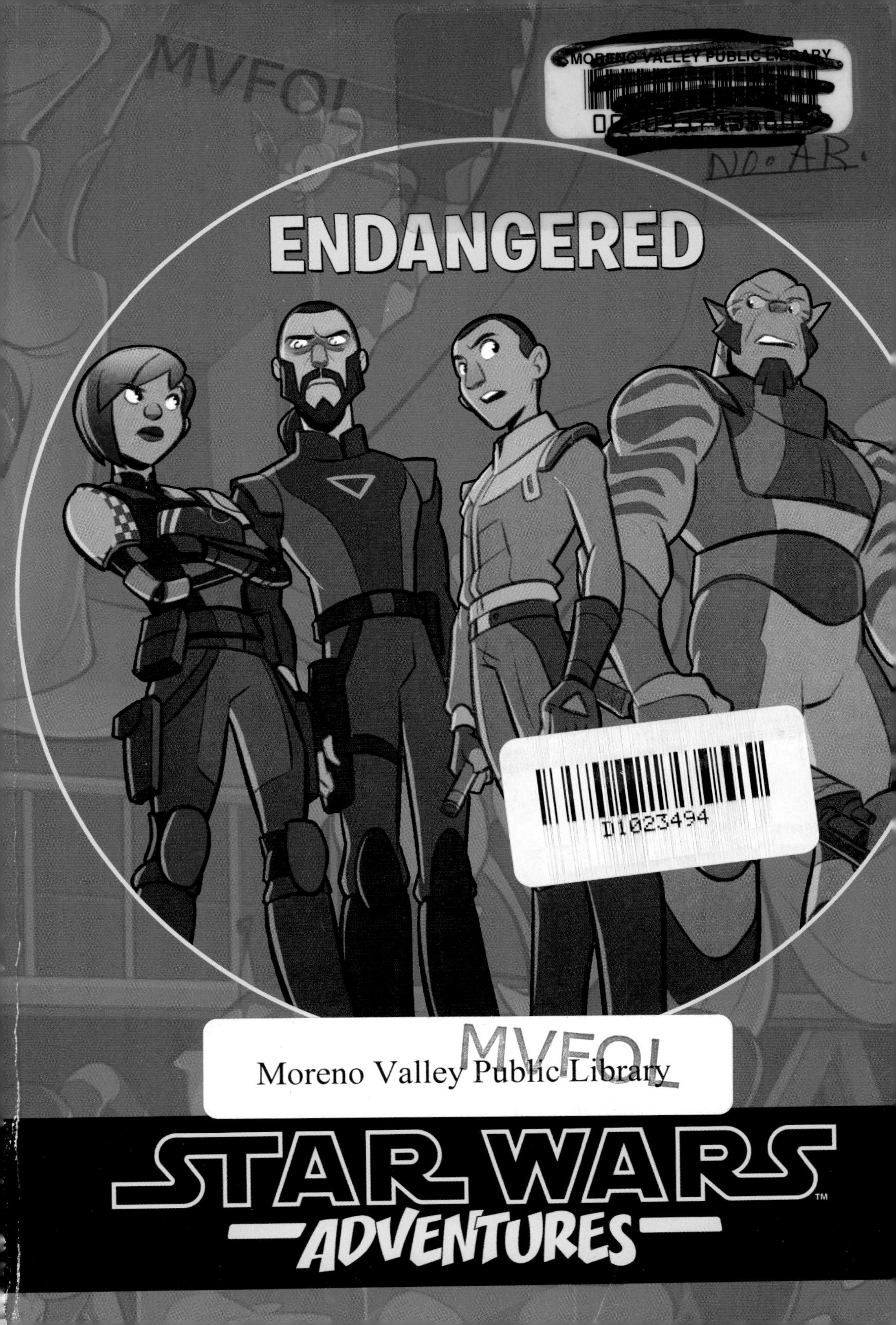
ENDANGERED
STAR WARS™
ADVENTURES

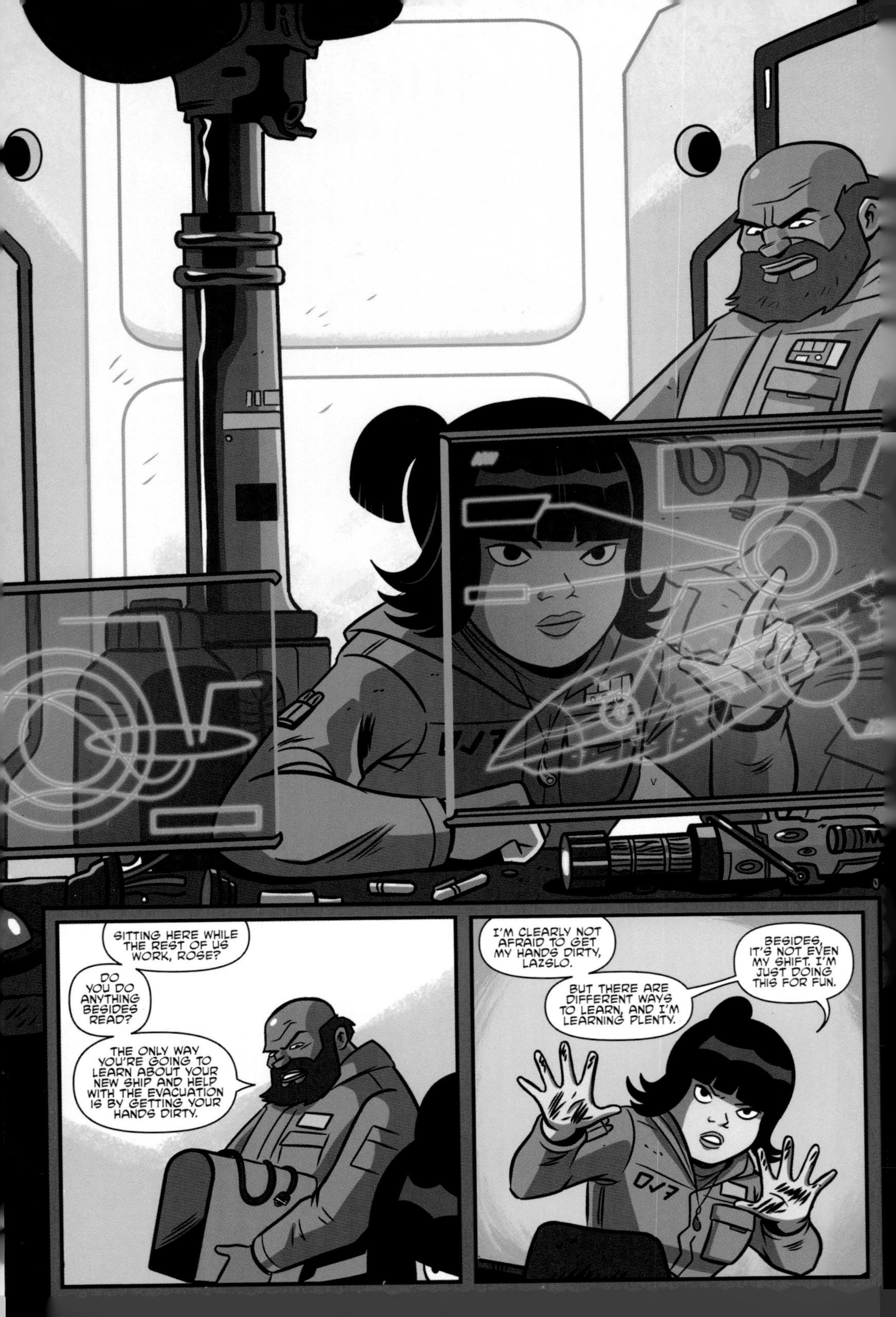
SITTING HERE WHILE THE REST OF US WORK, ROSE?
DO YOU DO ANYTHING BESIDES READ?
THE ONLY WAY YOU'RE GOING TO LEARN ABOUT YOUR NEW SHIP AND HELP WITH THE EVACUATION IS BY GETTING YOUR HANDS DIRTY.
I'M CLEARLY NOT AFRAID TO GET MY HANDS DIRTY, LAZSLO.
BUT THERE ARE DIFFERENT WAYS TO LEARN, AND I'M LEARNING PLENTY.
BESIDES, IT'S NOT EVEN MY SHIFT. I'M JUST DOING THIS FOR FUN.

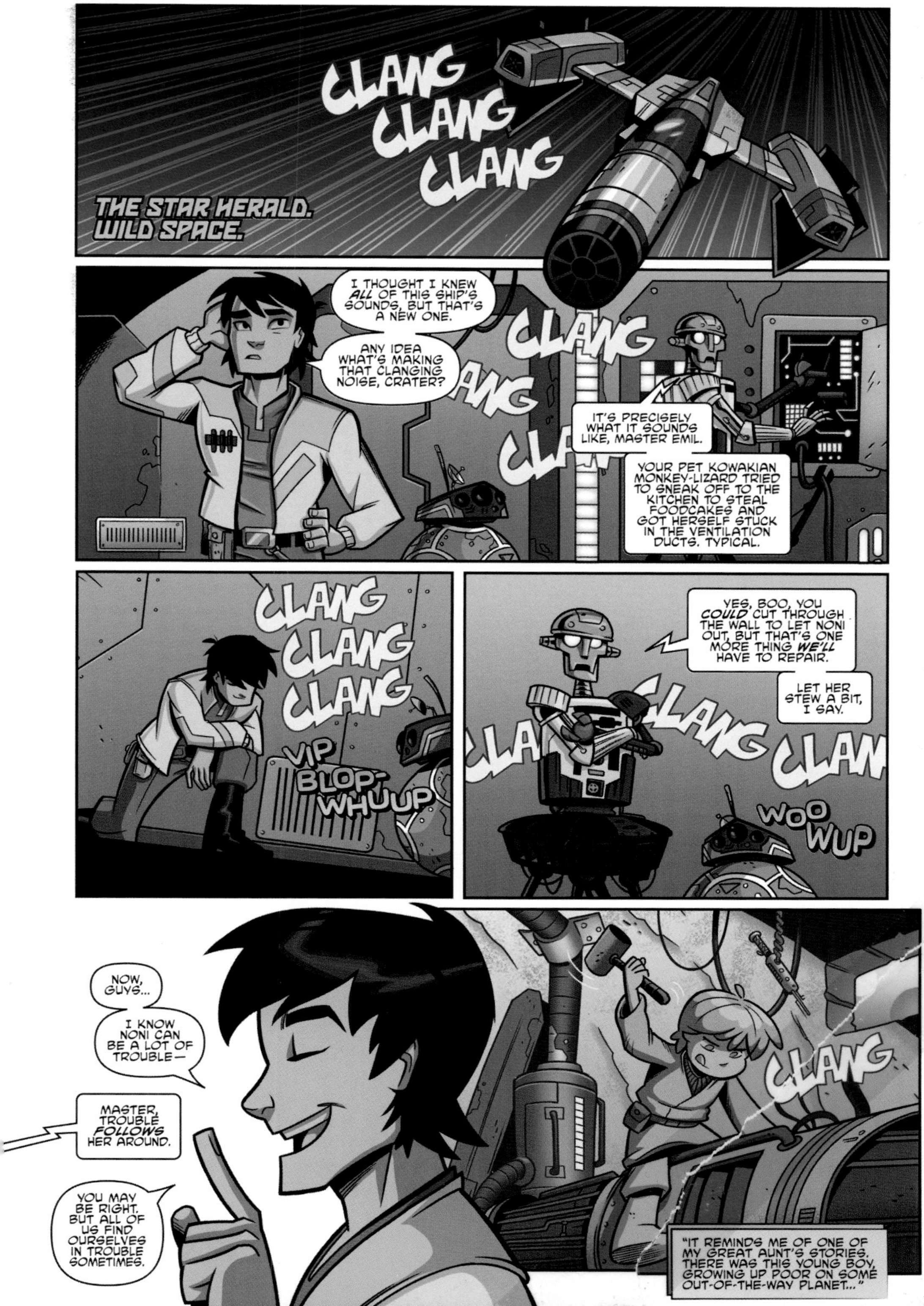
CLANG
CLANG
CLANG
THE STAR HERALD. WILD SPACE.
I THOUGHT I KNEW ALL OF THIS SHIP'S SOUNDS, BUT THAT'S A NEW ONE.
ANY IDEA WHAT'S MAKING THAT CLANGING NOISE, CRATER?
CLANG
IT'S PRECISELY WHAT IT SOUNDS LIKE, MASTER EMIL.
YOUR PET KOWAKIAN MONKEY-LIZARD TRIED TO SNEAK OFF TO THE KITCHEN TO STEAL FOODCAKES AND GOT HERSELF STUCK IN THE VENTILATION DUCTS. TYPICAL.
CLANG
CLANG
CLANG
VIP
BLOP-
WHUUP
YES, BOO, YOU COULD CUT THROUGH THE WALL TO LET NONI OUT, BUT THAT'S ONE MORE THING WE'LL HAVE TO REPAIR.
LET HER STEW A BIT, I SAY.
CLANG
WOO
WUP
NOW, GUYS...
I KNOW NONI CAN BE A LOT OF TROUBLE—
MASTER, TROUBLE FOLLOWS HER AROUND.
YOU MAY BE RIGHT. BUT ALL OF US FIND OURSELVES IN TROUBLE SOMETIMES.
CLANG
"IT REMINDS ME OF ONE OF MY GREAT AUNT'S STORIES. THERE WAS THIS YOUNG BOY, GROWING UP POOR ON SOME OUT-OF-THE-WAY PLANET..."

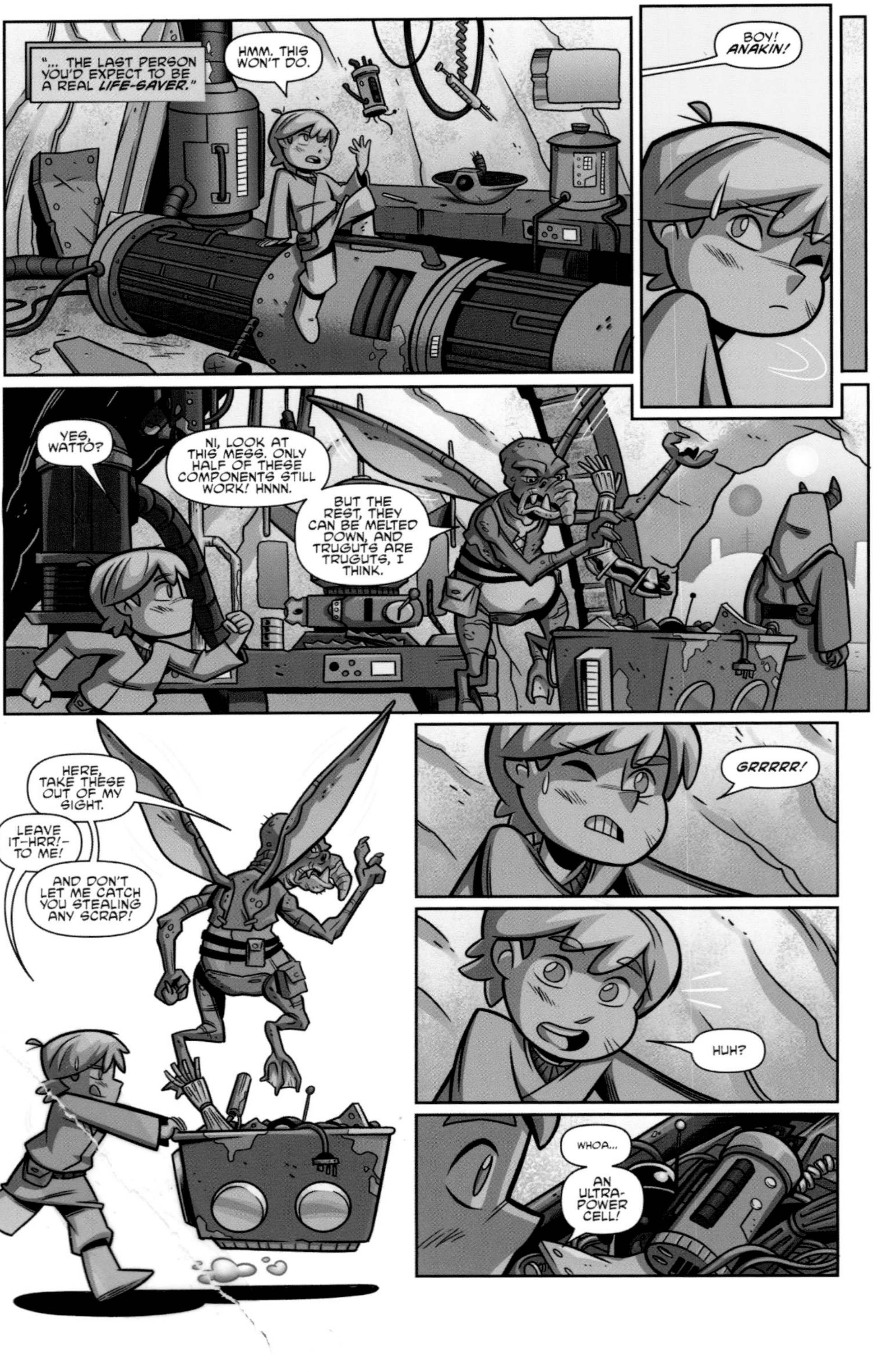

"... THE LAST PERSON YOU'D EXPECT TO BE A REAL *LIFE-SAVER.*"
HMM. THIS WON'T DO.
BOY! *ANAKIN!*
YES, WATTO?
NI, LOOK AT THIS MESS. ONLY HALF OF THESE COMPONENTS STILL WORK! HNNN.
BUT THE REST, THEY CAN BE MELTED DOWN, AND TRUGUTS ARE TRUGUTS, I THINK.
HERE, TAKE THESE OUT OF MY SIGHT.
LEAVE IT--HRR!-- TO ME!
AND DON'T LET ME CATCH YOU STEALING ANY SCRAP!
GRRRRR!
HUH?
WHOA...
AN ULTRA-POWER CELL!

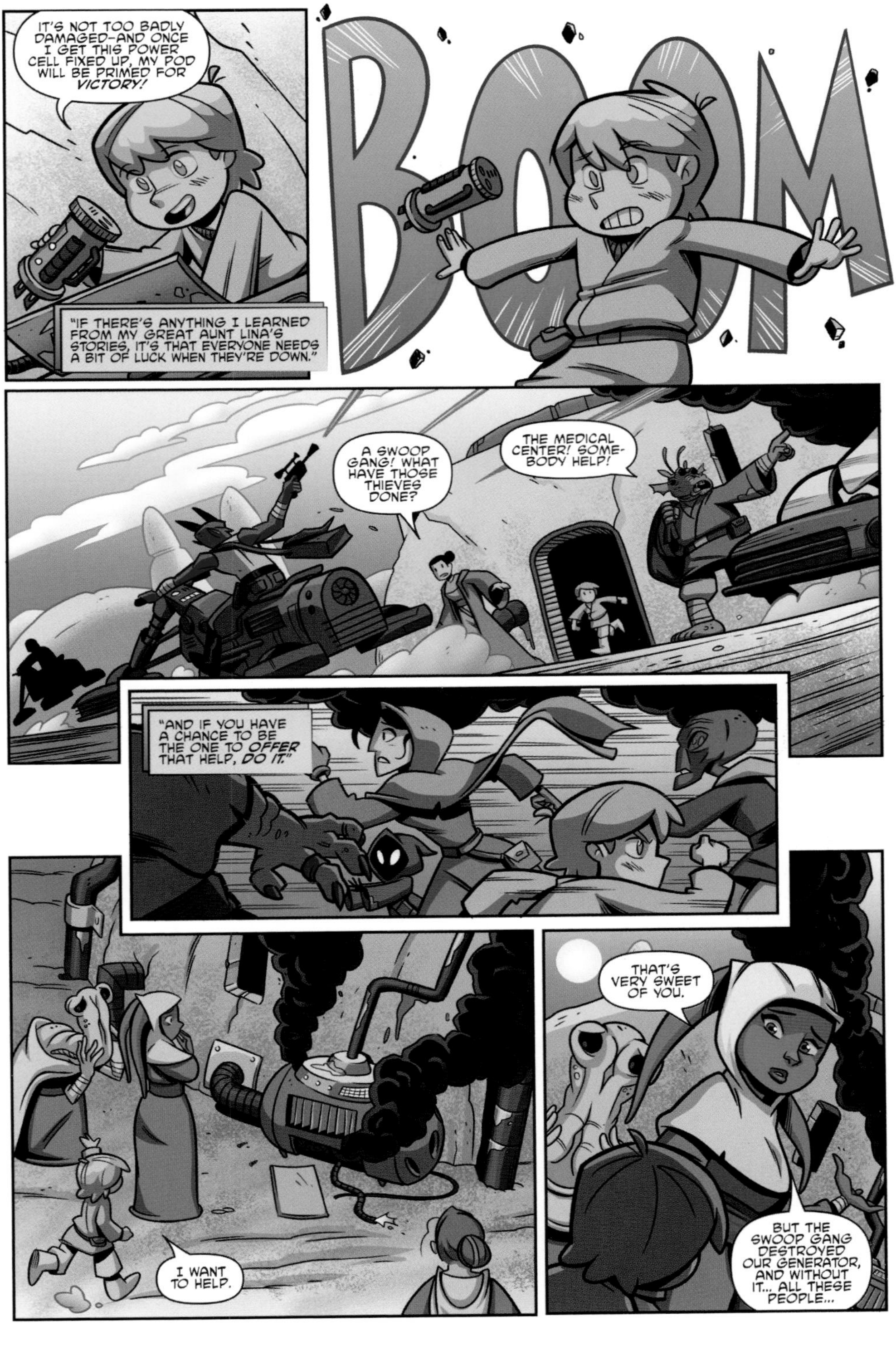
IT'S NOT TOO BADLY DAMAGED–AND ONCE I GET THIS POWER CELL FIXED UP, MY POD WILL BE PRIMED FOR *VICTORY!*
"IF THERE'S ANYTHING I LEARNED FROM MY GREAT AUNT LINA'S STORIES, IT'S THAT EVERYONE NEEDS A BIT OF LUCK WHEN THEY'RE DOWN."
BOOM
A SWOOP GANG! WHAT HAVE THOSE THIEVES DONE?
THE MEDICAL CENTER! SOME-BODY HELP!
"AND IF YOU HAVE A CHANCE TO BE THE ONE TO *OFFER* THAT HELP, *DO IT.*"
I WANT TO HELP.
THAT'S VERY SWEET OF YOU.
BUT THE SWOOP GANG DESTROYED OUR GENERATOR, AND WITHOUT IT... ALL THESE PEOPLE...

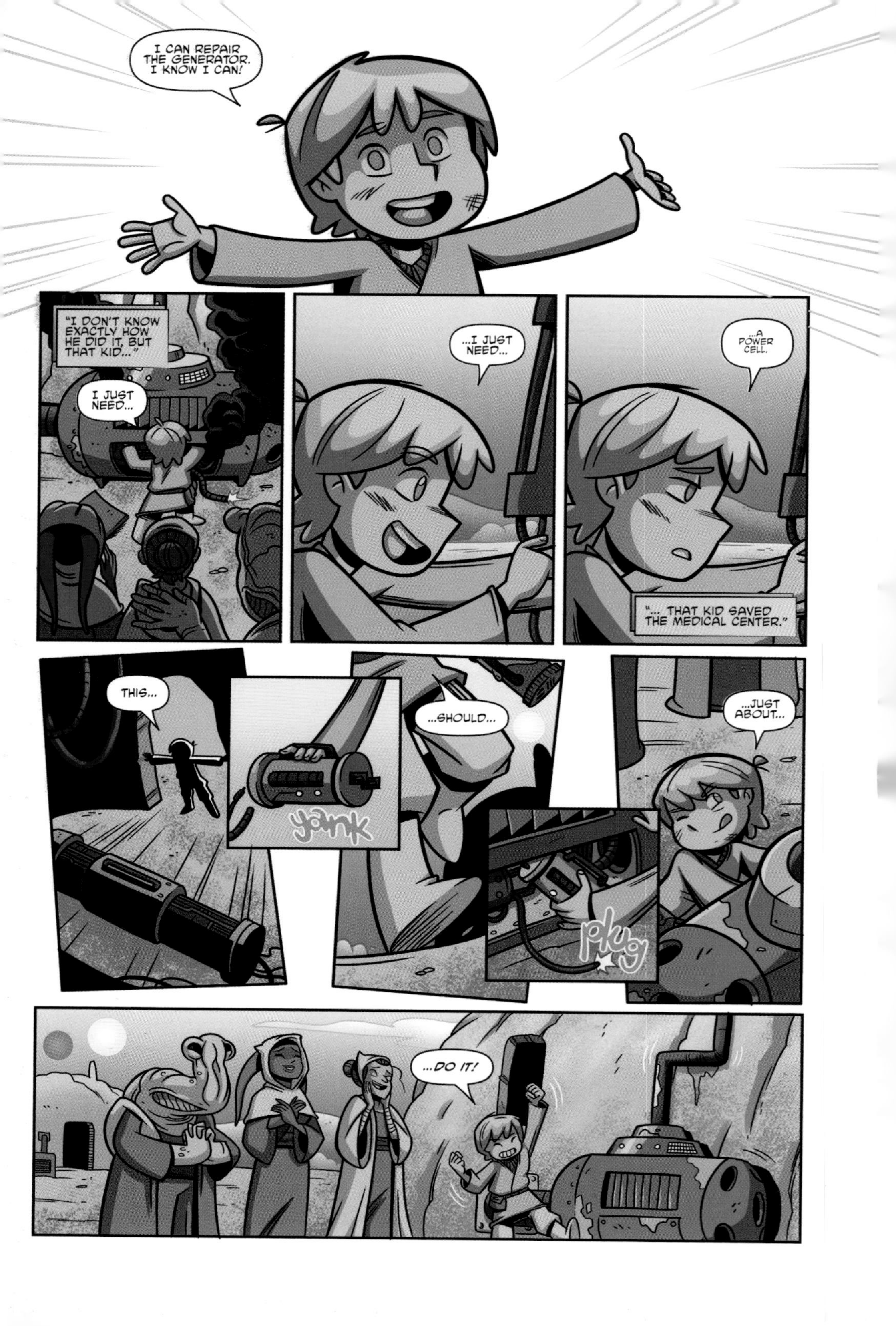

I CAN REPAIR THE GENERATOR. I KNOW I CAN!
"I DON'T KNOW EXACTLY HOW HE DID IT, BUT THAT KID..."
I JUST NEED...
...I JUST NEED...
...A POWER CELL.
"... THAT KID SAVED THE MEDICAL CENTER."
THIS...
yank
...SHOULD...
...JUST ABOUT...
plug
...DO IT!

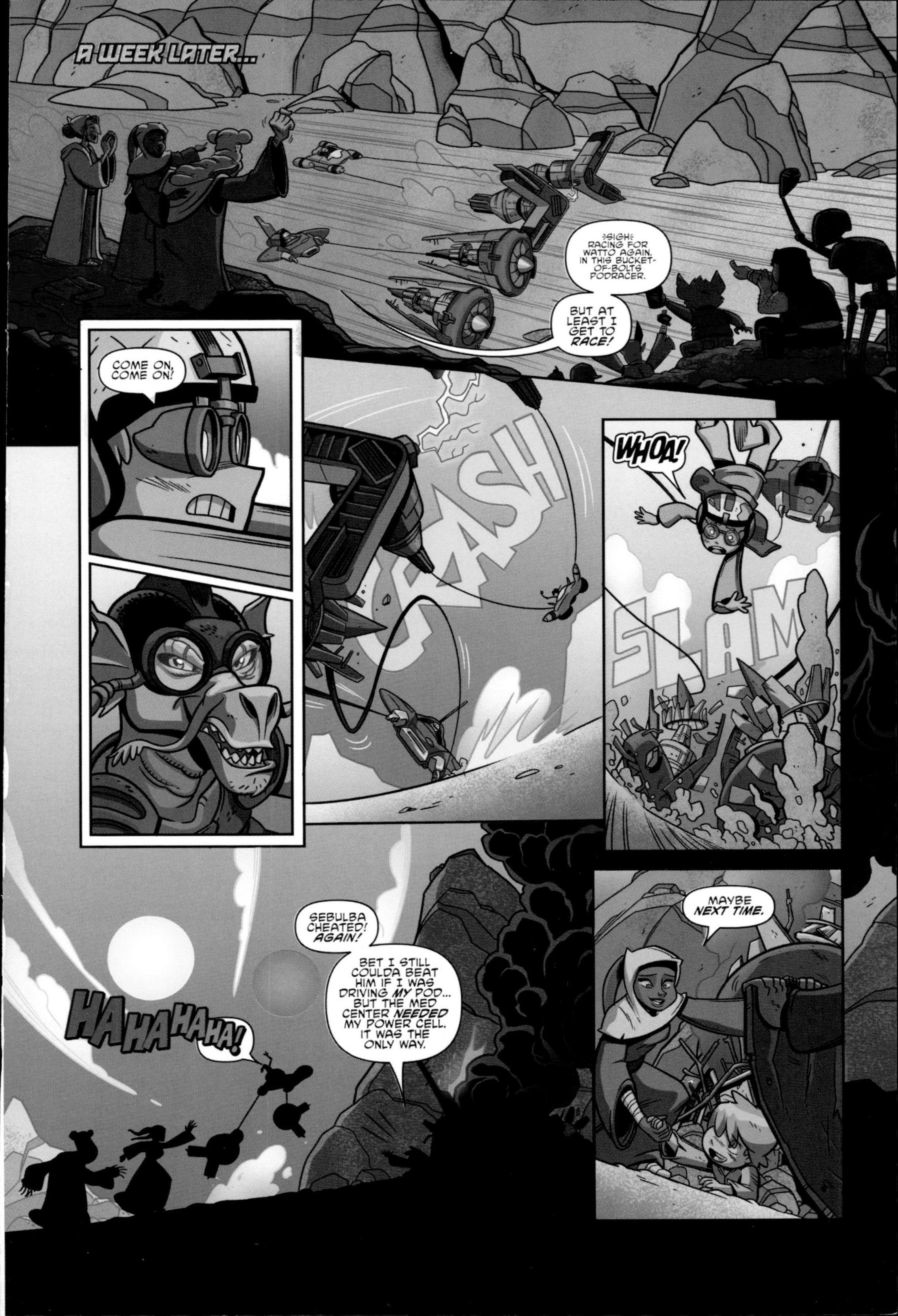
A WEEK LATER...
SIGH RACING FOR WATTO AGAIN. IN THIS BUCKET-OF-BOLTS PODRACER.
BUT AT LEAST I GET TO RACE!
COME ON, COME ON!
CRASH
WHOA!
SLAM
HAHAHAHA!
SEBULBA CHEATED! AGAIN!
BET I STILL COULDA BEAT HIM IF I WAS DRIVING MY POD... BUT THE MED CENTER NEEDED MY POWER CELL. IT WAS THE ONLY WAY.
MAYBE NEXT TIME.

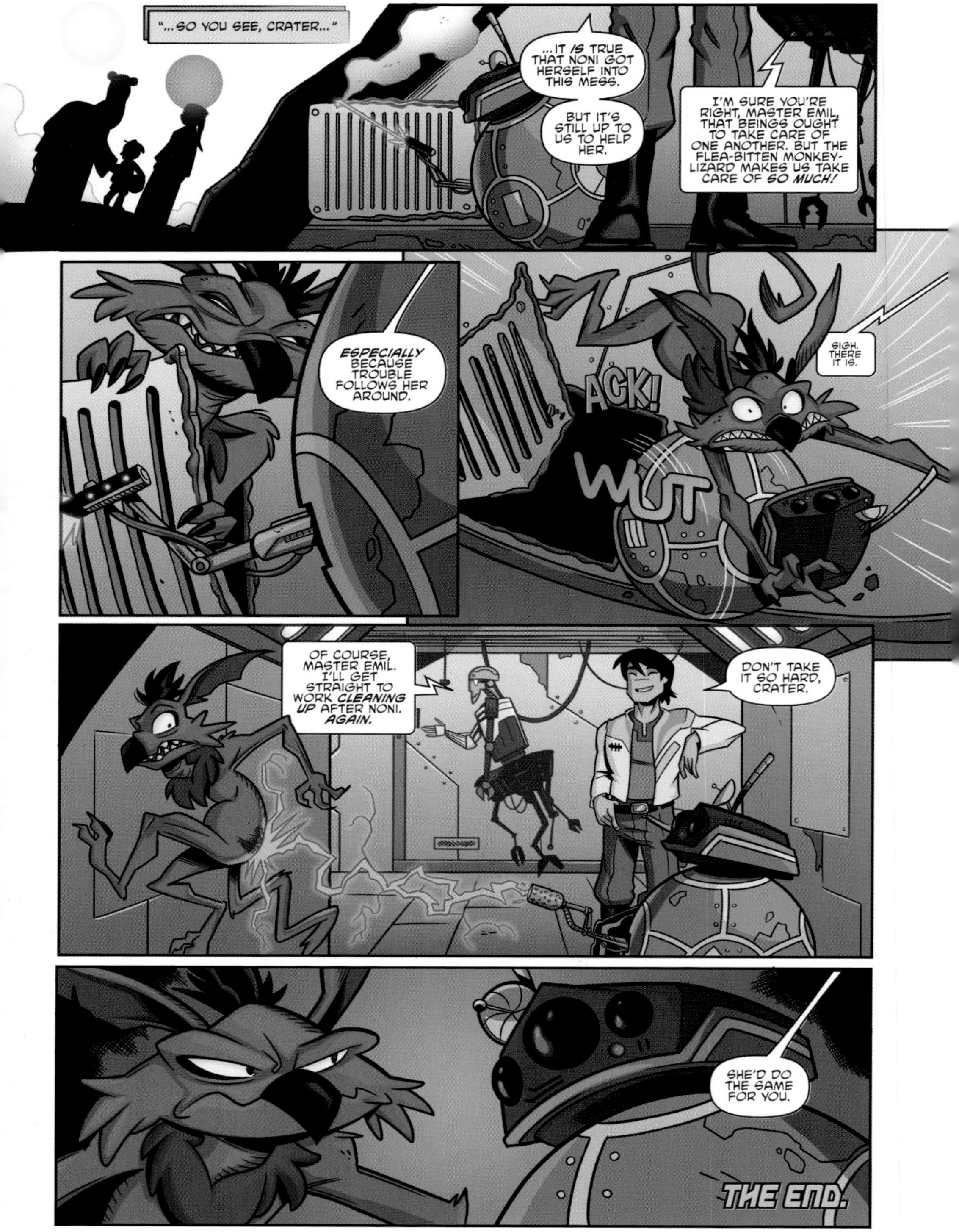
"...SO YOU SEE, CRATER..."
...IT *IS* TRUE THAT NONI GOT HERSELF INTO THIS MESS.
BUT IT'S STILL UP TO US TO HELP HER.
I'M SURE YOU'RE RIGHT, MASTER EMIL, THAT BEINGS OUGHT TO TAKE CARE OF ONE ANOTHER. BUT THE FLEA-BITTEN MONKEY-LIZARD MAKES US TAKE CARE OF *SO MUCH!*
ESPECIALLY BECAUSE TROUBLE FOLLOWS HER AROUND.
ACK!
WUT
SIGH. THERE IT IS.
OF COURSE, MASTER EMIL. I'LL GET STRAIGHT TO WORK *CLEANING UP* AFTER NONI. *AGAIN.*
DON'T TAKE IT SO HARD, CRATER.
SHE'D DO THE SAME FOR YOU.
THE END.

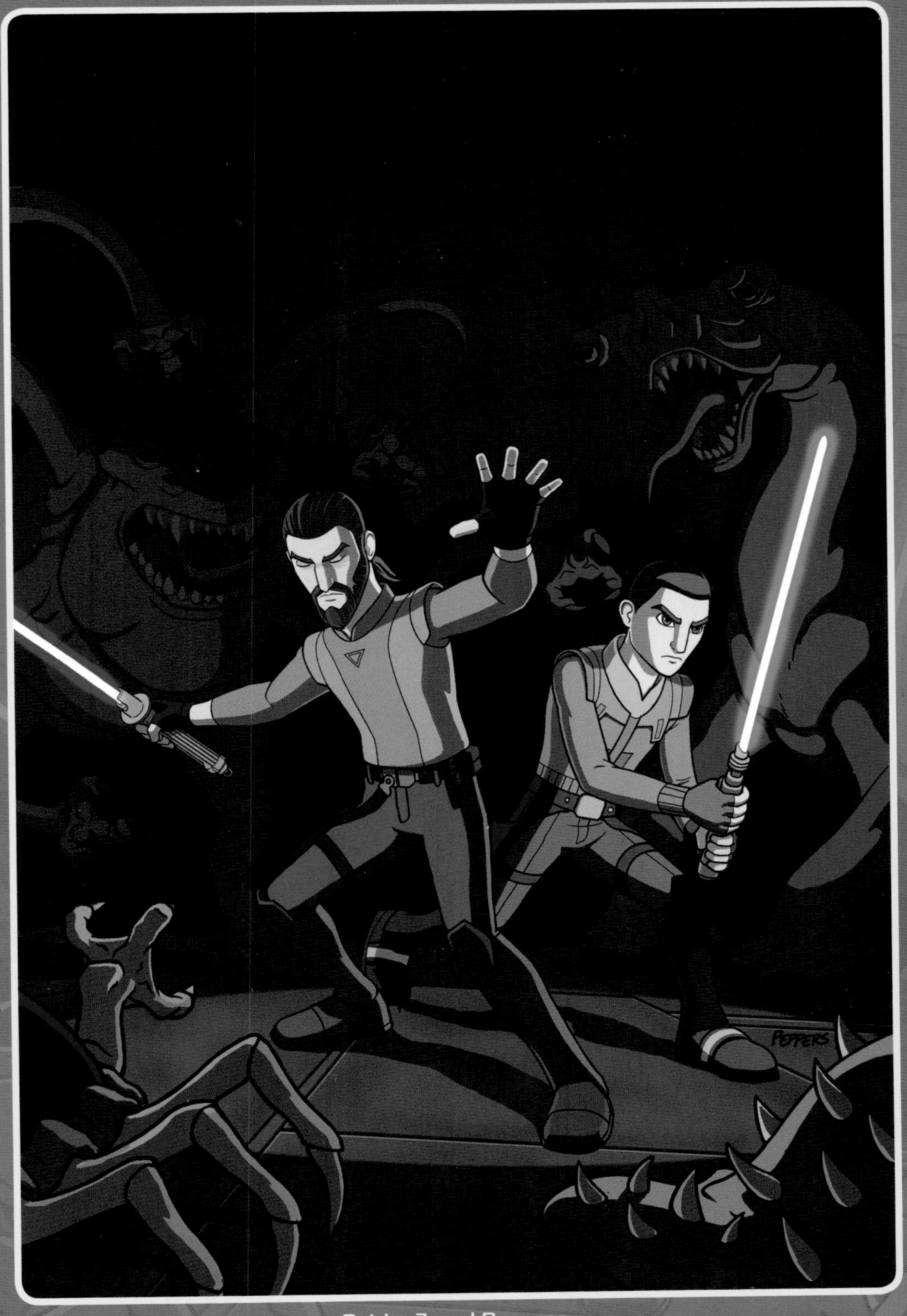
PEPPERS
Art by Jamal Peppers

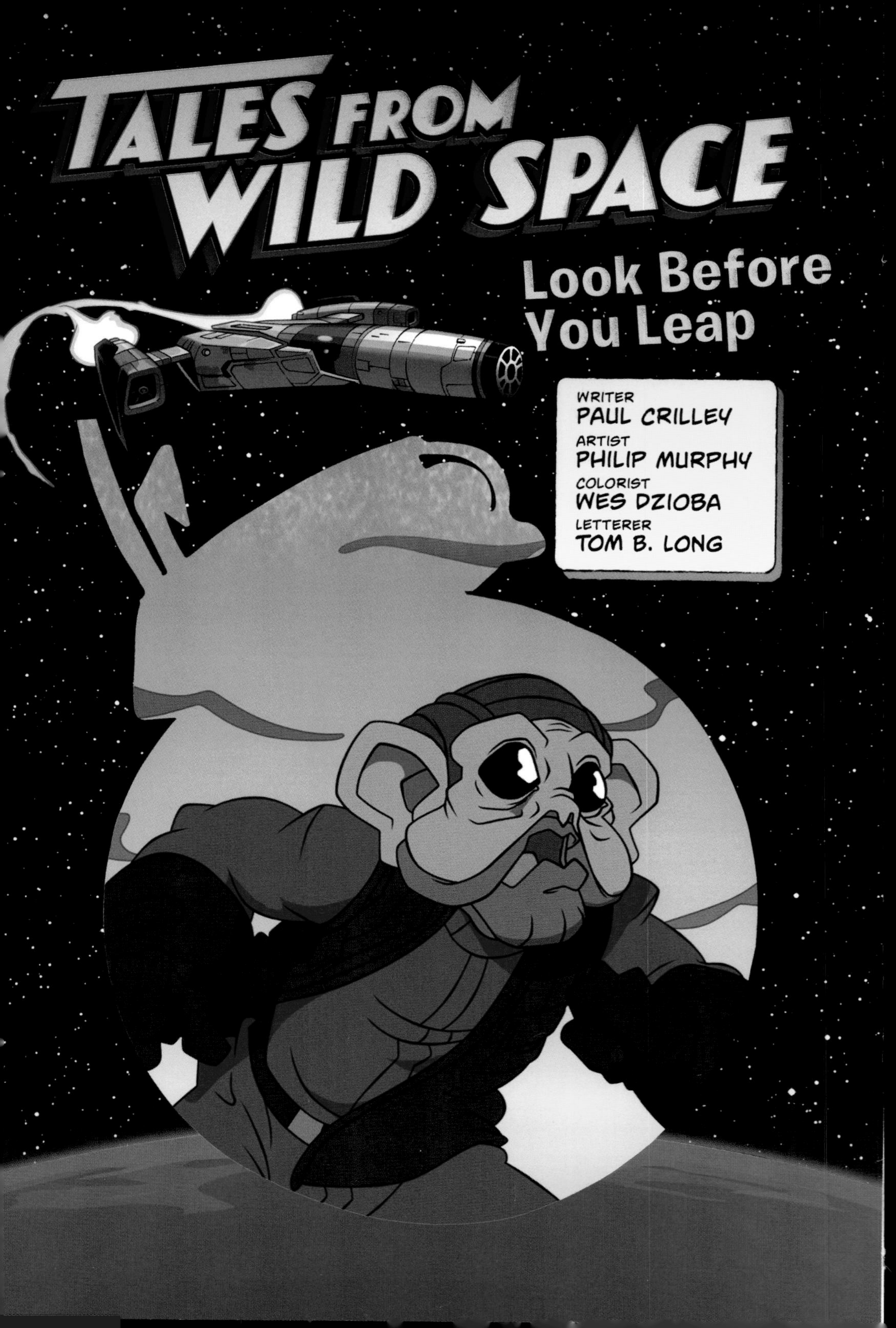
TALES FROM WILD SPACE
Look Before You Leap
WRITER
PAUL CRILLEY
ARTIST
PHILIP MURPHY
COLORIST
WES DZIOBA
LETTERER
TOM B. LONG

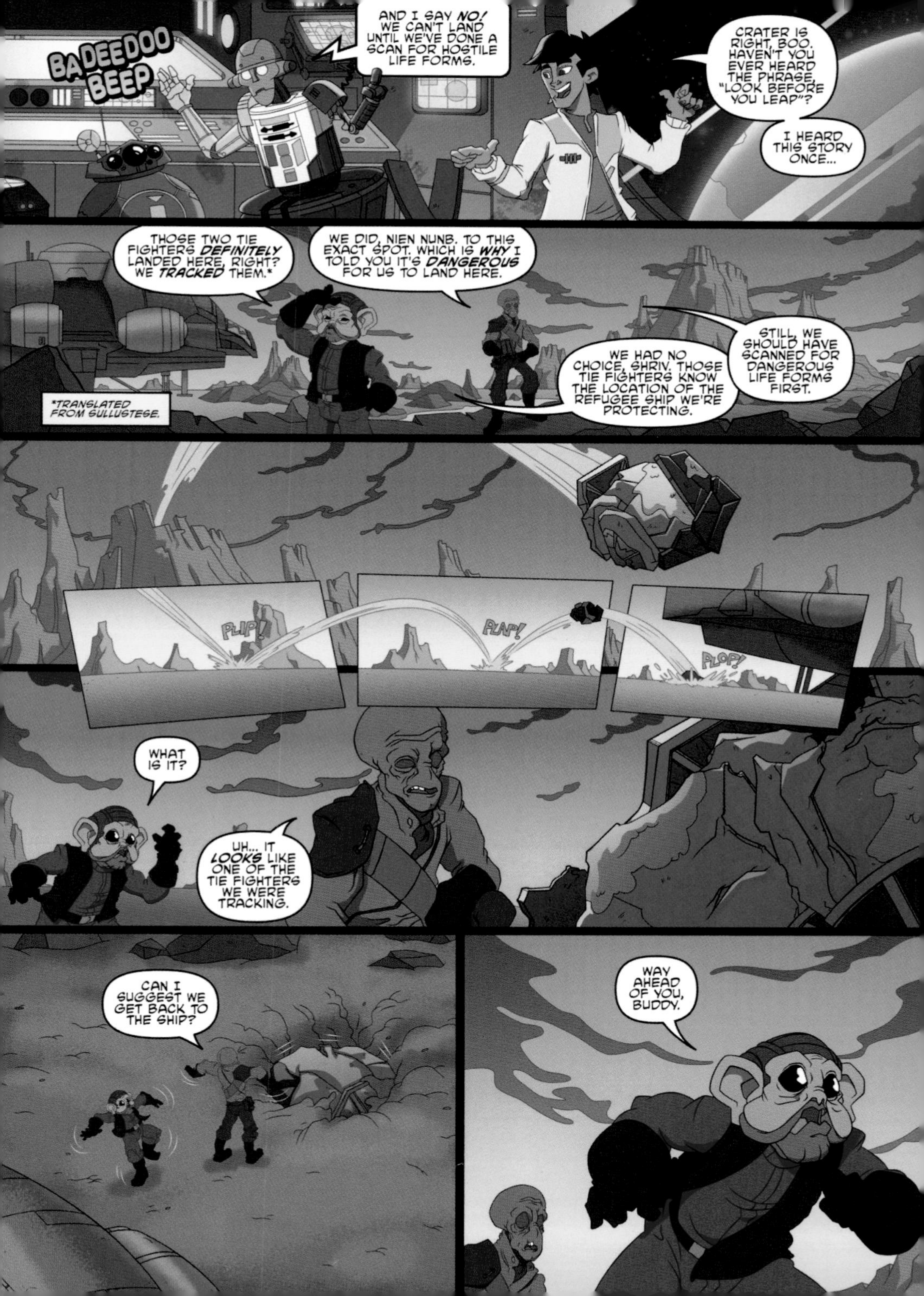

BA DEEDOO BEEP
AND I SAY NO! WE CAN'T LAND UNTIL WE'VE DONE A SCAN FOR HOSTILE LIFE FORMS.
CRATER IS RIGHT, BOO. HAVEN'T YOU EVER HEARD THE PHRASE, "LOOK BEFORE YOU LEAP"?
I HEARD THIS STORY ONCE...
THOSE TWO TIE FIGHTERS DEFINITELY LANDED HERE, RIGHT? WE TRACKED THEM.*
WE DID, NIEN NUNB. TO THIS EXACT SPOT. WHICH IS WHY I TOLD YOU IT'S DANGEROUS FOR US TO LAND HERE.
STILL, WE SHOULD HAVE SCANNED FOR DANGEROUS LIFE FORMS FIRST.
WE HAD NO CHOICE, SHRIV. THOSE TIE FIGHTERS KNOW THE LOCATION OF THE REFUGEE SHIP WE'RE PROTECTING.
*TRANSLATED FROM SULLUSTESE.
PLIP!
PLAP!
PLOP!
WHAT IS IT?
UH... IT LOOKS LIKE ONE OF THE TIE FIGHTERS WE WERE TRACKING.
CAN I SUGGEST WE GET BACK TO THE SHIP?
WAY AHEAD OF YOU, BUDDY.

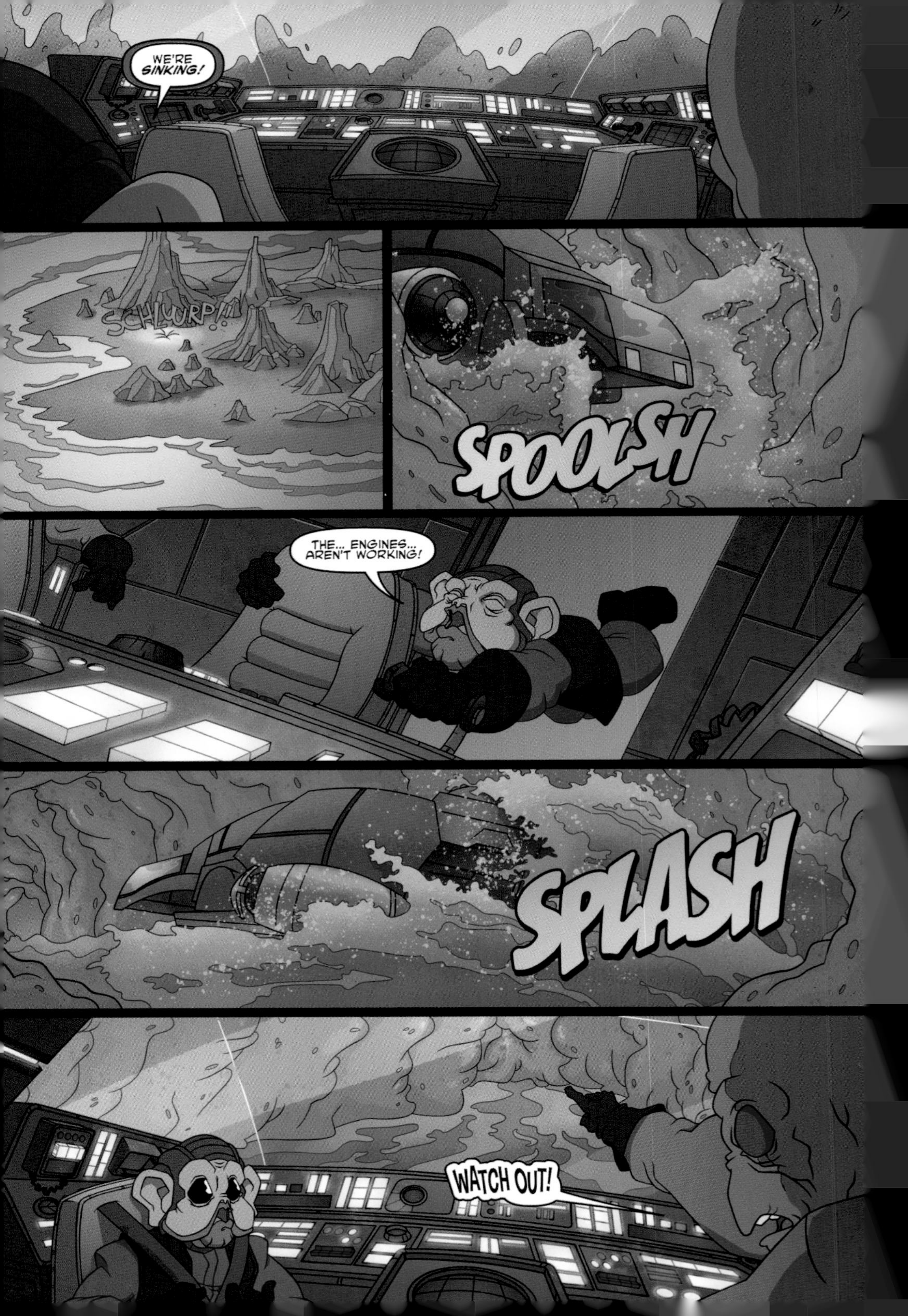

WE'RE SINKING!
SCHLUURP!!
SPOOLSH
THE... ENGINES... AREN'T WORKING!
SPLASH
WATCH OUT!

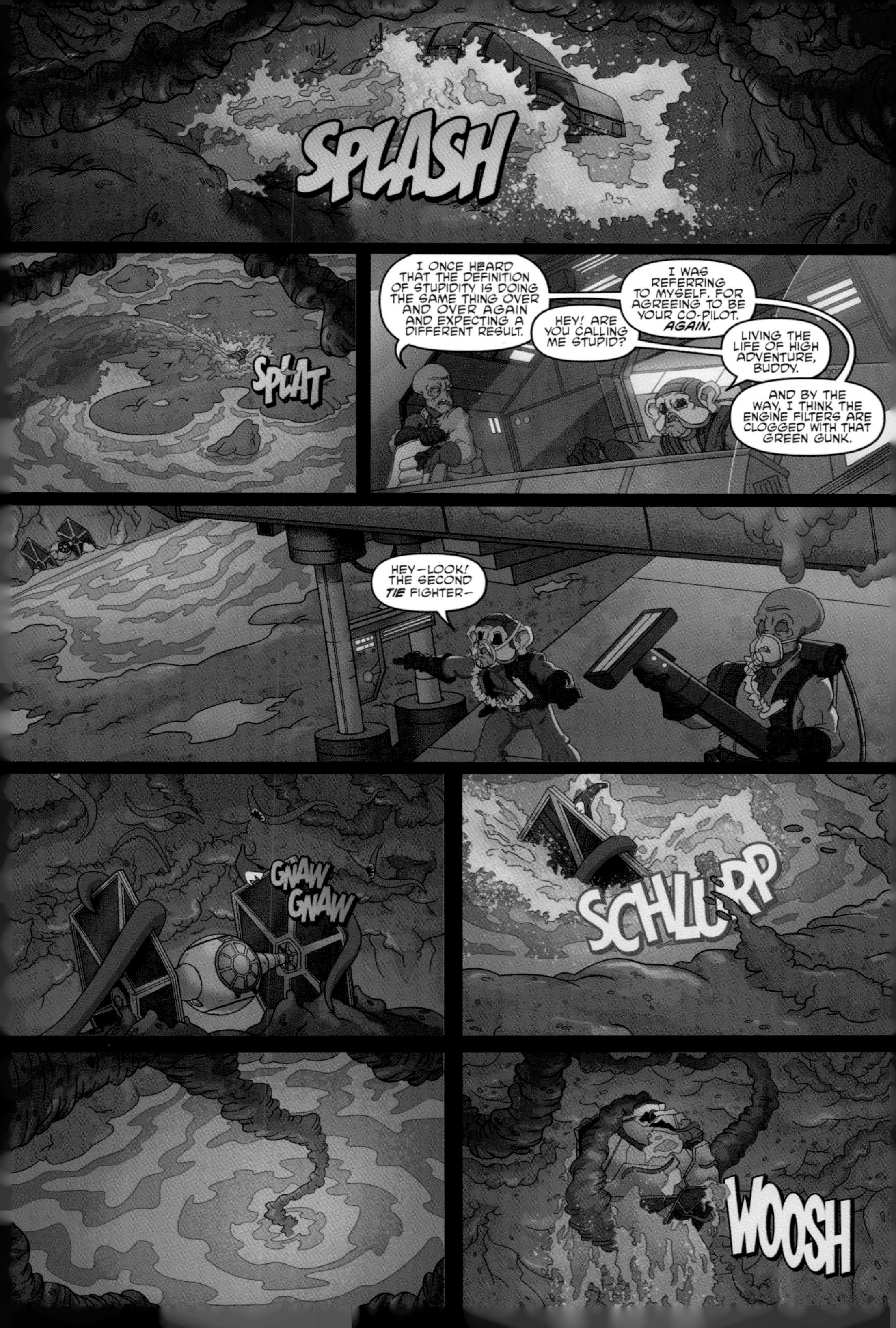
SPLASH
SPLAT
I ONCE HEARD THAT THE DEFINITION OF STUPIDITY IS DOING THE SAME THING OVER AND OVER AGAIN AND EXPECTING A DIFFERENT RESULT.
HEY! ARE YOU CALLING ME STUPID?
I WAS REFERRING TO MYSELF. FOR AGREEING TO BE YOUR CO-PILOT. AGAIN.
LIVING THE LIFE OF HIGH ADVENTURE, BUDDY.
AND BY THE WAY, I THINK THE ENGINE FILTERS ARE CLOGGED WITH THAT GREEN GUNK.
HEY—LOOK! THE SECOND TIE FIGHTER—
GNAW GNAW
SCHLURP
WOOSH

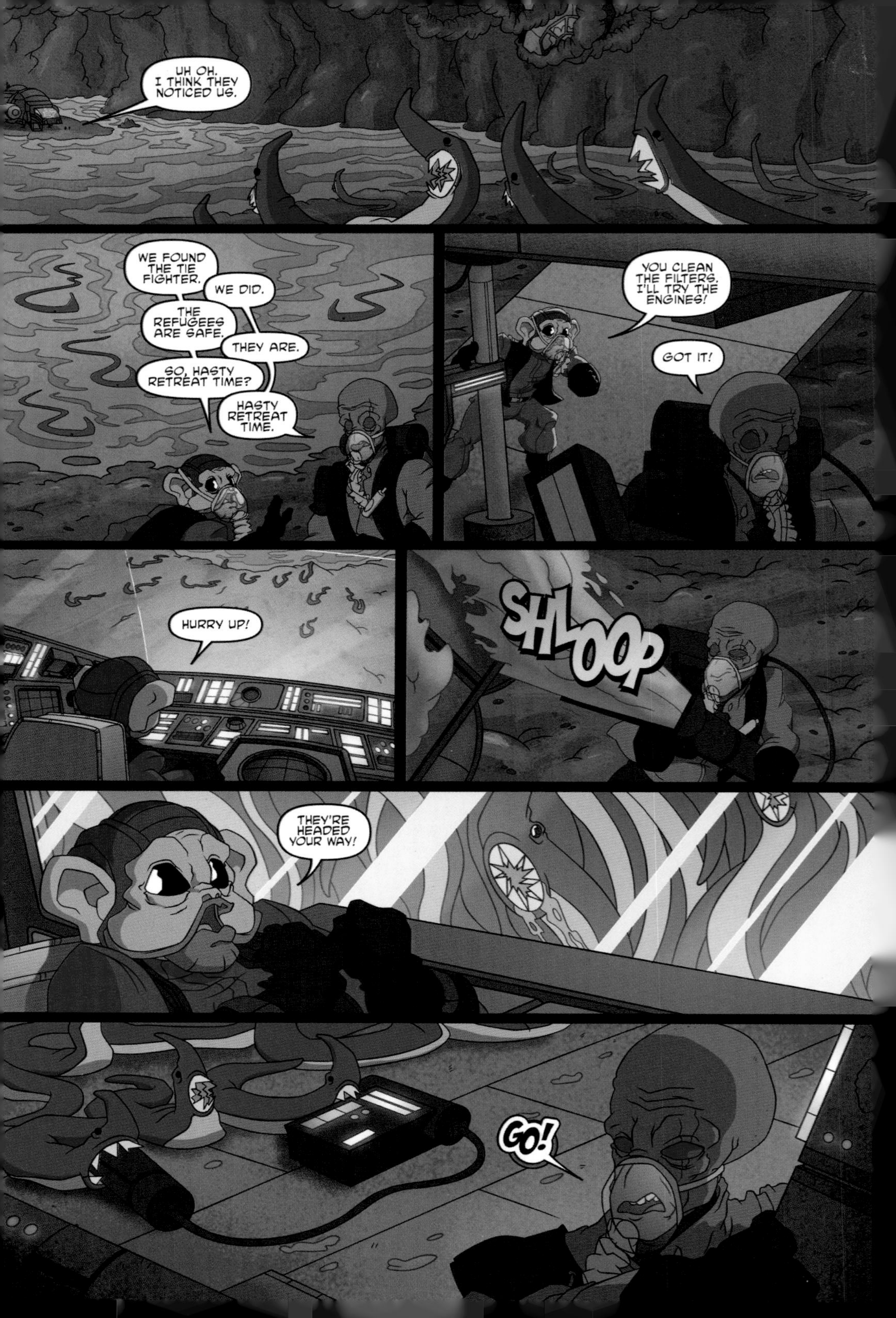
UH OH. I THINK THEY NOTICED US.
WE FOUND THE TIE FIGHTER.
WE DID.
THE REFUGEES ARE SAFE.
THEY ARE.
SO, HASTY RETREAT TIME?
HASTY RETREAT TIME.
YOU CLEAN THE FILTERS. I'LL TRY THE ENGINES!
GOT IT!
HURRY UP!
SHLOOP
THEY'RE HEADED YOUR WAY!
GO!

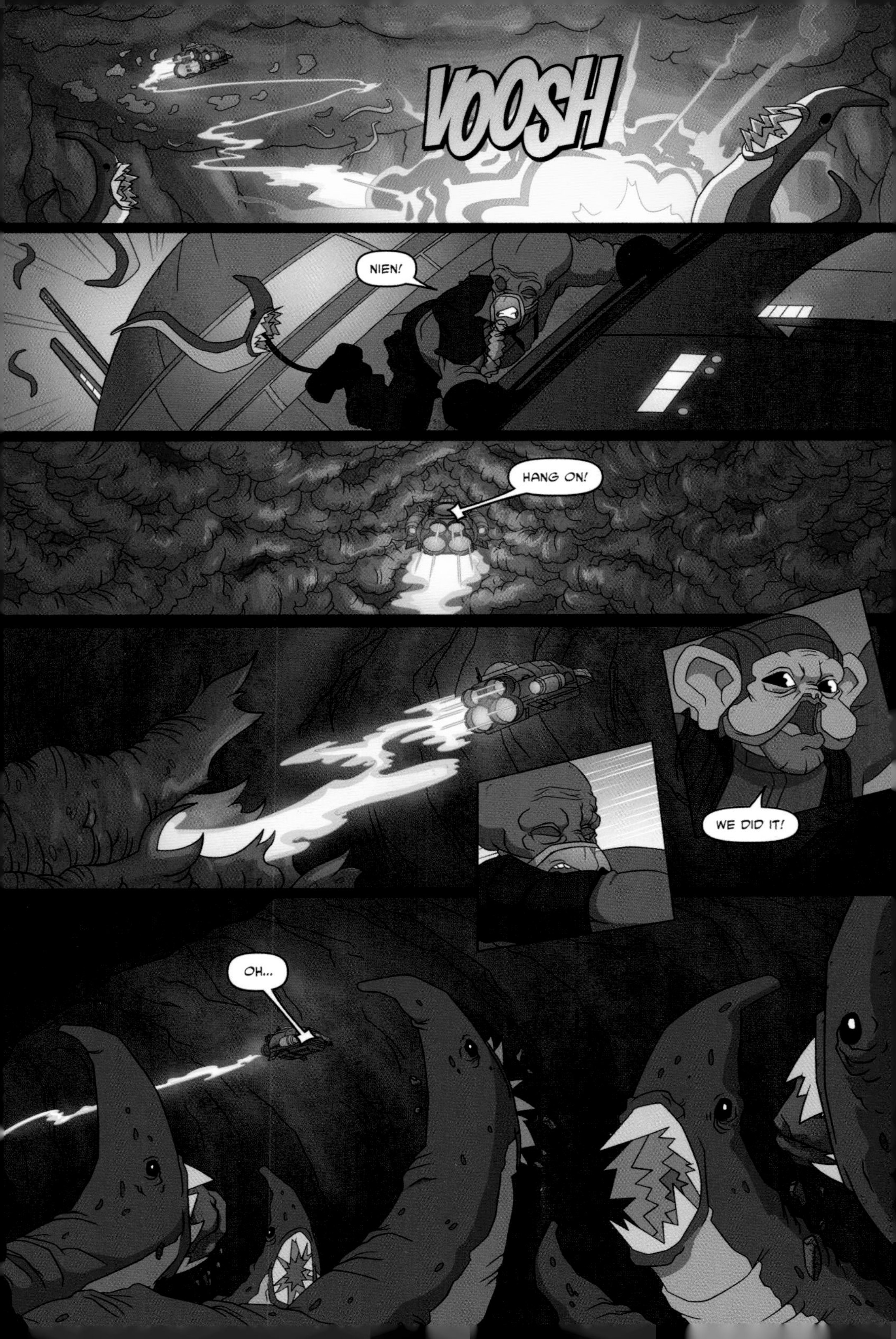
VOOSH
NIEN!
HANG ON!
WE DID IT!
OH...

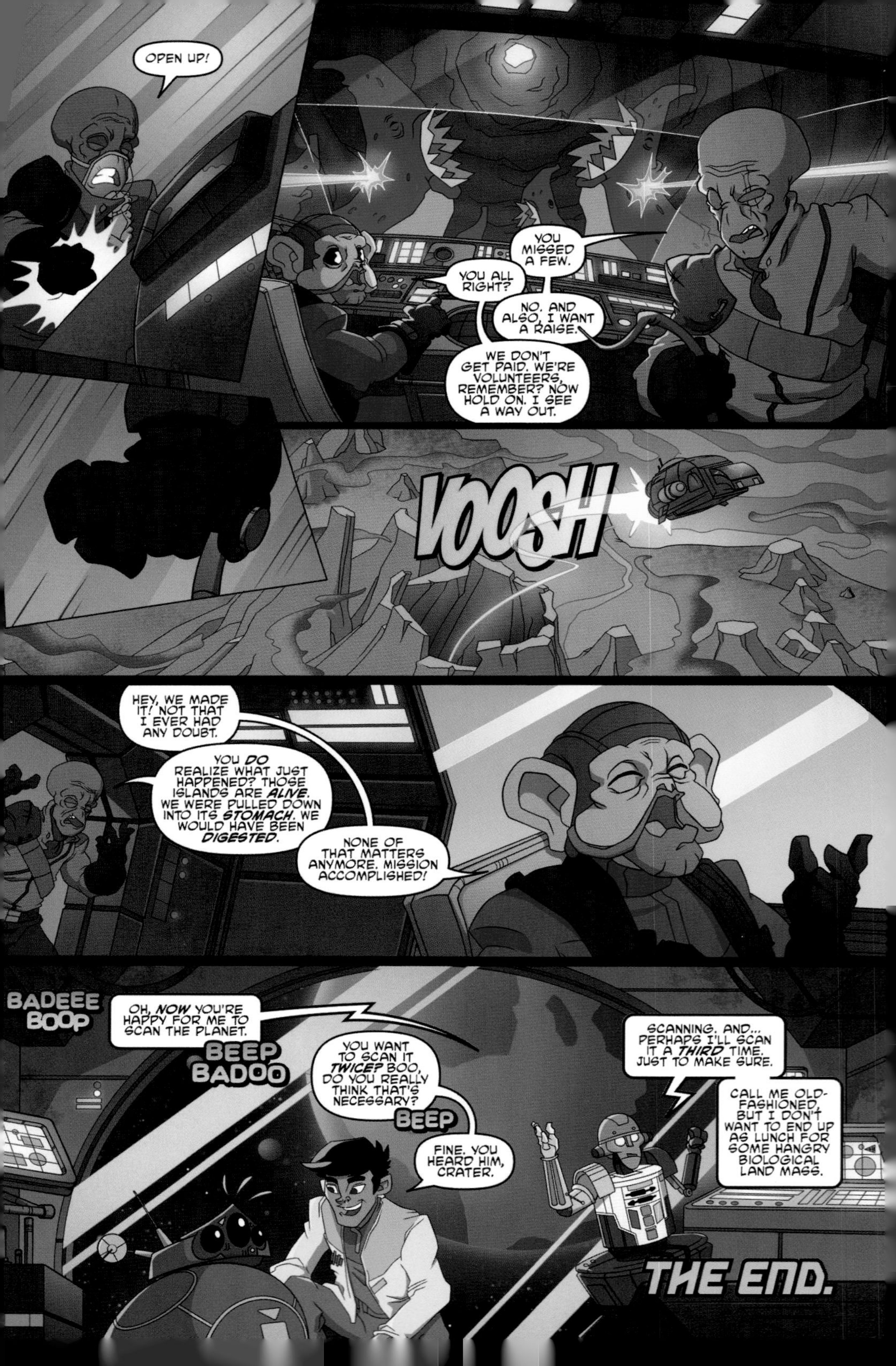
OPEN UP!
YOU MISSED A FEW.
YOU ALL RIGHT?
NO. AND ALSO, I WANT A RAISE.
WE DON'T GET PAID. WE'RE VOLUNTEERS, REMEMBER? NOW HOLD ON. I SEE A WAY OUT.
VOOSH
HEY, WE MADE IT! NOT THAT I EVER HAD ANY DOUBT.
YOU *DO* REALIZE WHAT JUST HAPPENED? THOSE ISLANDS ARE *ALIVE*. WE WERE PULLED DOWN INTO ITS *STOMACH*. WE WOULD HAVE BEEN *DIGESTED*.
NONE OF THAT MATTERS ANYMORE. MISSION ACCOMPLISHED!
BADEEE BOOP
OH, *NOW* YOU'RE HAPPY FOR ME TO SCAN THE PLANET.
BEEP BADOO
YOU WANT TO SCAN IT *TWICE*? BOO, DO YOU REALLY THINK THAT'S NECESSARY?
BEEP
FINE. YOU HEARD HIM, CRATER.
SCANNING. AND... PERHAPS I'LL SCAN IT A *THIRD* TIME. JUST TO MAKE SURE.
CALL ME OLD-FASHIONED, BUT I DON'T WANT TO END UP AS LUNCH FOR SOME HANGRY BIOLOGICAL LAND MASS.
THE END.

Art by Otis Frampton

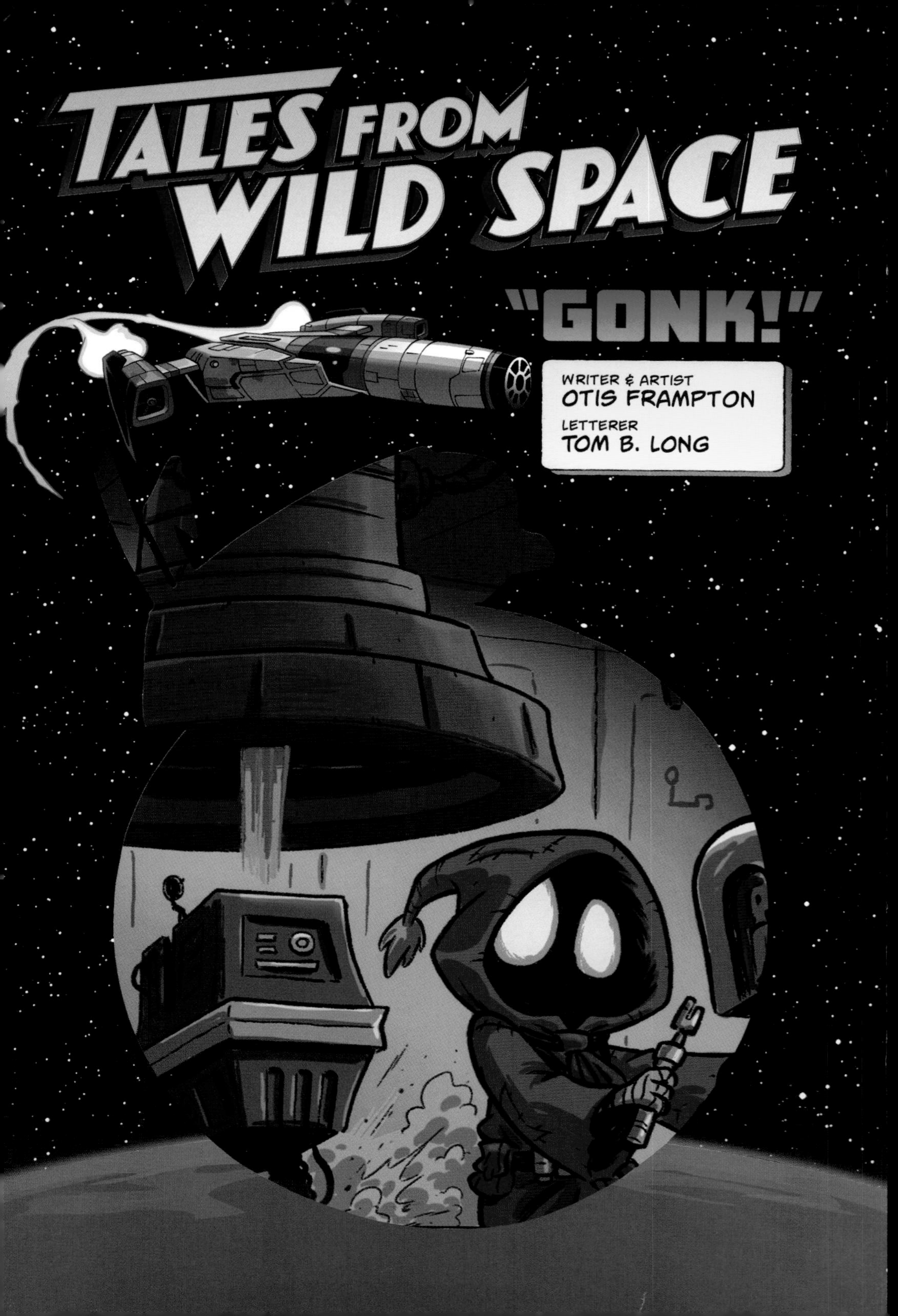

TALES FROM WILD SPACE
"GONK!"
WRITER & ARTIST
OTIS FRAMPTON
LETTERER
TOM B. LONG

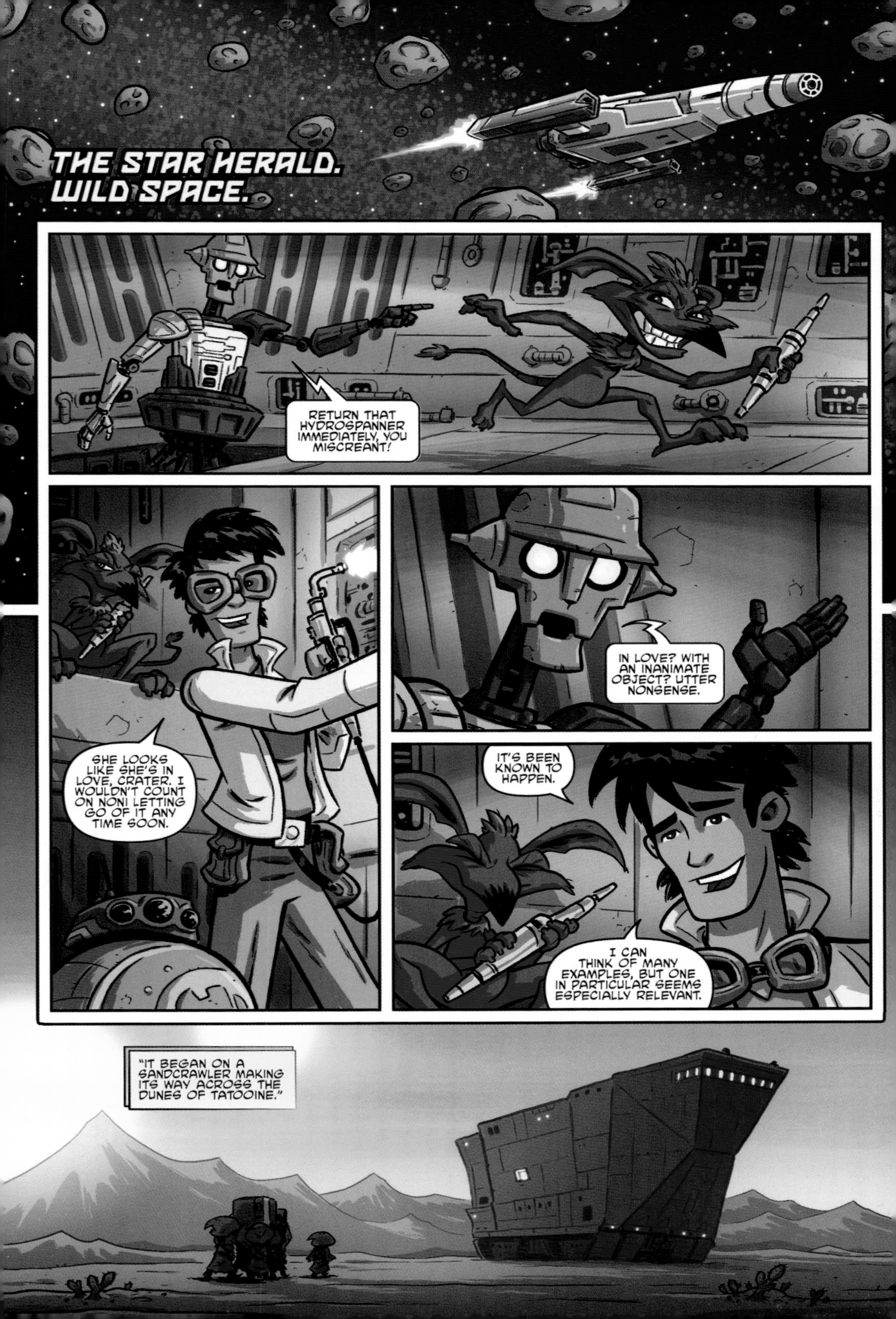
THE STAR HERALD. WILD SPACE.
RETURN THAT HYDROSPANNER IMMEDIATELY, YOU MISCREANT!
SHE LOOKS LIKE SHE'S IN LOVE, CRATER. I WOULDN'T COUNT ON NONI LETTING GO OF IT ANY TIME SOON.
IN LOVE? WITH AN INANIMATE OBJECT? UTTER NONSENSE.
IT'S BEEN KNOWN TO HAPPEN.
I CAN THINK OF MANY EXAMPLES, BUT ONE IN PARTICULAR SEEMS ESPECIALLY RELEVANT.
"IT BEGAN ON A SANDCRAWLER MAKING ITS WAY ACROSS THE DUNES OF TATOOINE."

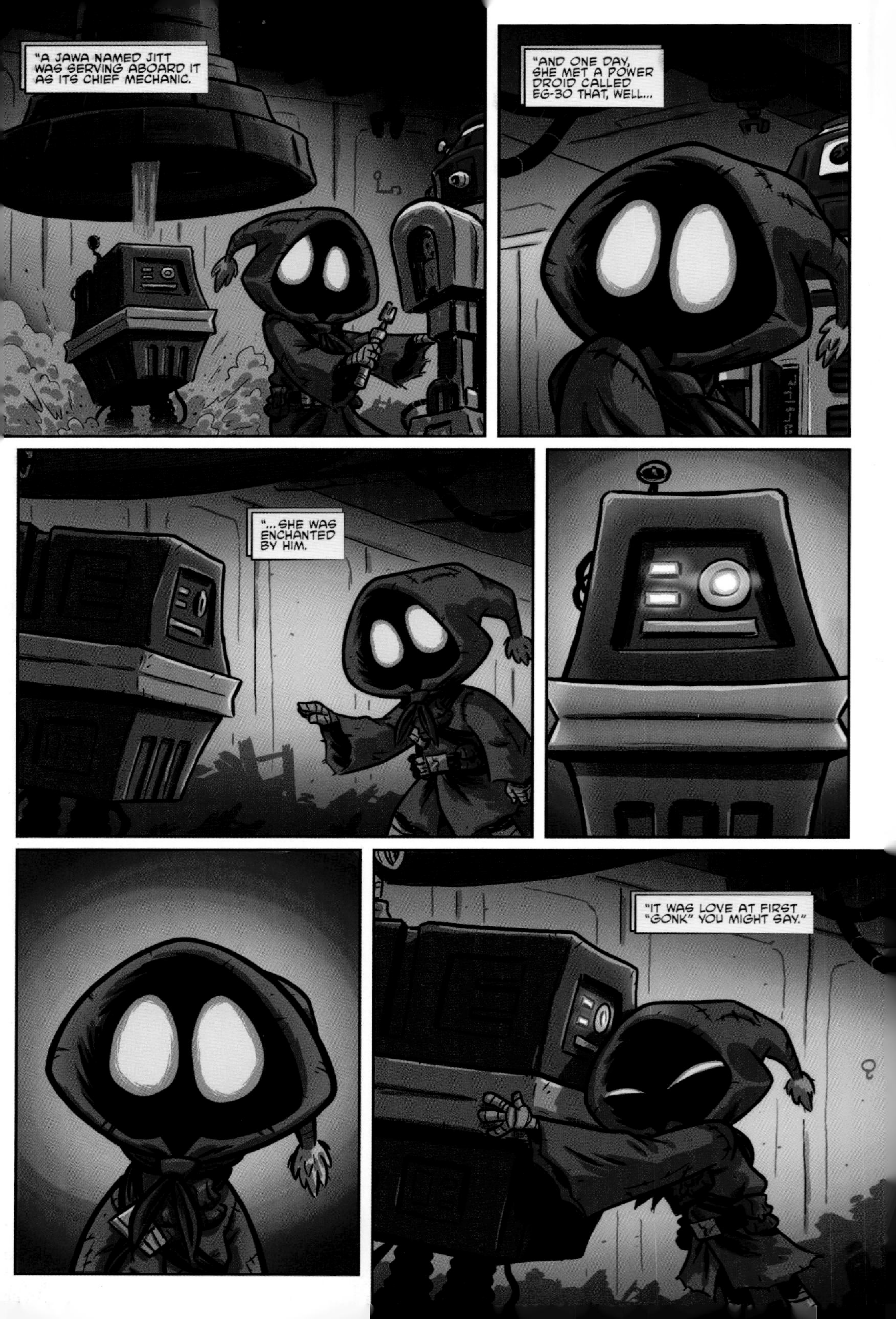
"A JAWA NAMED JITT WAS SERVING ABOARD IT AS ITS CHIEF MECHANIC.
"AND ONE DAY, SHE MET A POWER DROID CALLED EG-30 THAT, WELL...
"...SHE WAS ENCHANTED BY HIM.
"IT WAS LOVE AT FIRST "GONK" YOU MIGHT SAY."

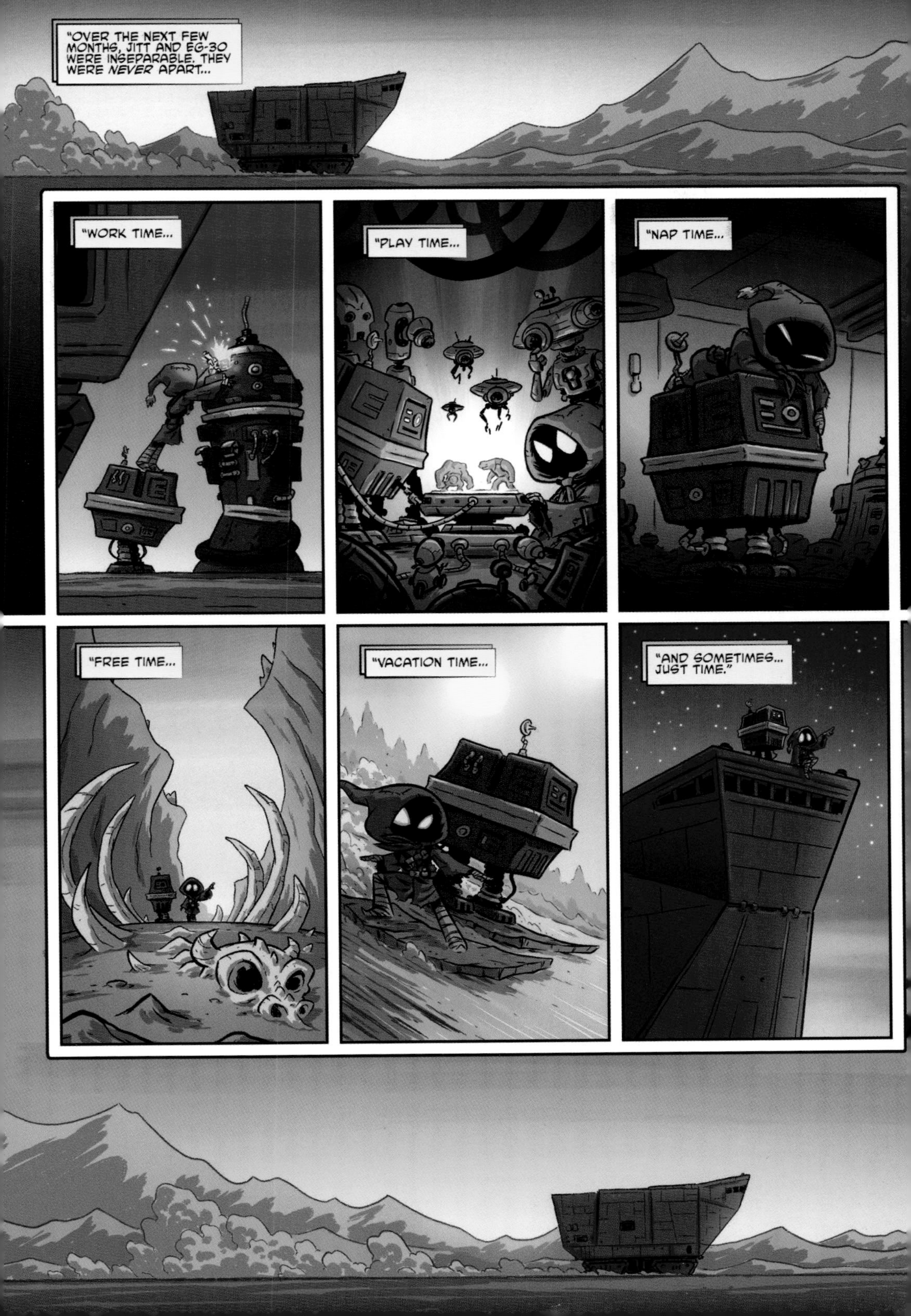
"OVER THE NEXT FEW MONTHS, JITT AND EG-30 WERE INSEPARABLE. THEY WERE *NEVER* APART...
"WORK TIME...
"PLAY TIME...
"NAP TIME...
"FREE TIME...
"VACATION TIME...
"AND SOMETIMES... JUST TIME."

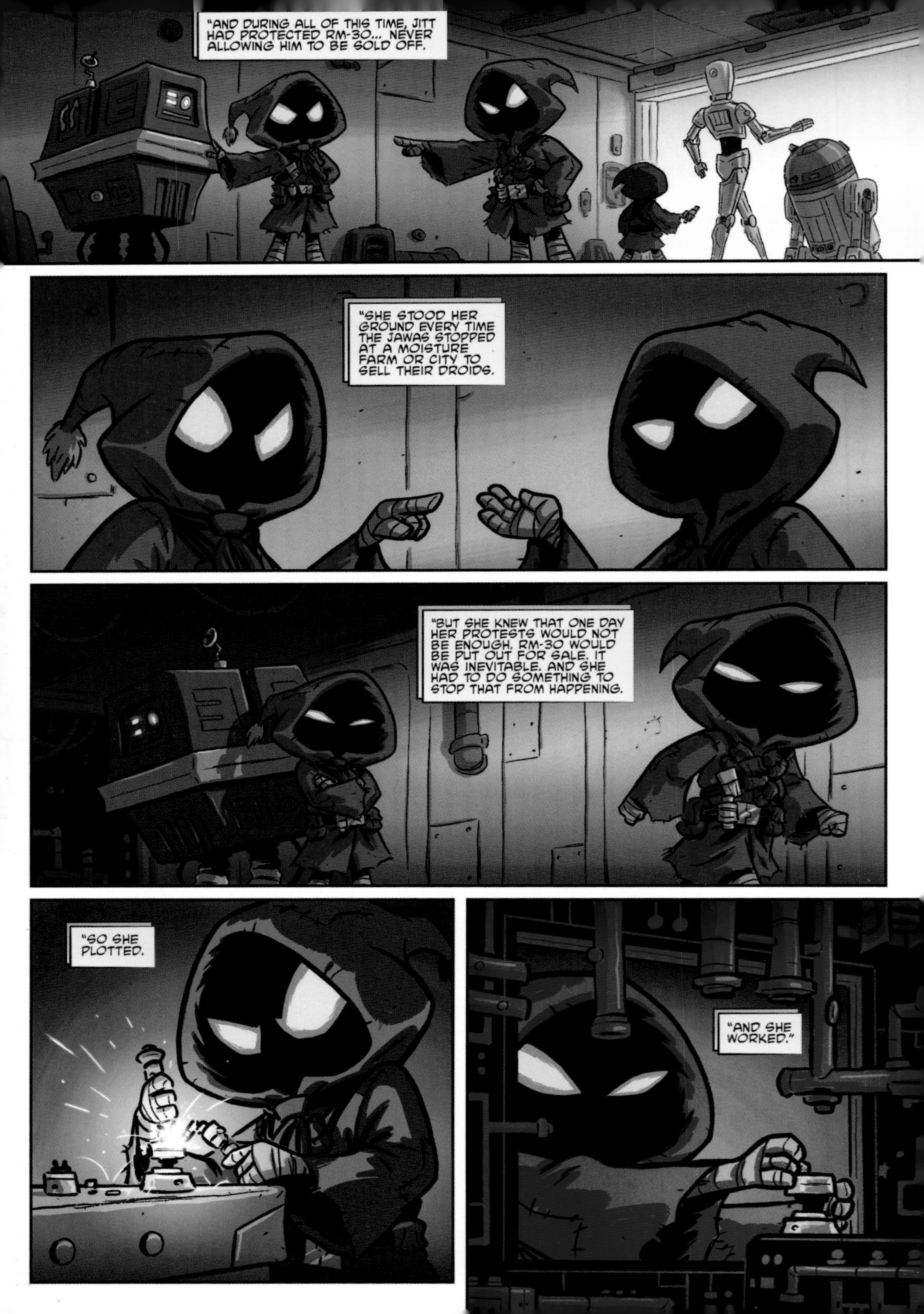
"AND DURING ALL OF THIS TIME, JITT HAD PROTECTED RM-30... NEVER ALLOWING HIM TO BE SOLD OFF.
"SHE STOOD HER GROUND EVERY TIME THE JAWAS STOPPED AT A MOISTURE FARM OR CITY TO SELL THEIR DROIDS.
"BUT SHE KNEW THAT ONE DAY HER PROTESTS WOULD NOT BE ENOUGH. RM-30 WOULD BE PUT OUT FOR SALE. IT WAS INEVITABLE. AND SHE HAD TO DO SOMETHING TO STOP THAT FROM HAPPENING.
"SO SHE PLOTTED.
"AND SHE WORKED."

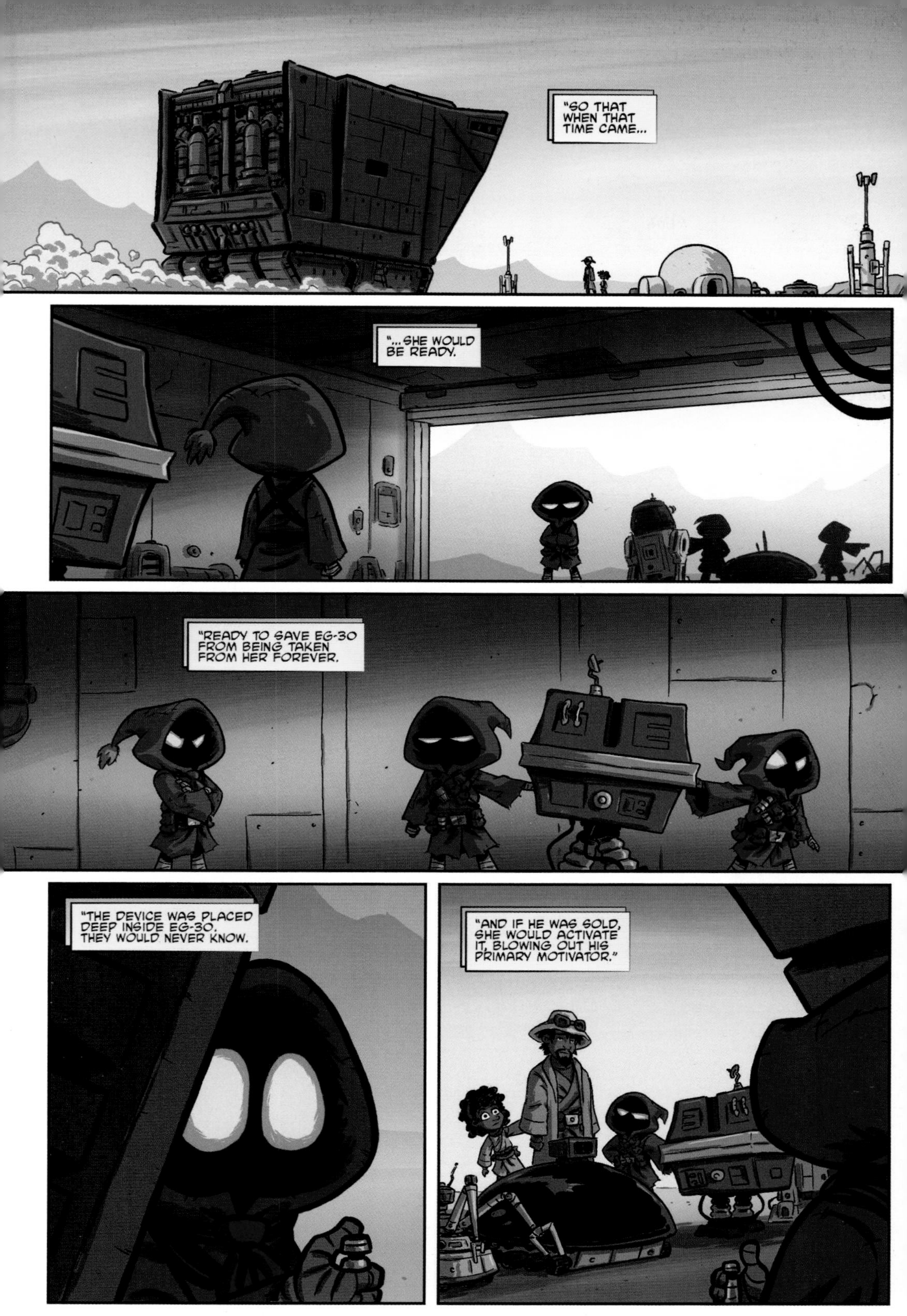
"SO THAT WHEN THAT TIME CAME...
"...SHE WOULD BE READY.
"READY TO SAVE EG-30 FROM BEING TAKEN FROM HER FOREVER.
"THE DEVICE WAS PLACED DEEP INSIDE EG-30. THEY WOULD NEVER KNOW.
"AND IF HE WAS SOLD, SHE WOULD ACTIVATE IT, BLOWING OUT HIS PRIMARY MOTIVATOR."

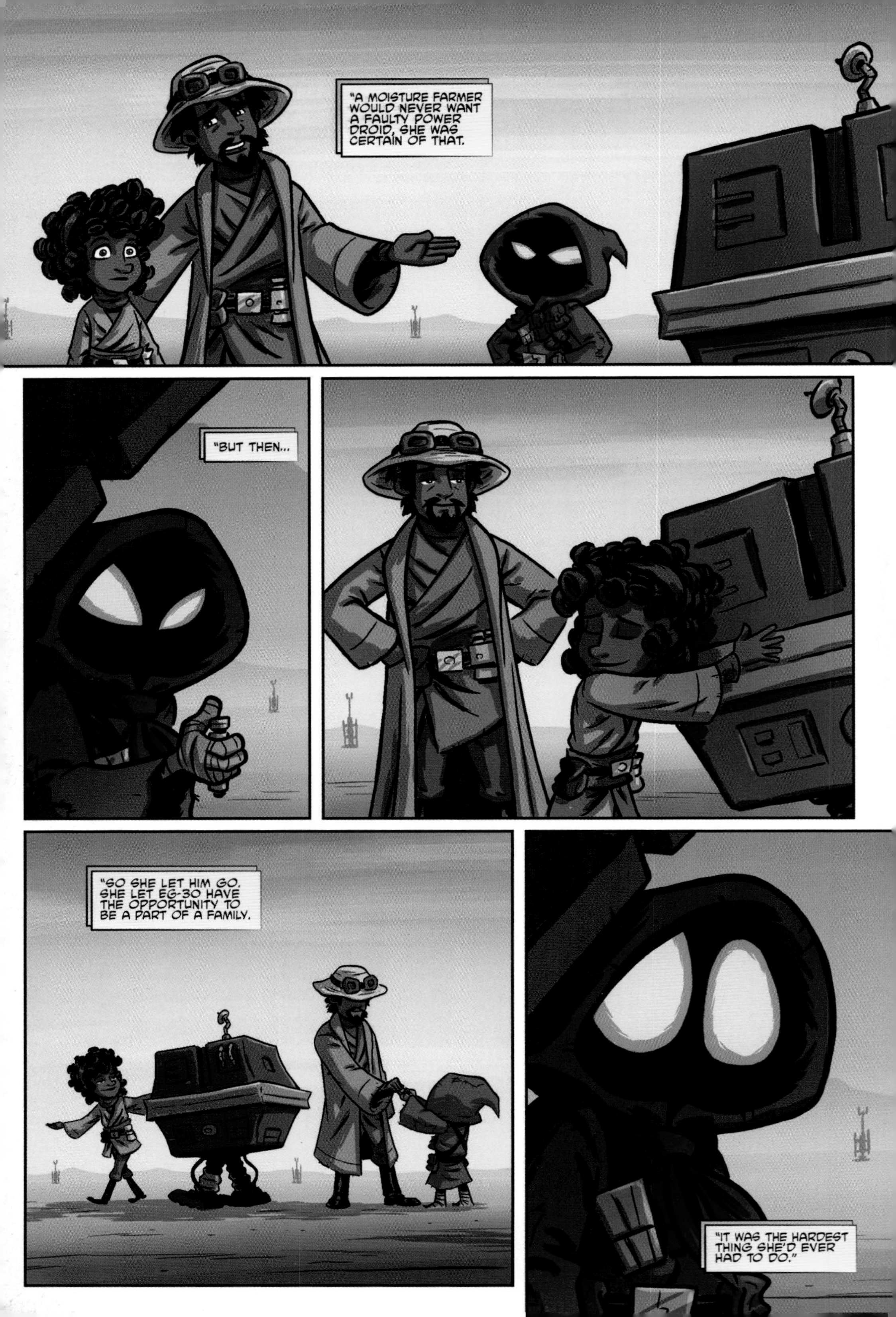
"A MOISTURE FARMER WOULD NEVER WANT A FAULTY POWER DROID, SHE WAS CERTAIN OF THAT.
"BUT THEN...
"SO SHE LET HIM GO. SHE LET EG-30 HAVE THE OPPORTUNITY TO BE A PART OF A FAMILY.
"IT WAS THE HARDEST THING SHE'D EVER HAD TO DO."

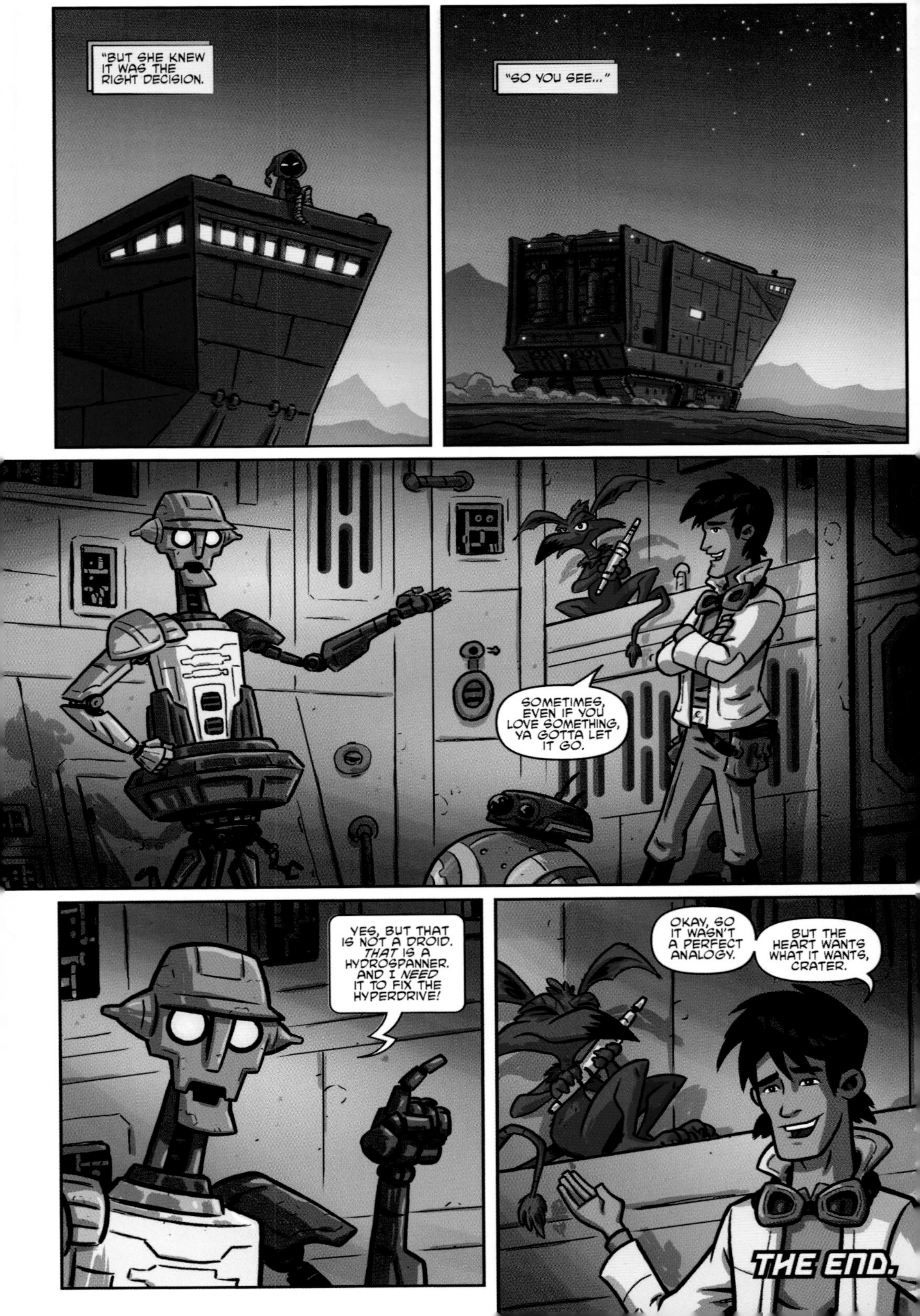
"BUT SHE KNEW IT WAS THE RIGHT DECISION.
"SO YOU SEE..."
SOMETIMES, EVEN IF YOU LOVE SOMETHING, YA GOTTA LET IT GO.
YES, BUT THAT IS NOT A DROID. *THAT* IS A HYDROSPANNER. AND I *NEED* IT TO FIX THE HYPERDRIVE!
OKAY, SO IT WASN'T A PERFECT ANALOGY.
BUT THE HEART WANTS WHAT IT WANTS, CRATER.
THE END.

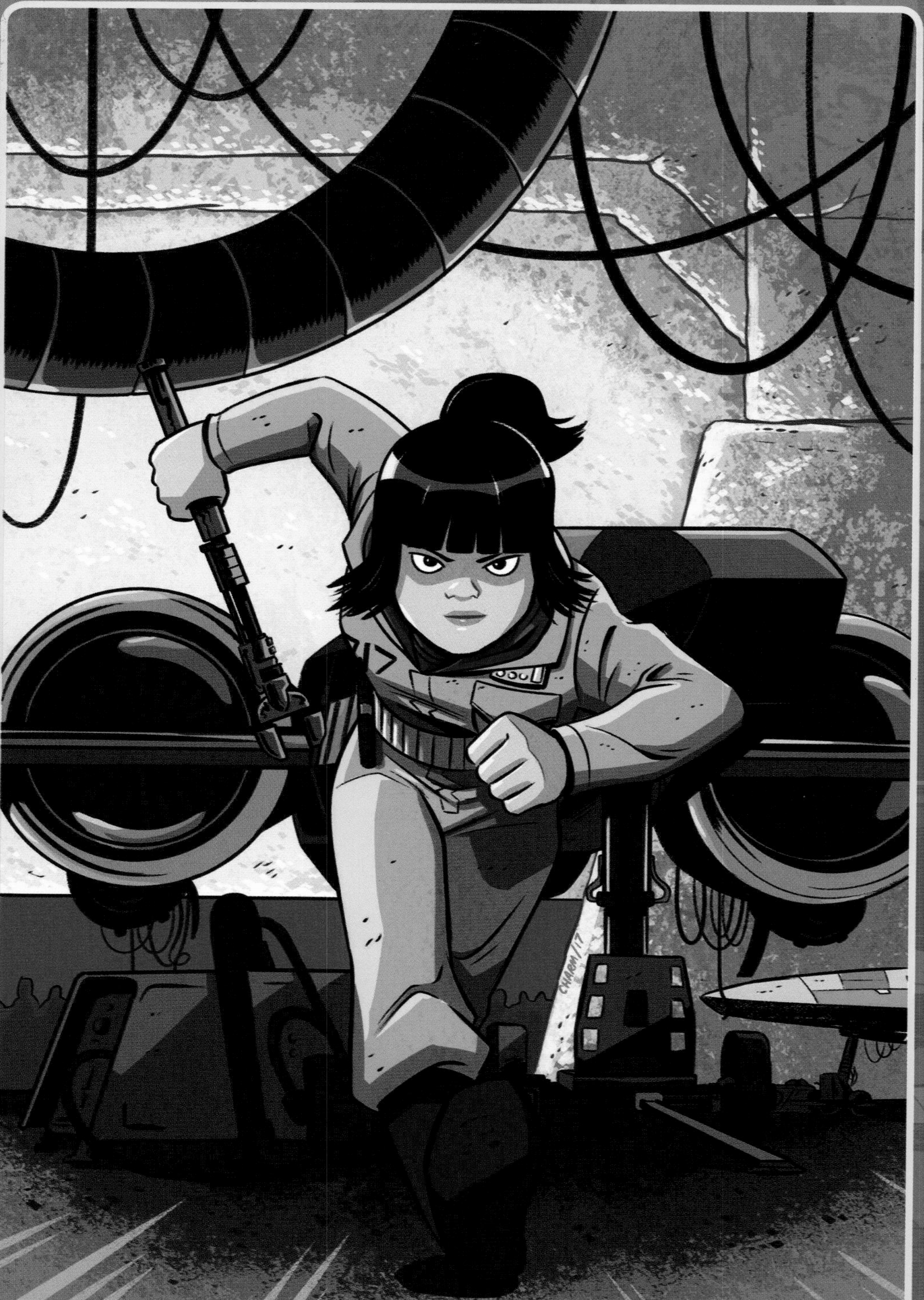
CHARM/17

Art by Derek Charm

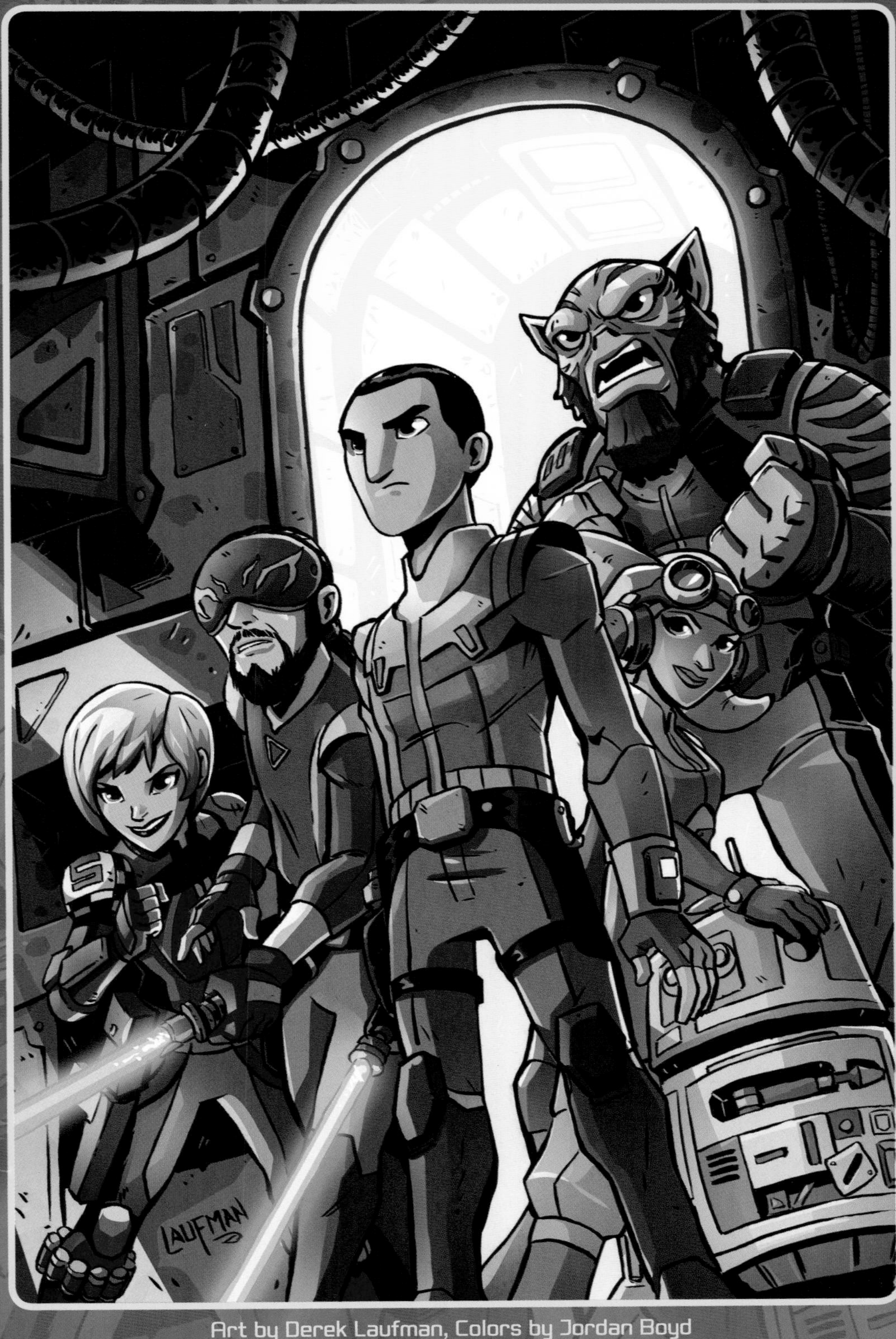
LAUFMAN

Art by Derek Laufman, Colors by Jordan Boyd

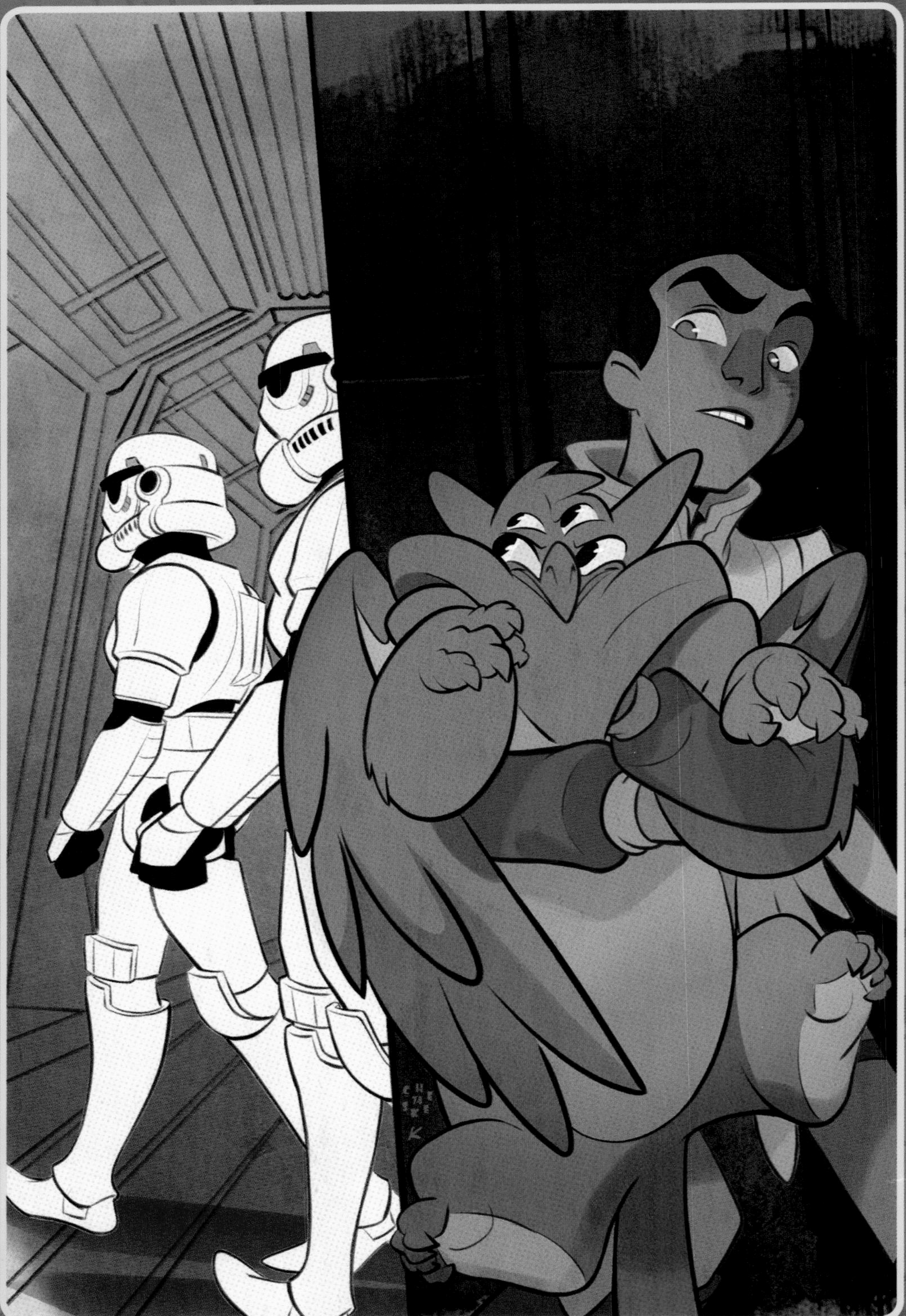

Art by Sean Galloway

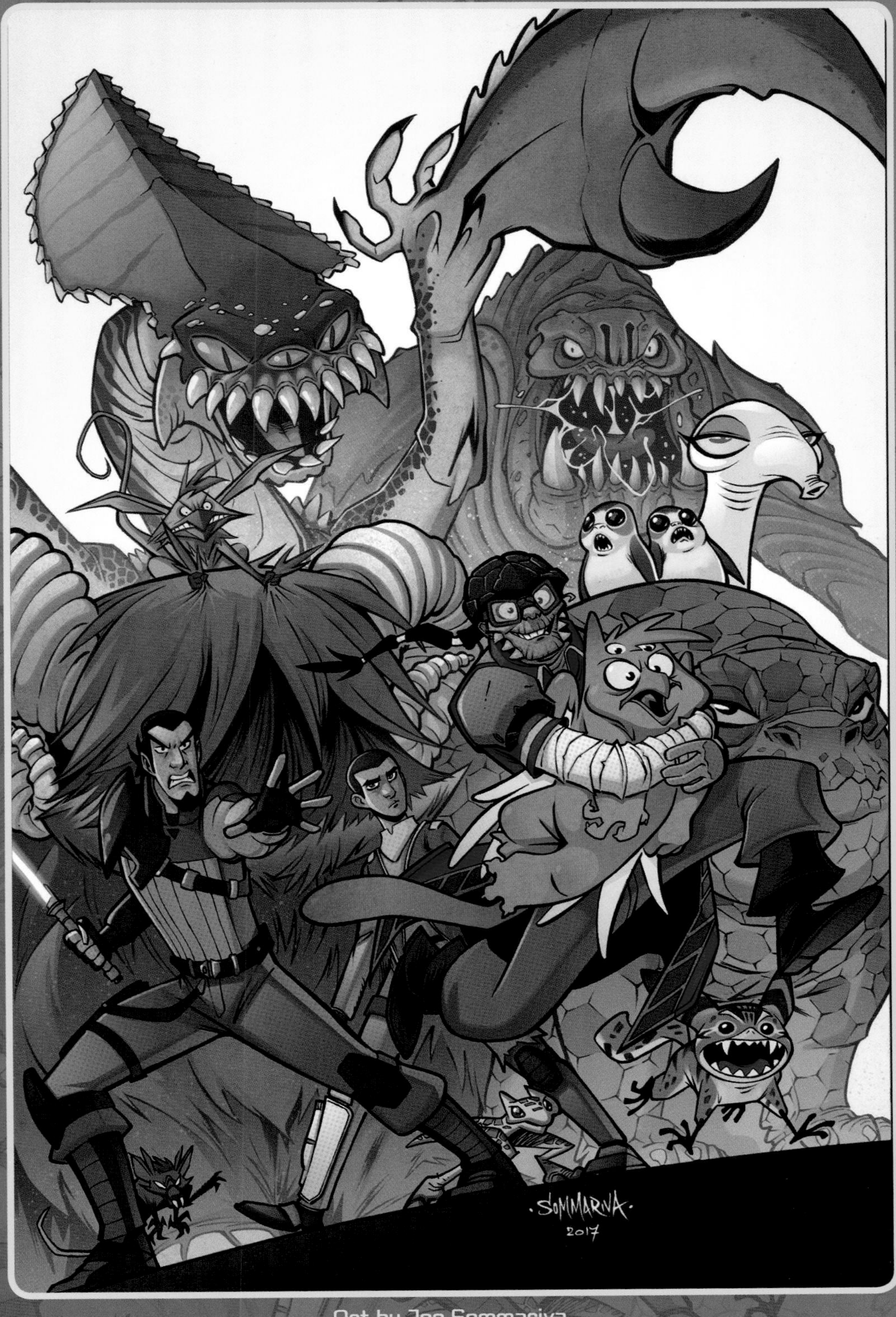
SOMMARIVA
2017

Art by Jon Sommariva